THE
BIRDDOG
TAPE

BARRY NORMAN is the highly popular presenter of the BBC television film programme. He has written numerous books about films and film stars, including *The Hollywood Greats* and *Talking Pictures: The Story of Hollywood*. His novels include *A Series of Defeats*, *To Nick a Good Body*, *Have a Nice Day* and *Sticky Wicket*.

By the same author

Fiction
The Matter of Mandrake
The Hounds of Sparta
A Series of Defeats
To Nick a Good Body
End Product
Have a Nice Day
Sticky Wicket

Non-fiction
Tales of the Redundance Kid
The Hollywood Greats
The Film Greats
The Movie Greats
Talking Pictures
100 Best Films of the Century

THE BIRDDOG TAPE

Barry Norman

CHAPMANS

Chapmans Publishers
141–143 Drury Lane
London WC2B 5TB

First published by Chapmans 1992
This paperback edition first published by Chapmans 1992

© Barry Norman 1992

The right of Barry Norman to be identified as the author
of this work has been asserted by him in accordance with
the Copyright, Designs and Patents Act 1988

ISBN 1 85592 082 4

Photoset by Rowland Phototypesetting Ltd
Bury St Edmunds, Suffolk

Printed and bound in Great Britain by
Clays Ltd, St Ives plc

For Diana and the girls, as always.
But also for Rick and Christine.

1

THE GIRL AT THE TABLE by the window had red hair and green eyes, and the word that came to mind was 'cute'. On her, since she can have been no more than twenty-three, cute was all right, but give her a few more years and it would swiftly become tiresome. Cuteness is for the very young and, give or take Goldie Hawn who has gone on being cute well into middle-age, no woman in the world has made it last much beyond her mid-twenties without discovering, after about ten minutes in any company, that she is being cute all by herself.

The girl with the red hair, however, was still a few years off that time and she was cute and she knew it and she was sticking with it. She did cute little things with her wine glass, she let her head droop prettily on its slender neck and her eyelashes were putting in a lot of work. What she was doing with her right foot was not, strictly speaking, cute but it seemed a safe bet that her companion appreciated it even more than all her other antics. She had slipped off her shoes and, as far as it was possible to tell from where I was standing over by the bar, she was resting her right foot in his lap and wiggling it about. Probably it was this as much as the whisky he was drinking that accounted for the high colour in his cheeks.

I knew the man she was with, at least by sight. Everyone knew him by sight. He was a game show host on one of the TV channels. It was a particularly mindless show and therefore particularly popular, and the host was always cropping up in the tabloids, delivering himself of some inane quote on various matters of the moment. There were a good many like him, models of mediocrity, men without any discernible talent and not even much charm but with the ability to smile continually while talking and, while talking, to keep their minds in neutral and their mouths in overdrive. As a skill this is comparable to being able to fart and chew gum at the same time but while the latter accomplishment can promote a man all the way to the White House, the former is only useful for hosting game shows on television.

Right now the game show host with the red-haired girl was smiling and talking while her foot did whatever it was doing to his groin. He must have been close to fifty, fighting hard against the flab that goes with the age, and over the years his hair, which had once been mousey, had turned prematurely black.

I watched them with mild curiosity wondering, purely on a theoretical basis rather than from desire, whether when I reached his age I, too, would be able to buy myself a girl like that. Probably not. I wouldn't be famous enough.

The barman drifted up and asked if I would like another Armagnac. I said I would. We had been celebrating that night, my two partners and I; a deal we had been nursing along had ripened sweetly and we were each about £60,000 better off. It was a property deal. We were entrepreneurs, the partners and I, which is to say we bought things and then sold them again – property when the market was right, shares when the market was right, gold and silver when the market was right. That sort of stuff. What we did was we took the money and ran. And then we did it again. We were speculators, really, and I could remember a time when 'speculation' was a dirty word and whenever you mentioned it you were supposed to wash your mouth out with soapy water. But that was then and this was now and we had laid the foundation of our business way back, early in the reign of the Empress Thatcher when speculators were her chosen people. To prove our fealty we bought the nation's gas, water, telephone system and anything else that was going and our chequebooks were always ready for the day when the government decided to privatise air and fire. Oh, there was plenty of gravy about and the partners and I could see no reason why we shouldn't dip our own slices of Wonderloaf into it. So we did. We had been doing it for a good few years and we weren't complaining because even in times of war and recession there was always money to be made if you knew where to look, and we did know. We had even got in on the Big Bang and got out before the Big Crash. So, at the very least, we were no burden on the state: we paid our taxes, the partners sent their children to fee-paying schools and we all contributed dutifully to private health schemes, thereby removing ourselves from any possibility of adding to the queues for what remained of the National Health beds.

Of course, if you wished to be critical, you could say that in almost every way we typified the New Britons – self-supporting, self-serving, well off and getting richer, and not doing much for anybody else. But what the hell, we only played where the goal posts were. And, besides, we weren't political animals. We had welcomed the idea of a new classless Britain when it was promised us some time back and though it hadn't happened yet we were still eager to join in when it came to pass.

It was after the barman had refilled my glass and we had done the weather and the latest deficiencies of the England cricket team and I had turned back to continue my surveillance of the near-empty bar area and the still-full restaurant that I saw the woman come in off the street. She was about forty, tall and elegant, and what attracted my attention was the expression on her face, at the same time both blank and utterly determined. Kamikaze pilots must have looked like that when they yelled 'Tora! Tora! Tora!' and turned the noses of their planes down towards the American aircraft carriers. This was a woman with a mission and the nature of that mission became clear when she walked straight up to the game show host and started beating him about the head with her hand-bag.

As the first blow ripped across his cheek he said, 'Jesus Christ!' As the second hit him on the ear he said, 'What the hell are you doing?' And as the third temporarily flattened his nose he said, 'She's my agent! She's my agent!'

I had to hand it to Michael, the maitre d'. The woman had hardly drawn back her arm for the first swipe before he had summoned up a couple of waiters and set off at a brisk trot in her direction. But if he was quick, she was quicker. By the time the Seventh Cavalry got to the scene, the game show host was bleeding from both cheeks and the bridge of the nose where the buckle of the handbag had torn the skin and his companion was wearing a spinach soufflé on the top of her head. I thought the colour scheme, the green a nice contrast to the red, rather added for a moment to her cuteness, though I doubt whether she would have agreed. And maybe she would have been right because the juice started coursing down her forehead and into her eyes and lines of green-black mascara stained her face like war paint.

When Michael and his cohorts grabbed hold of her the woman immediately stopped swinging and, without protest, allowed them to propel her gently back towards the door, Michael muttering soothing words into her ear. The odd thing about it was that throughout the whole incident she had said nothing. The game show host had yelled and cursed and the cutie had given a shrill yelp as the soufflé hit her but the older woman had been silent except for a curious hissing sound that she made between clenched teeth and lips that were drawn back into a rictus which, if you had ignored what she was actually doing, might have been taken for a smile.

Michael said a few more soft words to her and then she went out and I saw her pass the window, walking hurriedly back towards Piccadilly, wiping blood from her handbag with a tissue. The game show host and the wailing cutie got up from their table and headed towards the cloakrooms, while their fellow diners watched them with the whole-hearted pleasure of people who have seen total embarrassment visited upon others. Michael stood by the deserted table shaking his head sadly and then came over to me at the bar.

'Bloody idiot,' he said. 'I've told him God knows how many times not to bring that little tart here. His wife comes in two or three times a week to have lunch with her girlfriends. She was bound to find out sooner or later.'

'The wife,' I said, 'I imagine she was the one doing all the good work with the handbag?'

'Right,' he said, nodding.

'Nice action,' I said. 'Good swing and plenty of shoulder in it. You could say she telegraphs the blow a little too much but only a pro would notice.'

Michael nodded again. 'Stupid prat. Well, he asked for it.'

'That red-headed popsy with him, is she really his agent?'

'Is she fuck,' Michael said.

'Shame,' I said, 'because I was thinking if they hand out agents like that to everybody in show business you and I are in the wrong game.'

'Noticed the footwork, did you? Tickling his fancy with her tootsies? I could do with some of that.'

I asked him if he would like a drink. He said he'd better not because, the way things were shaping up, it looked like being one of those nights and it might be wise to keep a clear head. 'Enjoy your dinner?' he said. 'I see the partners have left you all alone.'

'Yes, well, they had to get back to their wives and families.'

'A lot to be said, I reckon, for not having wives and families to get back to.' He said this with some feeling as if he were speaking as one who had had more experience than he cared to remember of getting back to wives and families.

I shrugged. 'I wouldn't know. I've never had either.'

'Take my word . . .' He stopped, glancing over my shoulder towards the stairs that led to the lavatories. 'Excuse me. I'd better go and see to that arsehole and his bird.'

He went away to where the game show host and his girlfriend were hovering uncertainly near the restaurant's tiny vestibule. The girl had got most of the spinach out of her hair and washed her face and restored her make-up but she didn't seem happy. Her companion was now lurking behind a patchwork of sticking plaster that covered the cuts on his cheeks and nose, and he didn't look happy either. The girl was snarling at him in a low voice, her eyes slitty and her teeth bared, and he seemed unable to placate her. Mind you, it would have been hard, I imagine, to placate any girl in those circumstances, especially as everyone in the place was grinning at them. The couple moved hesitantly back towards their table by the window but Michael headed them off, doing his soft murmuring again, and after a few moments, presumably acting on his advice, they left.

'Thank God they've gone,' Michael said as he moved past me to take up his usual position beside the reception desk, a vantage point from which he surveyed the remaining diners with the cold eye of one daring anybody to disturb the peace of his evening again.

And it was at that point that Arnie Longbow came into the place.

He entered at a fast scurry, darting sharp suspicious looks around him, a thin little man in his mid-fifties with black hair that hung limply over his ears and was receding fast in front. He wore, as he always did, a black suit that needed pressing, with a matching black tie, and a white shirt that also needed pressing. He looked like an undertaker who was plying his trade in an area where nobody died. He paused briefly while he glanced about him and then went up to Michael and clutched at his sleeve. Arnie was always a great clutcher. They made a curious couple standing there: Michael, built on the generous lines of a Wodehouse butler, inclining his head courteously in the direction of this scraggy newcomer. A casual bystander might have supposed that Michael owned the place and Arnie had come in off the street looking for a handout.

Michael said, 'Mr Lennox?' He looked inquiringly over Arnie's head and in my direction and I nodded back to him. 'Yes, sir, Mr Lennox is over there at the bar.'

Arnie let go of Michael's sleeve and scuttled across to clutch mine instead. 'Bobby! Christ, there you are. Been looking all over for you, haven't I?'

'Are you okay?' I said. I hadn't seen him for a long time and in the interim he seemed to have declined physically in an alarming way. He had never been a healthy-looking man, having a permanent facial pallor which gave the impression that he had taken a skin transplant from the underbelly of a shark, but he had never looked positively ill before. Now he did. There was a light coating of sweat on his face, a pinched look about the lips, and he seemed even smaller and skinnier than I remembered.

'Of course I'm not bloody okay,' he said. 'That's why I'm here, isn't it?' It was a rhetorical question; most of his questions were. 'Christ, you're a hard man to pin down. Answering machine at your flat tells you sod all. I had to phone your mum to find out where you were likely to be and she gave me a bleedin' great list of pubs and clubs and restaurants. This is the fifth place I've tried.'

'Well, now you've found me,' I said. 'So calm down and have a drink.'

He stared longingly at the bottles behind the bar. 'Wish I could, believe me. Bloody ulcer won't let me, though. Do you suppose they'd give me a glass of milk?'

'I don't think they'd *give* you one, Arnie. They're not much in the business of giving things away here. But if we opened negotiations I reckon there's a fair chance they might sell us one.'

So I got him a glass of milk and he sipped at it and said, 'Can we talk? Private, I mean? Over there in the corner? There's nobody about over there.'

'If you like.'

We went to a table in the far corner of the bar. A waiter came across to us and I ordered another Armagnac for myself. I don't normally drink a great deal but I didn't want to sit there empty-handed watching Arnie sip milk. I was prepared to sit with him, though, because I was curious. It was about 11.30 and that was late for him. In the old days, when I knew him fairly well, he was usually in bed by ten watching one of his vast collection of video nasties with his big, plump wife, Vera, alongside him. So if he had been hunting around the West

End of London looking for me at this time of night it must be something important.

When the waiter had brought my drink and gone away again I said, 'What's your problem?'

'No problem.' He took a small gulp of milk. Either it was very cold or his ulcer was giving him a hard time because he winced a little as it went down. 'Least I don't think there will be. Just come to call in a favour, is all.'

'I don't owe you any favours, Arnie,' I said.

'Don't you?' His hard, cold, dark little eyes watched me carefully. 'I think you do. I think you owe me. I think you owe me twice.'

I sighed. 'Once, maybe, but certainly not twice. And I'm not even so sure about the once.'

'Yeah, well that's where we disagree, isn't it? I say twice, you say once – maybe. Tell you what, let's compromise. I only want one favour. You do that for me and we're quits. Can't say fairer than that, can I?'

I thought about it. 'What's the favour?'

He didn't answer immediately and when he did he spoke softly, though there was no need to. The only other drinkers in the bar were at least thirty feet away. 'I'm in for a job, a big job.'

'A hit?'

He made an impatient little gesture. 'Of course a hit. What did you think – I'd taken up painting and decorating in my old age?'

'Just wanted everything to be clear.'

'Right, so now it's clear, okay? It's a hit. Thing is, I don't know anything about it, except the money's good. I'm supposed to go see the bloke who's offering the contract tomorrow night, find out the details. Only I can't make it. Which,' he said, having a nibble at the milk again, 'is where you come in.'

I shook my head as determinedly as I knew how. 'I'm not doing a hit for you, Arnie.'

'Bloody right you're not. What am I, some kind of charity? I'm not offering you the job, Bobby, no way.'

'Well, that suits both of us,' I said, 'because I don't do that kind of work.'

He nodded. 'No. Not now. You don't do that kind of work now. But you used to, didn't you? That's how you got to owe me, isn't it? I can see you don't have to do that kind of work now, rich-looking bugger like you with your fancy suit and your fine old brandy. I can see that, all right. What do you do, anyway, to make a living these days?'

'Bit of this, bit of that. Me and my partners, we buy things, hold 'em for a while, sell 'em. That sort of caper. It's an honest living, Arnie.'

He snorted derisively. 'Honest living? You call that an honest living? Kicking old ladies out of their homes and then making a fat bleedin' profit? I'm surprised at you, Bobby. Worse than that – I'm ashamed of you. Whatever happened to your socialist principles?'

'I never had any, Arnie,' I said. 'Never had any Tory principles either. I just look out for number one and try not to screw anybody too hard on the way.'

Arnie shook his head. 'Typical. Typical of Britain today. Brutish, that's what this country's become. Brutish.' He looked truly disappointed in me. 'I always thought you was a socialist like me. Know what I am? Fully paid-up member of the Labour Party, that's what I am. Have been for nearly forty

17

years, unwavering. You got to have something to believe in.'

'Well, I can see that,' I said. 'But what I don't see is how killing people for a living fits in with all your socialist principles. I'm pretty sure the Labour leadership wouldn't approve, though I shouldn't like to speak for some of the other buggers in your Party.'

The waiter came back. Waiters are always attentive when it's a slow night in the bar. I ordered more Armagnac and more milk but when the drinks arrived I left mine untouched beside me. Like Michael I felt this could be an evening when I needed as clear a head as I could manage.

'About this favour,' I said.

'Yes, well, it's simple really. I'm supposed to see this geezer tomorrow night, half-past seven, in a little hotel off Piccadilly. Not far from here, matter of fact. But like I said, I won't be able to make it. So the favour is this: I want you to go along in my place, tell him you're me, find out the details and confirm the price. How bad? I mean, that's it – that's all you do and we're quits. You don't owe me any more.'

'Why can't you go?' I said, and for a moment he seemed embarrassed.

He fiddled about with his glass of milk and then he sighed and said, 'Because I've got to go into hospital, haven't I?'

'Ah. The ulcer, is it?'

He became even more embarrassed. 'No. Bleedin' hernia. Look, I had an operation a few months ago. I thought it was all cleared up but then, I don't know, complications or something. Anyway, I'm getting a lot of gyp and they want me in for a check-up. Gotta turn up tomorrow night, six o'clock. I'll only be in a day, maybe two, but it buggers everything else up, doesn't it?'

'Change the hospital appointment,' I said. 'Go in the day after tomorrow.'

'Don't be a twat, how can I? You know what the National Health Service is like these days. Cancel your appointment and you're lucky to get another one before next century.'

'That's the trouble with socialist principles. If you were an independent capitalist like me you'd have a private health scheme and go in whenever you liked.'

He sneered at me. 'It's people like you destroyed the NHS.'

'All right then, why not tell the bloke, your client? Why not rearrange the appointment with him for after you're released?'

Arnie looked exasperated, as if I were some particularly dull child. 'Well, two reasons, Einstein. First, I don't know where to contact him until seven-thirty tomorrow night and second, he's going to be well pleased, isn't he, he finds out he's giving a contract to a hitman with his balls in a sling? I mean, come on – be your age. Couple, three days I'll be fine, fit to do the job. I just want to stall him till then, is all.'

'Where did the contract come from, Arnie?' I asked. 'I mean, who put you and the punter together?'

'Donovan,' he said. 'Who else?'

'Who else indeed.'

It had to be Donovan. It always was Donovan. Or at least most of the time it was Donovan. I looked across at Arnie. He seemed to have grown even smaller, paler and sweatier as he sat there and the lines of pain were etched more sharply on his face. For a moment, remembering other times many years ago, I felt sorry for him.

'Okay,' I said. 'I'll do it. But as a favour, mind. I don't acknowledge any debt to you, but at the same time when I've done this you won't owe me anything either.'

'Bloody right I won't,' Arnie said. 'I was going to offer you two and a half grand, five per cent, just for subbing for me tomorrow night and you sit there, like Lord Muck, telling me I don't owe you nothing.'

Five per cent. Two and a half grand. A £50,000 hit. I was impressed. 'Tell you what,' I said. 'I'll be even more like Lord Muck. I won't take anything. I'll do it as a friend, just for you, for nothing. That way there'll be no misunderstandings. Whether I've owed you in the past or not, I most certainly won't owe you after tomorrow night. So tell me what I have to do.'

He told me. He told me the name of the hotel and the name of the man I was to ask for. I was about to write it all down on a paper napkin when he slapped me hard across the back of the hand.

'What the hell are you doing?' he asked angrily. 'Putting it down on paper? What are you, some kind of bleedin' amateur?' He shook his head. 'Yes, I suppose you are. These days you are. Was a time, though . . .'

I didn't contradict him. There didn't seem much point. We got the details straight and then as he slowly finished his milk, he said, 'You're still looking good, Bobby. Really fit, know what I mean?

And you've still got the same look, like old wotsis-name. You don't change a lot.'

I nodded. 'Well, I go to the gym three times a week, pump a bit of iron, hit the punchbags, that sort of stuff. I like it. I like being in good shape.'

'What's your weight these days, same as before?'

'Bit heavier. Five pounds, little more perhaps.'

He gave a small, wry grin. 'Not like me. I'm losing weight, God knows how. I've dropped nearly a stone this year. Must be all the worry.'

'Well, when you've got out of hospital and done the job give me a ring and I'll take you to the gym. They'll build you up. A few months working out and you'll be a regular little Sylvester Stallone.'

'That'll be the day.' He put his glass down on the table, thanked me for the milk and went home to Edgware and Vera and another video nasty. As he scurried out of the restaurant, stooping slightly, one hand clutched to his stomach he looked like a very old man.

2

THE HOTEL ARNIE HAD SENT ME TO was in a street off Piccadilly, up near Green Park. It had been constructed by knocking three large terraced houses together and it looked fairly new, very expensive and very discreet. I got there five minutes early and parked, with surprising ease, a few yards away. Getting to places early is something that's always happening to me; I have this obsession about punctuality. God knows how many hours I must have spent hanging around outside restaurants and people's homes waiting to arrive on time. Sometimes I think, the hell with it – this time I'm going to be late. And I still get there early and spend five minutes sitting in the car, listening to the radio, until – bang on time – I knock on the door and find my hostess with her hair in curlers and my host in his shirt sleeves, saying, 'Yes, I know we invited you for eight but we didn't think you'd *be* here at eight . . .' And then they let me in, give me a drink and go away to finish dressing while I'm left there feeling not like a man who had the courtesy to be punctual but like some desperate freeloader determined not to miss a single Scotch, a single pea-nut, a single tortilla chip or anything else on offer.

This time, while I waited for 7.30 to come around, I sat in the car thinking about what I was doing there anyway. In effect I was an accessory before a crime because indirectly I was about to help Arnie murder somebody. No doubt I should have felt bad about that but I didn't. My knowledge of Arnie's professional activities was pretty vague but I didn't think he was in the business of killing civilians. He liked, as it were, to keep death in the family, acting as final arbiter in disputes between incompatible criminals. Before last night I hadn't seen him for at least three years, so it was possible that he had widened his sphere of activities and was now pre-pared to hit anybody so long as the price was right. He was a greedy little bastard who, as his trade indicated, was prepared to do anything for money. But in the past, as far as I was aware, his victims were scumbags of one kind or another and no real loss to anybody, usually grasping and ruthless vil-lains who had been misguided enough to upset other villains quite as ruthless and grasping as themselves and even more powerful. I just hoped nothing had changed.

At 7.30 precisely I presented myself at the recep-tion desk and was told that Mr Jinks was expecting me. Second floor, room 205. It was a nice hotel, lots of dark wood and expensive carpeting, some good prints on the walls and plenty of indoor plants in elegant pots.

The man who opened the door of room 205 was in his late fifties, just above medium height and what the Americans would call heavy-set. Other people would say he was pretty fat but his was obviously rich fat. There's a difference between rich fat and poor fat. Poor fat speaks of junk food, chip butties, too much beer and a generally rotten diet. Rich fat is a testimony to years of tucking into three-star troughs and château-bottled wines. Poor fat has pimples and a rough complexion. Rich fat has smooth, pink skin. But perhaps the essential difference is not so much the quality of the fat as what it's dressed in and Jinks – though I was sure that was not his real name – was dressed in pale grey slacks, soft leather loafers with tassels, a heavy silk shirt and a pale pink cashmere sweater. Most of his head was bald and what little hair he had was grey and cropped. He wore aviator glasses with thin gold frames and he looked a bit like Erich Von Stroheim.

He said, 'Crossbow?'

'Longbow,' I said.

'Yeah. Right. Longbow.' He didn't say how do you do, nice to see you or even come in. He just turned away from me and walked back into the room, leaving me to follow. I got the swift impression that he didn't bother too much with social niceties.

'It's spelt L-o-n-g-b-o-w,' I said, closing the door behind me, 'not L-o-n-g-b-a-u-g-h.'

He glanced back over his shoulder, scowling. 'Why the fuck should I care?'

'It's not a matter of caring,' I said. 'It's more a matter of interest. You see, Harry Longbaugh, with the b-a-u-g-h spelling, was the real name of the Sundance Kid but I have a theory that both names come from the same root and perhaps the b-o-w variation was introduced because it's simpler. Now, if that's so, everybody of that name, however they spell it or pronounce it – and sometimes the b-a-u-g-h people pronounce it as in the bow of a ship – is related to everybody else of that name. Therefore the probability is that I am in some way descended from the Sundance Kid.'

At least I now had his full attention, though this wasn't necessarily all good news because I seemed to have upset him. Some people just aren't receptive to information and Jinks was one of them. He looked at me with distaste. 'You are some weird asshole, you know that?' He had a New York accent, neither particularly rough nor particularly cultured.

'Just presenting my credentials,' I said, trying to placate him. 'I thought, bearing in mind the task for which you are thinking of employing me, you might be reassured to learn that I was related, however distantly, to the Sundance Kid. After all, he was supposed to be the fastest gun in the West.'

He wasn't an easy man to placate. 'Jesus!' he said. The room was of reasonable size and furnished with discreet good taste. A navy blue cashmere blazer with big white buttons had been tossed casually onto the bed. On the dressing table were a Gucci briefcase, a bottle of Glenfiddich, a bowl of ice and two glasses. There were no other signs that anybody occupied the place, none of the bits and pieces that people usually spread around a hotel room to build a nest for themselves. Obviously Jinks had rented it solely for the purposes of this meeting.

He said, still giving me the scowl, 'Do I know you? You look kind of familiar.'

I adopted the modest expression I always use on these occasions. 'Michael Caine,' I said.

'What?'

'People tell me I look like Michael Caine. Before

he made all the money and put on the weight. Of course, there are differences. My hair is darker than his and I don't wear it curly like he's taken to doing lately. And you'll notice I don't need glasses – 20-20 vision, me. There are those who say I sound like Michael Caine, too, but I don't entirely go along with that. I mean, for a start I don't hit the aspirates as hard as he does. See, one of the big differences between him and me is that I had the disadvantage of an education and he didn't, which is probably why he's very rich and I'm not. But because of the education I've never had any trouble with aspirates while he drives them in with a sledgehammer so that nobody can ever accuse him of dropping an aitch again.'

Jinks said, 'What the hell is this? First I get a fucking history lesson, then you give me all this shit about Michael Caine . . .' He went over to the dressing-table and poured himself a big Scotch over ice. He didn't offer me one. 'In the first place,' he said when he'd taken a hefty gulp, 'if you look like Michael Caine I look like Meryl Streep. And in the second place, why would you want to look like a movie star anyway, a man in your line of work?' I don't think he was really interested in the answer. He was just trying to size me up and perhaps to recover his balance because, if nothing else, I seemed to have got him on the wrong foot.

'It's an advantage,' I said. 'If there are any wit-nesses – and naturally I try to make sure there aren't – but if there are any, what do they say? "Michael Caine did it," they say. And while the police are putting out an all points bulletin on Michael Caine I slip into my Harrison Ford disguise and take the first plane out of town.'

While I was talking he had put his glass down, opened the briefcase and slipped his hand inside. When it came out it was holding a little gun, a .22, and he was pointing it at me. I was astonished. 'What are you doing with that?' I said. 'You're not allowed to carry handguns in this country.'

'Easy now,' he said. 'Just ease off, okay? I'm getting a very bad feeling about this whole goddamn situation. I don't like you and I don't like your big mouth. Are you sure you're Harry Longbaugh?'

'No,' I said. 'I'm sure I'm not. I'm *Arnie* Longbow. Harry Longbaugh was the Sundance –'

'Shut up. Just shut up. Okay? I've had it with you and your crazy talk. I want you out of here. I don't know who you are, but whoever the hell you are I don't need you. I'll get somebody else . . .'

I stepped up to him and took hold of the gun. He resisted, glaring at me, but only for a moment and then his grip relaxed and I took the thing away from him. He stepped back, still glaring, though now there was fear in his eyes as well.

'You took a goddamn chance,' he said. 'How did you know I wasn't going to use that?'

'Because if you were going to use it, there'd be no need for me to be here in the first place, would there? If you had the guts to shoot me you wouldn't need me to do whatever it is you want done. You'd have the guts to do it yourself. Look, you're worried about me. You're not sure of me. All right, I can understand the caution; it's good. So let me put it simply: I'm Arnie Longbow and Donovan sent me because you went to Donovan and asked for somebody like me. Does that satisfy you? If it doesn't, call Donovan and check it out.'

And to my indignation that's what he did. He

called my bluff and I hadn't really thought he would. He gave a sort of grunt and eased around me, went to the phone beside the bed and started dialling. I put his little gun down on top of the briefcase and moved towards the door. Any minute now the shit would hit the fan and I didn't want to be caught standing underneath.

Into the phone he said, 'Donovan? Jinks.' I could hear Donovan squawking at the other end, though I couldn't make out the words. I leaned nonchalantly against the wall, with my fingers resting on the door handle. Jinks said, 'I just want to be sure, is all. How do I know who this guy is? You wanna descri . . . Okay, okay. *I'll* describe him.' He turned to look at me. 'About six foot, dark hair, blue eyes, around 170 pounds, give or take, very good condition, has some kind of London accent and talks like somebody who wanted to be a professor of English but flunked the course.' I didn't know whether Donovan would recognise me from that description but he sure as hell wouldn't recognise Arnie.

The squawking at the other end stopped for a moment, then started again. Jinks listened, said, 'Okay, if that's what you want,' and held the receiver towards me. 'He wants to talk to you.'

I took the instrument from him and, because he was hovering close, ushered him coldly away. He went over to the dressing-table and put more whisky and ice into his drink.

'Hello,' I said into the phone.

'Who the bleedin' hell's that?' Donovan said.

'Yes, that's right, boss, it's me,' I said.

There was a sharp intake of breath at the other end. 'Can he hear me?' Donovan asked. I said he couldn't. Jinks was standing roughly where I had been and it seemed a fair bet that if, from there, I hadn't been able to hear what Donovan was saying Jinks wouldn't be able to either.

'Bobby!' Donovan said. 'I thought it must be you. What the fuck are you doing there?'

'Right,' I said. 'No problem, boss.'

'Where's bloody Arnie?'

'Of course I'm sure,' I said. 'No problem at all. Mr Jinks and I have just been getting to know each other.'

There was another pause at the other end. 'All right,' Donovan said, 'all right. But there'd better be a bloody good reason why you're there and Arnie's not.'

'I told you: there's no problem. It's cool.'

Donovan said, 'Listen to me carefully. There'd better be no problem because there are some very important people involved here. You taking this in, are you? Some *very* important people, who can become very *nasty* if they're fucked about and I don't want 'em fucked about. Do you understand what I'm saying to you?'

'Every word,' I said. 'In whatever order you use them I understand them.'

'Good. So put Jinks back on.'

I waved the phone at Jinks. 'He wants to talk to you again.'

He swallowed his Scotch and grabbed the receiver from me. I took his place by the dressing-table and poured myself a drink. Jinks said, 'Yeah, okay. Look, I'm sorry, all right? I just can't afford to take any chances and this is a very weird guy you've sent me. You say he's okay, then he's okay but he's not what I expected, is all.' He hung up. To me he said, 'Donovan says you're okay.'

'Well, of course he does,' I said. 'So now we've got that settled, who do you want hit?'

He lowered himself onto the bed, first moving the cashmere blazer away from his buttocks. Rich people may be careless about their clothes but not so careless that they sit on them. 'The smart question is not who but where.'

I sighed. 'Okay, I'll bite. Where?'

'California,' he said. 'LA. Hollywood. Beverly Hills. That kind of area. Do you have any problem with that?'

'No.' I shook my head. 'I do have one question, though: why do you want me? Why not use local talent, someone who knows the neighbourhood?'

He gestured to me to pass the whisky bottle, a casual, imperious gesture as if in his everyday life there was always someone around to carry out onerous tasks like picking up whisky bottles for him. I poured a generous slug into his glass and added a couple of cubes of ice with my fingers. He frowned – in his everyday life people probably did that with silver tongs – but he didn't say anything. 'I'm a careful man,' he said. 'I want somebody hurt very badly –'

'Dead is about as badly hurt as you can be,' I said, in my philosophical way.

He ignored that. '– and when this goes down there's going to be one hell of an uproar. The cops will be charging around like their balls are on fire. So when that happens I don't want whoever has done the job to be even in the same country, let alone the same town. Does that satisfy you?'

'Yes. So I ask again: who do you want hit?'

'Right now that's none of your business.'

'It's entirely my business,' I said. 'If you're

putting out a contract on a little old lady who lives in a remote shack in the Hollywood Hills, that's one thing. But if the mark you have in mind is a six-foot six-inch, 220-pound, black-belt karate expert with a sawn-off shotgun tucked down his jockstrap, then we're talking something else again. I have to know these things.'

He nodded slowly. 'I take the point. Let me think about that for a while. Meantime, here's the deal . . .' He got up, took a long white envelope from the Gucci briefcase and carried it back to the bed. 'In here there's 500 dollars. That's just expenses. You take it away with you tonight. Plus I'll fix for you to pick up a return air ticket to LA and I'll book you into a hotel somewhere around Sunset Boulevard. When you get out there I'll contact you again, give you names, addresses, anything you need and that's when we'll arrange about payment.' He set his mouth in a firm line and gave me the kind of hard stare that probably intimidated everyone in his business life, whatever that was. I was unimpressed. In my former trade I had been used to taking hard stares from people much more frightening than he was. And besides I had a pretty good line in hard stares myself.

'You prick,' I said. 'Now I'll tell *you* the deal.' I gave him my own hard stare and it worked. He held my gaze only for a few seconds and then he looked down at his shining, tasselled loafers.

The effect of that stare always surprised me. For a long time I'd had no idea how chilling it could be but one night at a charity dinner in a London hotel I overheard two people talking about me. They were quite unaware that I was around and one of them said, 'Bobby Lennox? Christ! Tell you the truth, that man scares me. He has the coldest eyes I've ever seen.' I was amazed. The first thing I did was go to the men's room and examine my eyes in the mirror. They looked like nice, warm eyes to me – blue and friendly and amused. Then I put on the hard stare and I saw how they changed. The man was right – they were cold. But what he didn't know was that there was nothing personal about it. It was just a professional trick, one that everybody in my trade used.

So I gave Jinks the full, 100-watt, blue-ice glare and said, 'One, I'll take the 500 dollars as a gesture of good faith. Two, I want a first-class return ticket to LA – no economy crap. Three, the fee is 50,000 and if we're not talking sterling here we're not talking anything at all. Four, I want half the money upfront. Five, I have to know now who I'm going to hit.'

And at this point we started haggling. He didn't want to give me half the money in advance because how did he know he could trust me? How did he know I wouldn't just take it and run? I refused (on Arnie's behalf, let us remember) even to contemplate the job without the fifty per cent upfront because how did I know I could trust Jinks? I could end up on Sunset Boulevard, I said, with a lousy 500 dollars in my pocket to discover that while I was halfway across the Atlantic he had changed his mind and I would never hear from him again. And what was I supposed to do, stuck in Hollywood, with a lousy 500 dollars? Go to Disneyland? Do the Universal Studios tour? Visit Knottsberry Farm? I'd done all that once before and didn't want to do it again, and so what if I hadn't seen Magic Mountain? I could live without it. So we compromised. I would take the 500 dollars and the first-class air ticket and he would book the hotel. But if there wasn't another 10,000 dollars waiting for me when I checked in I would check right out again and catch the first plane home. The day after I arrived, he said, he would contact me and we would meet and he would give me the rest of the advance money, plus the name of the intended victim.

I agreed to most of that but . . . 'No more meetings,' I said. 'This will be the first and last time we meet.' After all, I wasn't going to LA: Arnie was and Jinks had never seen Arnie. 'If there's a screw-up I don't want any connection between you and me. When I get to LA you send me the name, address and money by post, special messenger, whichever you reckon is safest.'

He considered this carefully. 'Okay. But let's say I send you half the ante, you do the job and then I vanish and don't pay the rest of the money. What do you do then?'

'Consider it from the other angle,' I said. 'What if I get to LA, pick up the 10,000 dollars and then go straight home? What would you do in those circumstances?'

He gave me a vicious little grin. 'I got contacts in LA. I got people, I give them the right kind of money, they'll find you and hurt you bad. For the job I have in mind I don't want to use them because it's going to cause too much heat. But for dealing with someone like you, no problem.'

'Good,' I said, 'because I've got contacts, too. I know Jinks isn't your real name. I don't care right now what your real name is – it doesn't even matter. But if you double-cross me I'll have your name, address and inside leg measurement within twenty-four hours and twenty-four hours after that I'll be coming round to visit you. Do we understand each other?' To be frank I had no clear idea what I was talking about but it sounded good to me and it must have have sounded good to Jinks because he seemed to believe me. He nodded soberly and said, 'Yeah, I guess we understand each other.'

'So. When do you want me in the States?' I hoped it would not be too soon because I didn't know what kind of condition Arnie would be in when he got out of hospital.

To my relief Jinks said, 'Well, I got some business to do here in Europe, maybe take a few days. Then I'd like to get back to California a day or two before you arrive, arrange a few things, make sure the money's waiting for you. What's today – Thursday? Right. Thursday. Okay, by tomorrow night, maybe Saturday morning, I'll have my schedule worked out. Is there any place I can contact you Saturday, around noon?'

I gave him the name and number of a wine bar I use in Kensington. He said he'd call me there between twelve and one on Saturday and got up as if the meeting was over. I stayed where I was, leaning against the dressing-table and sipping my drink.

'I still have to know who I'm going to hit.'

'And I'm not going to tell you,' he said. 'Not till you get there.'

'You *are* an exceedingly cautious man,' I said, 'and I appreciate that. But I can't go into this thing blind. I have to know the kind of person I'm supposed to deal with.'

He thought about that for a few moments. Then: 'No names. Not yet. Not till you're someplace I can keep an eye on you. But . . .' He took a deep breath. 'I'll show you a picture.' He went to his briefcase and took out not one but two photographs.

'*Two* people?' I said. 'If I'd known that, the price –'

'We made a deal, remember? Besides, it should only be the difference between one bullet and two. When the time comes you'll find them both in the same place.'

He gave me the photographs. The first was of a man in his early forties. It was hard to tell from a photo but he gave the impression of being fairly tall. He certainly looked lean and fit but I'd have said he was swimming and tennis fit rather than martial arts fit. I didn't think he would scare me too much. He was standing beside a pool, wearing a friendly grin and expensive, casual California clothes. The other picture was of a woman. She was a few years younger than the man, blonde and very beautiful and rather grave. She had been photographed in a street somewhere, possibly, I thought, Rodeo Drive, and her clothes – a simple white top and a short, dark blue skirt – looked very expensive, too.

'Who are they?' I asked, as he took the pictures away from me again.

'You'll find out. Do you think they'll give you any trouble?'

'From the look of them, no. Why do you want them dead?'

'You don't have to know that. Not now, not ever.' He put the photographs back in his briefcase, locked it, took the empty glass out of my hand and eased me towards the door. 'I'll call you Saturday,' he said. And then I was back in the corridor again.

I went down the stairs, out onto the street and along to my car and waited there. Half an hour passed and Jinks didn't emerge. I went back into the hotel and attracted the attention of the receptionist, a superior young man in a dark suit. 'Mr Jinks,' I said, 'I think I left my glasses in his room.'

'Mr Jinks is no longer with us, sir,' he said. 'He checked out a quarter of an hour ago. But I'll ask the housekeeper to look for your glasses. Could you describe them for me?'

I wasted another ten minutes while the housekeeper went into room 205 to search for a nonexistent pair of horn-rimmed spectacles. Not that time mattered any more. Jinks had been long gone before I returned to the hotel.

'Is there another entrance to this place?' I asked.

'Yes, sir,' said the receptionist. 'It's in the street behind us. Mr Jinks left that way, as a matter of fact.'

The housekeeper phoned down to say she couldn't find my glasses.

'You wouldn't have a forwarding address for Mr Jinks, would you?' I said. 'He may have taken my specs with him.'

'No, sir. Mr Jinks was only with us for a short time and left no word as to where he was going.'

'That kind of place, is it?' I said bad-temperedly. 'You can rent rooms by the hour, can you?'

He looked at me with cold disdain. 'Certainly not. Mr Jinks paid the full daily rate. Where he went from here is none of our business.' Nor, he implied, mine either.

I returned to my car and drove away from there and I was not in a happy mood. I was disturbed, I was shocked and I was very worried. What I had done since leaving Jinks had not been for Arnie but for me. Because I knew the woman in the photograph. Her name was Beverley Timkins and I had once killed a man for her.

3

THE MAN I KILLED was the debt that Arnie claimed I owed him. Or one of the debts. Donovan was involved in it. Donovan was involved in much of my life in those days. I had first met him when I was about twelve years old. My father had just died and my mother had decided to move herself and me back from the Essex village to which the old man had taken us when I was a baby to the street where she had been born, where she had met him and where they had continued to live for a few years after their marriage. It was in London, south of the Thames, not far from the Elephant and Castle and though, naturally, it had a name it was known to its inhabitants simply as The Street. Most of them, like my mother, had been born there or at least had lived there for most of their lives and they formed a small, close community, almost like a village, which was responsible for considerably more than its share of London's petty crime and, in some cases, major villainy as well. It was – still is – a long, narrow cul-de-sac, but it has changed a lot since my mother took me back there. A good few years ago the local council moved in and improved it. They bought and tore down the rows of little terraced houses and replaced them with tower blocks. Almost overnight the two-storey slums were replaced by multi-storey slums. That was progress. In my time The Street was a no-go area for the police unless they patrolled it in pairs. Now it's a no-go area even for cops in patrol cars with riot gear. That's progress, too, I suppose.

My father took me and my mother away from there – not because he thought it was an unsuitable environment for a baby but because he was a sour, embittered man who believed The Street had let him down. Life had been a continual source of disappointment to him since the Second World War broke out. He was about nineteen then and had just become the getaway driver for a team of armed robbers who operated out of The Street. They had knocked over a couple of post offices in north London and were working their way up to their first bank job when the war started and my father was called up. Donovan was part of that team, the man who carried the shotgun. I don't know what the hierarchy is in a team of armed robbers but I imagine the man with the shotgun ranks a little higher than the getaway driver, though you would never have thought so to hear my father talk. Anyway, he was called up into the army and so was one of the other partners in the enterprise. Donovan, who was a year older than my father, somehow managed to stay out of the services as did the leader of the team, a man in his early thirties. I don't know how they arranged it but I suspect they were shrewd enough to give the right amounts of money to the right people.

My old man hated the army and so did his mate. They each tried to desert twice, hoping to be able to return home proudly boasting dishonourable discharges, and resume their interrupted business careers. But the army unsportingly refused to let them go, sending them instead to the glasshouse and then to the front line. The other fellow was killed at El Alamein and my father lost his left arm in the Normandy landings, which turned out to be a more effective way of getting out of the forces than anything he had tried before. When he got back to The Street he discovered that the original leader of his gang had been murdered by three American GIs in a pub brawl in Soho and Donovan was now in charge of everything.

The war had been very kind to Donovan. He had got in early on the black market and built up from there. By the time my old man returned he was already running several books, a couple of gaming clubs and an expensive brothel in Mayfair. He had also bought a lot of property in the West End, arguing that the value was bound to increase once the bombing stopped, and he was masterminding the activities of two or three teams of hold-up men. My father, who had always regarded himself and Donovan as competitors, was bitterly jealous of all this power and affluence and the jealousy turned to hatred when he went to his erstwhile colleague and rival to get his old job back and was told that, even in such a time of manpower shortage, there was very little demand for one-armed getaway drivers.

It was a rebuff from which the old man never recovered. Years later, when the automatic gearbox was invented, he used to complain that he had been born before his time. 'If I was a young man now,' he would say, 'by Christ, I'd be the best getaway driver in the business. You only need one arm with them things.'

But in the cars available towards the end of the war, two arms were a minimum requirement. In the end my father grudgingly accepted that and volunteered to do something else. He wouldn't mind, he told Donovan, taking part in the raids themselves, brandishing a shotgun or the service revolver he had stolen when he left the army. But Donovan was not keen on that either.

'A one-armed hold-up man', he said, 'is going to stick out like a boil on a stripper's arse. Forget it.'

For old times' sake he found my father various odd jobs to do but even that didn't work out too well because my old man had been fairly well back in the queue when they were handing out the brains and there wasn't a lot, aside from physical action, that he could cope with. That's one reason why I could never really understand why my mother married him, which she did around that time. I know from the family photo album that he was a very good-looking young man, with or without both arms, but he was undeniably on the thick side, while my mother was very bright indeed. I suppose she must have felt sorry for him; the maternal thing perhaps. In any case they married and stayed on in The Street until just after I was born, at which time my father's uncle died and left him a two-up, two-down cottage in one of the drabbest, ugliest villages in Essex. And my old man took us there into exile because his jealousy and hatred of the increasingly rich and influential Donovan had become insupportable.

In Essex he sat back, went into premature retirement and did virtually nothing until the day he died. My mother, who had taught herself shorthand, typing and book-keeping, earned whatever income we had, the old man's contribution to the family fortunes being restricted to a bit of one-armed shoplifting whenever we went into Southend or Colchester. He didn't like me much. By a lucky stroke of fortune I had inherited my mother's brains along with his looks and I don't think he really understood me because we had hardly anything in common. I would often catch him looking at me with a sort of puzzled scowl, as if I'd been dropped into the nest by some passing cuckoo. As I got older we barely talked to each other at all except when he'd had a few down at the village pub and then he would expound the curious philosophy that he had developed over the years.

'We was short-changed, us servicemen,' he would say. 'Went off to the war, do our bit for the country. "Don't worry," they said, "your jobs'll be waiting for you, you come back." And what happened? Eh? I ask you, what happened? I come back, short of an arm that's probably still hanging about on some beach in Normandy, and what do I find? Eh? Do I find me bleedin' job still waiting for me? Do I bloody heck. "Don't need you," they said, "one-armed git like you. Nobody needs you." Short-changed, that's what we was. I blame that bastard Donovan.'

And then he died, quite suddenly, quite young, of a stroke. It's an awful thing to say but neither of us mourned him much. My mother sold the cottage and then took us both back to The Street to live with her own mother and that's when I met Donovan. I had heard so much about him from my father, none of it good, that I greeted him at first with trepidation. He was a pretty big-time villain by then, not perhaps as big as the Richardsons or the Krays – though later on he was to become bigger than either and to last even longer – but he still lived in The Street, probably so as not to draw attention to himself. God knows what kind of income he admitted to the Inland Revenue but, living where he did, it could have been very small and still have seemed credible. He had a shop in The Street, a grocery business, and I imagine he declared himself as a grocer on his tax returns. In any event he took my mother on to run the shop and do the books for it while he conducted the rest of his activities from the two houses on either side. He doesn't live there now, of course. When betting shops and gaming clubs became legal he moved openly into both businesses, using nominees at first so that nobody would wonder where all his money had suddenly come from. And a few years before the council took over The Street he shifted out to Hampstead, a small flat to begin with, then a bigger one, then a house, then an estate in Norfolk as well. But he did things gradually and no doubt he always declared an income that was just about commensurate with his lifestyle. Donovan was ever a keen student of history, or at least the kind of history that was pertinent to his professional affairs. 'Never forget,' he said to me, not once but many times, 'it wasn't the Filth brought down Al Capone, it was the bleedin' Inland Revenue. Stupid bastard lived like a king and declared a pauper's income. Don't ever make that mistake, young Bobby.'

To me, a twelve-year-old, he was an awe-inspiring figure, a tall, burly, strong-looking man with a big Irish head and a thick mop of curly, ginger hair. He didn't speak like an Irishman and he always denied that he was one. 'I was born here, in The Street,' he said, 'and my old man was born in Aldgate. I'm a Cockney, not a bloody Mick.' But he was proud of his name and when a pop singer came along who was also called Donovan, he grew quite irate and one night, when he'd had a few drinks, talked of sending a couple of the boys round to the singer's house to break his legs for him. 'Fucking liberty!' he said. 'Taking my name, *my* name, and using it to promote that pop crap.'

But the mood passed and the singer was allowed to pursue his career without grievous bodily harm. In any case the outburst was unusual; Donovan rarely did anything in anger, still less in drink.

Anyway, he took me and my mother into his patronage. I think at one time he must have fancied her rather a lot and maybe still did because he had an obvious affection for her and I benefited from that, too. It took me some time to be accepted by my peer group in The Street because I was the only kid in the neighbourhood who went to grammar school. All the others attended the local secondary modern – or they did when they felt like it, which wasn't often – and spent most of their time there writing graffiti on the walls, terrorising the teachers and trying to burn the place down. I'd have been happy enough helping them but my mother wouldn't have it. When I passed the eleven-plus she insisted that I was to have a proper education, one that would leave me with loftier ambitions than to be a getaway driver like my father.

The other boys in The Street regarded me as a kind

43

of toffee-nosed freak and used to beat me up regularly in a fairly dispassionate way as if they were performing some kind of necessary public service.

One day Donovan caught them doing it and though he didn't interfere he came up to me after they'd left me sitting in the gutter, bleeding from nose and mouth, and said, 'What you want to do, son, you want to learn how to fight. Get yourself fit, build up some muscle. Then you can give those little shits some of their own medicine.'

The next day I joined the boys' club in the next borough and pretty soon I was in the boxing team. I had a talent for it and a hunger, a need to do as Donovan had suggested and give those little shits some of their own medicine. It worked, too. I never exactly walked up to the biggest bully and challenged him to a fight. I wasn't that dumb because he was about three years older and twenty pounds heavier than I was. And besides, the opportunity could never have arisen because they always attacked me mob-handed. But after a while they began to realise that they, too, were coming away from our regular encounters with bloody noses, black eyes and loose teeth and gradually they stopped picking on me. And later, when I started winning local and then London and eventually national schoolboy and boys' club championships, they left me alone entirely and even became rather proud of me. I was still a freak but I was a freak who could fight and that counted for a lot.

When I was sixteen I started working for Donovan at weekends and in school holidays and that added to my street cred. I didn't do a lot – running errands mostly – and I don't think I did anything illegal, although quite often I found myself carrying strange packages from one part of London to another. I never knew what was in them and I never tried to find out; in The Street it wasn't exactly healthy to enquire too closely into Donovan's business. But at least I was pretty sure I wasn't carrying drugs. Donovan had a violent antipathy to the drug trade because his own nephew, his sister's son, had OD'd at the age of nineteen on heroin and after that Donovan declared war on the dealers. Any of his own people found to be trafficking on the side were punished severely and I know of at least one big-time drugs baron who, having been charged, tried and acquitted on some legal technicality, had a fatal accident visited upon him the following day by Arnie, whose fee was paid by Donovan in the guise of philanthropist. To Donovan the money spent was indeed a kind of charitable donation, even though he could hardly charge it against his income tax. Later on, when he had become a respectable businessman, he sat on official anti-drugs committees, often alongside high-ranking policemen who had been in his pocket for years.

At eighteen I went to university – not Oxbridge but one of the good newer places in the Midlands – to read English literature. And by then I was in love with Beverley and she, I think, was in love with me. She was a couple of years younger than me, she lived at the other end of The Street and she was a prostitute. No, I didn't love her *because* she was a prostitute – I have my faults but I'm not that kinky. I loved her in spite of it. In any case, no kind of moral judgement was involved; with her family background she could hardly have been anything but a prostitute. She came from a line of whores that stretched back through her mother and her grandmother and probably way beyond that. I doubt if there was a female member of her family for the last hundred years who knew the identity of her own father. Bev's mother put her on the game when she was fourteen, by which time she was already tall, leggy and remarkably well-developed. That was when I first became aware of her, though it was not for another year that we started going out together and I didn't sleep with her until she was sixteen. Come to think of it, ours was a bizarre courtship and it must have made her practically schizophrenic. On the one hand she was turning tricks for any man with the price in his pocket, and on the other she was being escorted in her spare time by me, who treated her like an underage (which she was), virginal schoolgirl (which she certainly wasn't).

And yet when we finally went to bed together, on the night of her sixteenth birthday, she behaved as if it was the first time for her. I wasn't totally inexperienced but I was hardly the greatest swords-man south of the Thames and she must have known more about the mechanics of sex than I could even imagine. But she let me take the lead and I felt strong and masterful and protective and great because she had reached the age of consent and what we had done was legal and now, at last, she was truly my girlfriend. All right, at that time she probably made the bulk of her living by pre-tending to be a virgin while fat, middle-aged per-verts snorted and grunted all over her but I believed then, and I still believe now, that what she felt with me was different, was genuine.

The day after she reached sixteen Donovan took her into one of his houses in the West End. This was a neat stroke of business on his part because she was a very good-looking girl but it was also, to give him credit, altruistic. Before then he had refused to have anything to do with her for fear that if one of his tame coppers suddenly became overambitious and mounted a raid on one of his premises, the discovery of an underage girl doing naughty things with an MP or a captain of industry or whatever might lead the courts to view him, Donovan, with particular disapproval. But she needed somebody like him. At fifteen, and with only her boozy mother to look after her interests, she had had a lot of difficulty with prospective pimps, had acquired a police record and at one time had been in the care of a probation officer. Donovan, who always looked after his own – which is to say the people who lived in The Street – had seen off the pimps, no trouble, but there was little he could do about the other, legal problems. It was, in part, to save her from any repetition of these that he had recruited her into his house in Mayfair.

I hated to see her go there but then I hated her profession anyway, not that we ever really discussed it. She didn't like to talk about it, and God knows I didn't wish to hear what other men did with her. Once, though, I was supposed to be taking her to the movies but when I called to pick her up she was all rigged out in her tart's uniform – hair in pigtails, white shirt, tiny gym slip, stockings, suspenders and high-heeled shoes. She looked like the nymphomaniac captain of some school hockey team.

She said, 'Bobby, I'm ever so sorry. I've got to work tonight. The motor show's on, hundreds of randy car salesmen in town and they want all the girls in.'

Just for a moment there I almost hated her. I certainly hated Donovan. I said, 'For Chrissake, do you have to do this? Why can't you get a decent job?'

But she just shrugged and said, 'Well, it's better than working at Woolworths.' In a sense, of course, she was right – financially it was a lot better. And she was right in another sense, too, because a job at Woolworths or on a production line was probably the only alternative for her. I don't mean she was stupid: she was anything but. She was bright and shrewd and street smart and she had a lot of common sense but she had no academic ability. Unlike me she wasn't an exam passer and I suppose the best she could have hoped for in the world of 'respectable' employment was to become somebody's typist.

But she didn't want that. She had dreams of her own. What she wanted was to be a dancer, to land a job in the chorus of a big musical and be discovered there and swept away to become the Ginger Rogers to some latterday Fred Astaire. A lot of the money she made from hooking went on dancing lessons and by the time we became lovers she was regularly attending auditions for West End shows. One day I went with her. She wasn't too keen on my being there and she made me creep into the auditorium and sit unobtrusively at the back while she did her stuff. Obviously I was biased but it seemed to me that she danced quite as well as any of the others and was a whole lot sexier. But when the audition was over she came back to me and said, 'Oh well, another unscheduled disaster.'

'You didn't get the job?'

She gave me a wry little grin. 'Got to hand it to you, Bob, you grasp things quick.' I was still groping around to find some way to comfort her when she said, 'The choreographer wants me to have a coffee with her. Will you come?'

'Sure,' I said.

So we went together to the café next to the theatre where the choreographer was waiting. She didn't seem particularly pleased to see me though she shook hands politely enough. 'Are you a dancer, too?' she asked. I said I wasn't and from then on she ignored me. But she was nice to Bev, telling her that technically she was good but that there was something missing, that she didn't seem to feel the music enough, that she didn't move as if dancing was the natural, instinctive way for her to get from one place to another. It was probably a load of crap but it sounded impressive to me and at the end she said, 'I can teach you. I can make you better.' Bev looked doubtful and the woman said, 'I know, you're worried about the cost. Well, there's no need. The first couple of times you come to me we'll see how it goes and after that, if we both feel it's worth continuing, well, we'll already have worked out the payment, won't we?' Bev mumbled something and the woman said, 'Well, look, here's my card. That's my home number at the bottom. Call me there.' Then she patted Bev gently on the cheek, paid for the coffee and left.

I said, 'That sounds like a pretty good offer. You'll take her up on it, won't you?'

Bev shook her head.

I said, 'Why? D'you think it's some kind of con? Get you there and make you sign on the dotted line? I'm sure it won't be like that.'

She looked at me with all the wisdom of her profession in her eyes. 'Of course it won't be like that.

She won't charge me any money and she sure won't give me any dancing lessons. She's a dyke, Bobby. She was sitting there groping my thigh. It's a good job I'm wearing jeans or she'd have had my knickers off. All she wants is to get into my pants and she's not going to because I don't fancy dykes.'

That happened during my first summer vacation from university. My going away hadn't seemed to damage our relationship at all. We wrote to each other every week and a few times she came up to the Midlands to spend the weekend with me. Instinctively she dressed exactly right for the occasion, just like the girl students. And they liked her because although she was younger than they were, she seemed older and wiser. Well, let's face it, she was in the right trade to make a girl older and wiser before her time. So they went to her for advice on their love life and whatever she told them must have been good because for days after one of her visits I'd have women coming up to me, saying, 'Is Bev going to be here at the weekend? There's something I want to talk to her about.'

The male students fancied her desperately but that didn't cause any problems because she had a way of brushing them off without hurting their feelings, although there was one occasion when a lad with a title and money in his family and a history of getting everything he wanted came on a little too strongly even for her. But that was where The Street came in handy. I watched him pawing her and I sized him up and, though he was big and hefty, I knew I could handle him. So I took him outside and using methods that would have had me disqualified and probably banned for life if I'd tried them in the ring I made it clear to him that there were some things you didn't do to a lady, even if the lady was a hooker. Not that he, or any of them, had the faintest idea that Bev was a hooker. Anyway, I gave him a few thoughts to meditate upon while a couple of his friends helped him back to his room and they had to help him because, temporarily at least, he couldn't walk straight any more.

During my second year at university Bev was raped. The man who raped her was a probation officer named Anderson, a fellow in his mid-thirties with a wife and a couple of kids. He had not been Bev's probation officer but he had come into contact with her when she was busted at fifteen and the authorities had taken a brief interest in her welfare. At that time he had found opportunities to get her on her own and try to touch her up. She hadn't taken much notice then because men were always trying to touch her up. But one night in the summer when she was seventeen and walking home after a day shift at Donovan's whorehouse he had come by in his car and grabbed her and taken her to some disused site on an industrial estate south of the river and there he had done things to her that even newspapers like the *Sun* or the *News of the World* would have found themselves too decorous to mention. He had been particularly inventive with a beer bottle and Bev told me later that she was pretty sure he would have killed her if a courting couple hadn't parked nearby and distracted him enough for her to get out of the car and stagger into a busy high street round the corner. Somehow she had managed to get home where she found her mother dead drunk and asleep and because she felt defiled she had burnt her thin summer dress and bathed and scrubbed herself and gone to bed.

In the night she began to haemorrhage badly. Her mother, who had now recovered enough to be useful, phoned for an ambulance and Bev was taken to hospital. Because of the nature of her injuries a policewoman was called and questioned her and Bev blew the whistle on the probation officer.

So he was charged and there was a trial and I came home for it. Bev was a loser from the start because there was no forensic evidence on her side. It was her word against his. The dress had been destroyed, the underwear Anderson had ripped off her in the car was never found and the traces of semen inside her could have belonged to a couple of million men. In the witness box, Anderson was immensely plausible. Yes, he knew the girl. He had met her several times two years ago when she was the client of a colleague of his. In fact, she had made advances towards him which, naturally, he had rebuffed, though he had felt even then that she was building a grudge against him because of it. His wife gave evidence, too, telling the world what a faithful husband and devoted father he was. I watched her carefully in the box and it seemed to me that she was terrified of the man but the court didn't appear to notice. What really told against Bev, though, was the cross-examination when she had to reveal why she was in the care of a probation officer in the first place. A hooker? Shit! That was more than enough for the judge, who belonged to the traditional school of the judiciary and saw women as either respectable and fragrant or disreputable, stinking and evil. Prostitutes were not fragrant and in his summing up he went after Bev like a hellfire preacher with the result that Anderson was dismissed without a stain on his character and with profuse apologies from the court for the awful embarrassment and inconvenience he had suffered.

I took Bev home with me that night and sat consoling and soothing her for hours. She slept, alone, in my room while I went to what had, until her death a few months earlier, been my grandmother's bedroom and lay awake for hours planning revenge against Anderson. But what revenge?

The next day I consulted Donovan about it and he said, 'I know what you mean, Bobby. I'm fucking livid about this. Bev's one of my people. But this is not the time. Anything happens to that bastard Anderson, the police are going to *know* who did it. It's got to be me, you, Bev, friends of hers – somebody close to her anyway. There's nothing we can do. He's got away with it.'

I think Anderson knew that, too. Because six months later he tried to rape her again. Again he grabbed her, physically, off the street and this time she got away by leaping out of the car when he slowed down to take a corner. She turned up, dishevelled and nearly hysterical, in the Red Lion, the pub on The Street where Donovan held court in the back room. He was there alone at the time and she told him what Anderson had said: that as far as she was concerned he was in the clear and would always be in the clear. That the court had decided she was a liar and would never believe her, whatever charge she brought against him. That he could do whatever he wanted to her, whenever he wanted, and the law couldn't touch him. That she was filthy, wicked, a slut, a bitch, that he was going to punish her and that if he wasn't able to punish her enough that night he would punish her again and again and again.

I heard about this an hour or so later when Donovan had sent her home escorted by a couple of minders and I called in to the pub to have a drink with him. He said, 'Something's got to be done this time, Bobby. The guy's a maniac. He's going to kill somebody some day, probably Bev.'

'I know that. I told you that last time. So what can we do?'

He said, 'If only Arnie was here . . .' Arnie was out of town at the time, even out of the country, I think, God knows where but obviously slaughtering somebody for money.

'Why wait for Arnie?' I said. 'I'll do it.'

'You?' Donovan looked at me dubiously. 'I don't think it's that easy, Bobby, killing somebody. You got to have the instinct for it.'

'In this case I've got the instinct,' I said. 'Besides, we can't afford to wait for Arnie. This bloke could have another go at Bev any time. Get me a gun and I'll see to it.' I knew about guns – rifles, shotguns, handguns – because there was a shooting club at the university and I was a fairly keen member of it. I wasn't exactly a marksman but I was good enough. 'Just one thing, though, when it's over I don't want Bev to know who did it. Tell her anything you like but don't tell her it was me.'

Donovan looked astonished. 'Why not? She'll love you for ever she thinks you did a thing like that for her.'

'Maybe. On the other hand she might not want to spend the rest of her life with a killer. Better she doesn't know.'

'Like that, is it?' Donovan said. 'Are you really sure? I mean, you're both a bit young to be talking about the rest of your lives. You're what, Christ, you're only nineteen and she's seventeen. Long time to go yet.'

'I hope so but that's our business, isn't it?'

He looked at me then for quite a long time and finally he smiled and shook his head. 'You know what I like about you, Bobby, why I've always taken an interest in you?'

'No.'

'You're not like your bloody father. I mean, you look like him but you're not like him. He was, and I say this with no disrespect, he was a total idiot, your old man. If brains were shit he didn't have enough for a wet fart. But you, you're like your mum and that's a very bright lady, too bloody bright for him anyway.'

It occurred to me then to ask him what, if anything, there had been between my mother and him before my father came along and then took her off into exile in gloomiest Essex, but I didn't. Donovan wouldn't have told me anyway. He said, 'Okay. I'll get you a gun. And Bev will never know anything.'

For the next couple of weeks he insisted that Bev stay at home or at least within the confines of The Street where he and his people could keep an eye on her and that was a wise precaution because Anderson's car was seen a couple of times cruising around the house in Mayfair where she usually worked. And it was spotted because Donovan had men following it, working out the pattern of his movements. What they discovered was that twice a week Anderson went to a pub a couple of miles from where he lived in Loughton and played darts. He wasn't much good at darts but he went to the pub because he was screwing one of the part-time barmaids. Every Wednesday and Friday he would leave the pub just before closing time and wait in his car for her to join him.

Donovan said, 'I think you should do it this coming Friday, Bobby. He follows normal procedure he'll come out about ten minutes before last orders, she'll come out ten minutes after they close. Give you twenty minutes to do it and be gone. Can you manage it?'

'I think so.'

'Good. Only don't take no chances. There's any possibility somebody's going to see you, forget it, we'll do it another day. Okay?'

As it turned out, Friday was perfect. It rained hard all evening but the pub was still crowded and when Anderson arrived a little later than I'd expected the car park was nearly full. The only space available for him was way out at the back and in near darkness. By then I had already been waiting an hour, sheltering under an oak tree at the other side of the car park, and I was soaked through. As Anderson drove in I started moving swiftly towards the one remaining space, using the other parked cars for cover. I know he didn't see me and neither did anyone else because in that rain there was nobody else about. So I thought, why wait till closing time? Do it now. I watched him get out of his car, pull up the collar of his raincoat and start to lock the door. Then I moved up behind him and said, 'Mr Anderson?'

He turned and said, 'Yes?' He was bigger than I had remembered, fatter, more florid.

'Mr Laurence Anderson, the probation officer?'

He said, irritably now, 'Yes. Yes, that's who I am. What do you want?'

I said, 'Bev says hello, Mr Anderson.' And then

I shot him between the eyes. The gun had no silencer but it didn't make a lot of noise. He looked at me with a curious, baffled expression on his face and I suppose anyone would be baffled who had just been shot by a complete stranger and then he slid down the side of his car and lay on his back in a puddle. His eyes were open and he was certainly dead. I rolled him over quite gently with my foot until he was under the car and then I walked away.

I had parked the Ford Donovan had provided by the station. As far as I knew nobody had seen me leave it there and there was certainly nobody around to see me drive it away again. When I had crossed the river I drove down among some warehouses and threw the gun out into the middle of the Thames. Nobody saw me do that either because the rain was sheeting down by now. I went back across Blackfriars Bridge and left the car, which one of Donovan's people had stolen earlier that evening, in a street off the Strand. Then I walked to Leicester Square and got a cab home. I had had a shower and a change of clothes and was having a Scotch with Donovan in the Red Lion before it was closing time in Loughton.

Donovan said, 'Everything go all right?'

I said, 'Fine,' and we never talked about it again, though the next day Donovan turned up at my house in a white MGB, secondhand but in marvellous condition, handed me the keys and said, 'Present for you.'

'It's not hot, is it?'

'Course not,' he said indignantly. 'It's absolutely kosher.'

'Then thanks very much,' I said.

4

I HAVE NO IDEA what you're supposed to feel after killing somebody. I felt nothing, certainly not remorse. The night I shot Anderson I had a few drinks and slept well and in the morning I felt good. I daresay it would have been hard to get Anderson to agree with me but in my opinion the world was a better place without him.

Donovan and I, the only two people who knew what I had done, kept quiet until the murder was announced on TV at lunchtime on the Saturday and then I went round to Bev's house and said, 'I've got great news. Anderson's dead.'

She said, 'What?'

'He's dead. Somebody shot him last night outside a pub in, I don't know, Essex somewhere. One of the barmaids found the body a bit after closing time.'

Bev said, 'Thank God. Oh, thank God! Isn't that marvellous?' And she threw herself at me with more passion than she had shown for months. 'I feel like it's Christmas. Let's go out somewhere, let's do something, let's celebrate.' And that's what we did. I took her up to the West End in my new car and we had lunch in Soho and drank to the death of Anderson.

Bev was curious about the car at first, wondering how I could have afforded it but I told her Donovan had offered me a special deal because I'd been such a good boy, running errands for him and carrying his mysterious packages about, and she accepted that. The police accepted our stories, too. They spent a few days sniffing suspiciously around The Street because of the rape case but I don't think they ever really believed Bev had killed Anderson, although they weren't so sure about Donovan. He had no criminal record – he doesn't have one now – but the cops are not fools and even those he didn't own had a pretty shrewd idea of the kind of things he got up to.

They couldn't break his alibi, though, nor Bev's, and I never claimed to have one which, curiously, seemed to work in my favour. If you think about it, innocent people usually don't have alibis; they don't need them. Besides, the police were just going through the motions really when they questioned those of us in The Street. The rape case had been some while back and the second attack on Bev had never been reported, and without knowledge of that there hardly seemed a strong enough motive for murder, especially when they found out about Anderson's affair with the barmaid. From what I read in the tabloids, the cops gave the woman's husband a hard time for a couple of weeks but eventually they abandoned that and the investigation ended up as dead as Anderson.

Anyway, that was the first favour that Arnie thought I owed him. By his reckoning it should have been his hit and therefore I had robbed him of his lawful fee. It was Donovan who told him I had done it. God knows why, though it was safe enough to do so. Arnie, of all people, was not about to tell anybody else. I think what happened was that they had fallen out over money. Arnie was asking for a rise in line with inflation or something. I couldn't say what economic criteria hitmen use when they want an increase in pay but whatever it was, Donovan lost his temper and told him about Anderson and how all I had got for the job was a secondhand MGB. I think it was this that upset Arnie most. For a while he seemed to regard me as a kind of scab or blackleg, going around undercutting honest professionals. It was the sort of thing that would offend his socialist principles.

Several months had passed, though, before Arnie learned these things and by then Bev had gone out of my life. Her going was a shock but not, by the time it happened, a surprise. For several weeks after Anderson's death she and I were closer than ever but then something changed. Her letters became less open, less affectionate and she found reasons not to come and see me at university. When I phoned her she was friendly enough but evasive. What was wrong? Nothing was wrong. She was fine, everything was fine, she loved me, she would see me soon. But there was no conviction in any of this. And then one day I had a letter from her. She had got tired, she said, of waiting for a chance in a West End musical and had taken a job with a dance troupe that was touring the Middle East. She didn't know when she would be back but she would keep in touch. In the event, she never came back and she never kept in touch.

Why she had gone nobody could tell me, not Donovan, not her mother. Indeed her mother never forgave her for walking out.

'Give up a good job, she did, little mare,' the woman said. 'A bleedin' good job. She'll never find anyone else looks after her like Donovan did, ungrateful little cow. What's going to happen to me with her gone, eh? What am I going to do?'

In fact, Donovan took care of her urgent needs, which amounted to little more than money for rent, food and booze and he didn't have to do that for long, because a couple of months after Beverley left her mother tried to leap aboard a moving bus in Ludgate Circus and, being smashed out of her mind, missed it completely and fell under the wheels of another bus right behind it. 'Typical of her fucking luck,' they said at the funeral wake – more of a piss-up, really – that Donovan gave for her in The Street. 'Bad enough being run over by a bus in the first place but the *wrong* bus . . .'

When I graduated from university with a respectable BA (Hons.) Donovan asked me to work full time for him. I didn't want to do that. Until now I had not knowingly – give or take a single murder – done anything criminal. But if I joined Donovan I would have to and I didn't fancy it, though not for any moral reasons: in the environment in which I had lived since I was twelve, crime was a natural way of life. I just wanted something else. The truth is that though I was fond of Donovan and was back on good terms with Arnie, I had very little in common with my contemporaries in The Street and didn't want to spend the rest of my life with them, robbing banks or running brothels or whatever Donovan might have had in mind for me.

So I became a schoolteacher in the same secondary school my mother had refused to let me go to as a student. By now it had become a comprehensive and a truly vicious place, which was one reason why I took up boxing again. It was a question of self-defence. I hadn't been there a month before some great, hulking kid came at me with a knife. There were a few anxious moments before I was able to bite his thumb to the bone and then step back and break his nose with a left jab. That night his father was waiting for me outside the school gates. He was even bigger and nastier than his son but he was also overweight and slow and by working vigorously to his body I had him on his knees within five minutes. I didn't throw a single punch at his head: you can break your hands doing that.

Oddly enough, those two incidents brought back my appetite for the ring. There had been no boxing club at my university and I hadn't fought under the Marquess of Queensberry rules for three years. But I had trained and kept fit because I liked it and I had filled out a lot. I was now six feet tall and a natural middleweight. So I joined a good amateur club and discovered that, along with the instinctive defensive skills I had always had, I'd developed a knockout punch with my right hand and a pretty good wallop with my left.

I gave up my teaching job after one term and went back to running errands for Donovan to make a little money. He was very disappointed in me.

'I can't understand it,' he said. 'Bloke with your education doing this kind of crap. I got fellows here earning five times as much as you and they got shit for brains. Why don't you join me proper?' He paused. 'Properly.'

This was something I'd noticed with Donovan lately: he was trying at last to get some kind of grip on English grammar. And he was also affecting a most curious accent, though not with his own people – just with outsiders. It seemed to be his idea of standard, or anyway traditional, BBC English and it sounded as if his adenoids had taken over the work of his larynx. It led me to suspect, rightly as it turned out, that he was preparing to move away from The Street and blend inconspicuously with the nobs in some posh suburb. Fortunately, he discovered soon after he had made his move that he was probably the only person in the world who spoke like that and he quickly reverted to his original accent, though his grammar did get better over the years, except sometimes when he was excited.

I told my mother, who was still running his grocery shop, about Donovan's offer.

'Don't even consider it,' she said. 'He's a crook. We've always known that and he's a very clever crook. It could be he'll get away with it for ever but it could be he won't and if he doesn't he's going to spend a lot of time in prison and anyone who's been close to him is going to spend just as much time in the next cell. It's not worth it, son.' So I ran errands and I boxed and I tried not to think too much about Bev.

After a lot of hard and patient work I had identified the agency that had sent her out with the dancing troupe to the Middle East. But by then she had moved on to somewhere else and the agency no longer had knowledge of her whereabouts. Donovan had also tried to help, asking around among various international whoremongers of his acquaintance to see if she had returned to her old profession but that turned out to be a dead end, too. She had simply vanished.

The boxing went well, though. I won the London middleweight championship and then the national – the Amateur Boxing Association – title and this gave me a place in Britain's Olympic team that year. I came back with a bronze medal, having been out-pointed in the semi-final by a Cuban who went on to win the gold. And it was then that Morrie Abrams came into my life.

Morrie was a very fly old boxing manager who was always prowling around the amateur scene, poaching the better prospects, and I was one of those he poached. He turned up at my mother's house one day, about a week after I returned from the Olympics.

'I can make you a champion,' he said. 'World champion? Who knows? Maybe not. But British champion very likely, European champion possibly.'

And I thought: what the hell? I didn't want to work for Donovan, I'd hated being a teacher and I couldn't think what else I could do with a degree in English literature. Newspapers, radio, television? I didn't much fancy any of them even if they would have had me.

So I signed up with Morrie and, on the whole, he handled me well. He picked my opponents care-fully and I started off with sixteen straight wins, nine of them inside the distance. Then he made his first mistake by putting me in too early with the British champion, who beat me pretty comprehen-sively over fifteen rounds.

'Sorry,' Morrie said to me afterwards, as I lay on

the massage table aching everywhere and with my right eye nothing more than an angry slit surrounded by a lump of puffy flesh the size of a snooker ball. 'Sorry, son, my fault. I thought he was over the hill, I thought he was gone.' Morrie was a tubby little man with the kind of ugly-attractive face that might have resulted from mating Edward G. Robinson with an intelligent frog. 'We'll take him next time, though. Couple of years, few more fights, get you back close to the top, then we'll take him.'

In fact, we – or rather I, who naturally did the fighting for both of us while Morrie did the talking and the wheeling and dealing – never did take him. I had a few more fights and won those and while I was still waiting for another shot at the British title, Morrie got me in through the back door for a European championship bout. The original challenger, a Frenchman, had gone down with flu a few days before the fight and I was accepted as a last-minute replacement. I lost that one, too. Well, it was against an Italian in Rome and, ask any British boxer, if you're fighting an Italian in Italy you're lucky to sneak a draw if he throws in the towel in the first round. To be honest, though, it was a close contest and could probably have gone either way wherever we fought.

But that, my second defeat, set me back again and by the time I had my next attempt at the British championship there was a new holder, an unbeaten KO specialist who was thought to be our best world title prospect for years. Morrie was full of encouragement.

'Don't worry about him, Bobby,' he said. 'So he's a big hitter, so what? You've got a great defence and a nice punch of your own. Jab him, son, jab him. Hit and run, that's the way.' So that's what I did. I jabbed his head off for five rounds and then knocked him out in the sixth with a perfect right hook. Morrie wasn't too pleased. It turned out that despite all his professed faith in me he had actually bet on the other fellow.

But that fight was the start of a good spell for me. I knocked out the world title prospect again in a return bout, at which point it was pretty obvious that he had everything going for him except a chin strong enough to take anything much harder than a love tap from his girlfriend. Then I took the Commonwealth and European championships, won a Lonsdale Belt outright with another success-ful defence of the British title, knocked over a couple of ageing but still respectably ranked Ameri-cans, and defended the European championship by stopping a German in the tenth.

It was after this that Morrie came to me with his big news. 'Oh boy, have I got something for you,' he said. 'Have I got something for you! Who are you fighting next? Tell me, who are you fighting next?'

'How the hell should I know?' I said. 'You're the manager – you tell me.' But I knew from his excite-ment who it had to be. 'All right,' I said, 'all right, enough of the guessing games already. Willie Slate. Tell me I'm right.' When you spent enough time around him Morrie's speech pattern became con-tagious.

He nodded vigorously. 'You're right. Willie Slate it is. Three months from today, Wembley Stadium – and for the world title. How do you feel?'

'My nose is bleeding already,' I said.

Willie Slate was a black American from Harlem, who at that time had been world champion for three years and had never even looked like losing to anybody. He wasn't just a good middleweight, he was a great middleweight – a superlative boxer who never really needed to box much because he punched so hard that few of his opponents got beyond the third round.

'I think it's a mistake,' I said. 'I'm the best in Europe but I'm not in his class.'

'What's this I'm hearing?' Morrie said, indignantly. 'Defeatist talk? Am I hearing defeatist talk? I don't want to listen. Look . . .' He put his arm around my shoulders, which wasn't easy because he had to reach up a fair way, and led me out of the gym where I'd been working out on the heavy bag. 'Look, all right, I agree – you're not in his class. But neither is he.'

'Pardon?' I said.

'He's not the man he was. He's lost it, he's over the hill.'

'You said that once before, Morrie, and I've still got the bruises.'

'So? So I was wrong before. This time I'm right. Believe me. You can take him.' We'd gone into a little anteroom off the gym, which was above a pub in south London. There was a kind of hospital bed in the middle and another of Morris's fighters was lying there, having a massage. He was a chunky little guy with an appendage almost as big as a third leg hanging from his groin. 'You know him?' Morrie said. 'Jackie Breslin? What am I saying? Of course you know him. The next bantamweight champion and when I say champion I'm talking world champion.'

'Bantamweight?' I said. 'Has it occurred to you that if you cut that thing off him he'd be a natural flyweight?'

'Don't think I haven't thought about it,' Morrie said. He took me into the far corner of the room and began talking in a low, urgent, persuasive tone. 'Listen to me. I know Slate's manager, an old friend. He's worried. Willie's legs have gone. He can't do the championship distance any more.'

'He's never had to,' I said. 'His opponents don't last that long.'

Morrie nodded wisely. 'True. I can't deny it. But that was then, this is now and now he's an old man. For a fighter he's an old man. He's how old, who knows, he's thirty-two going on thirty-five maybe? His time is over. What he's looking for, he's looking for a good, big, final payday and he could get it here, in London, against you. You're a big draw, Bobby, he's a big draw. Between the two of you you pack Wembley Stadium, we get a piece of the TV rights, Willie gets a fat cheque and says goodbye and you get the title.'

'Does Willie know all this?' I asked.

'He doesn't have to know. His manager knows. Who cares what a fighter knows?'

'Thanks.'

He patted me on the shoulder. It was easier for him now because I was sitting down. 'You know what I mean. Willie's never fought anybody like you. You're quick, you got great moves, you look good going backwards and that's what you do with Willie. You go backwards, six, eight rounds you keep out of his way, then his legs go and you've got him.'

'Simple as that, huh?'

'Exactly. Trust me.'

I said, 'Have you got a deal going, Morrie? Is he going to throw this fight? Because if he is I don't want any part of it.' Real *Boy's Own* stuff and yet I meant it. I wanted to be the champion of the world, every fighter does, but I didn't want my manager buying the title for me. Morrie put on his pained look. I think it was about Look 47 in his repertoire.

He said, 'You don't make deals like that with Willie Slate. He's a proud man. When he goes down he'll go down fighting and you're the man who's going to put him down because his time is over and your time has come.'

So he persuaded me. Three months later I got into the ring with Willie Slate at Wembley Stadium for the middleweight championship of the world and he beat hell out of me for fifteen rounds. I think I shared the first two while he was still warming up and maybe I took the eighth with a lot of pretty good counter-punches and I certainly took the ninth when I actually made his knees wobble with a hard right hook. But he had me down in the sixth and the tenth and he broke one of my ribs in the eleventh and my jaw in the thirteenth. The only thing that really surprised me was that he didn't finish me off. He had the chances, God knows, but always at the crucial moment he seemed a little hesitant and I was able to recover enough to make it to the bell. After the tenth when I wasn't entirely sure where I was, what date it was or even who I was, I remember mumbling to Morrie: 'Pull me out. I've had enough.'

He said, 'Pull you out? What are you saying? You've got him – his legs are going.'

I said: 'Go and tell him that. It might help.' I

couldn't breathe too well and my lips felt like a couple of very old and very worn spare tyres.

You know, there's a myth about boxing that says you don't feel the pain when the punches hit you; that pain comes later, on the stool between rounds and, especially, the next day when your blood's running cooler and your body has stiffened up; that when the punches actually land all you feel is the thump of them hitting you and a slightly woozy sensation, as if you'd had too much to drink. But the people who believe this are the guys in the ringside seats, not the fellows in the ring. Oh, sure, I was woozy, all right; I was so woozy I might as well have been on a three-day bender. But I felt the punches, too, every one of them, and when the rib went crack it was as if the pain was coming with sound effects.

'This is a world title,' Morrie said. 'Pull you out from a world title? I wouldn't insult you.' So he sent me back again and Willie Slate broke my jaw and practised some fancy glove work on my head and body and I stuck in there until the end of the fight, at which point he was given the unanimous decision and when I'd stopped reeling around as if I was pissed out of my mind I was taken to hospital.

Morrie came to see me the next morning as I lay in bed, hurting everywhere, with my jaw wired up. 'What can I tell you?' he said. 'I made a mistake. I'm sorry.' I grunted at him. 'How are you feeling?' he asked. This time I didn't even grunt. I just gave him the cold stare I'd developed for psyching out opponents in the ring. He ignored it.

'You know what I'm thinking?' he said. 'I'm thinking return fight. You know what you are today? You're a national hero. You seen the papers?'

'Fuck the papers,' I said.

'A return, three months from now.' He looked closely at me. 'Maybe six. Wembley again. It'll be another sell-out.' He glanced at his watch. 'Think about it.'

'I've thought about it,' I said, moving my lips like a third-rate ventriloquist. 'The answer's no. I'm retiring.'

'Don't make a hasty decision. There's money involved. Listen, do me a favour – keep an open mind. We could clean up.' Another look at his watch. 'I got to go, plane to catch. Jackie Breslin's fighting for the European title in Madrid in five days' time. You want me to give him a message?'

'Yeah. Fuck him,' I said. I wasn't feeling well.

'I'll tell him you wish him luck. Okay, I'm going. I'll be back, less than a week. Meantime, do what I'm doing – think return. You and Slate, it's a natural. Trust me.' And then he was gone.

Donovan turned up in the afternoon with a couple of the minders he'd lately taken to trailing around with him, big muscular fellows with faces like well-used battering rams. His attitude was not friendly.

'How you feeling?' he asked, though he didn't sound as if he cared much one way or the other. I couldn't believe the question. How did he think I was feeling, lying there with my ribs strapped up, one eye closed, lips like a couple of pounds of calves' liver and my jaw in a sling?

'Great,' I said. 'I'll be fighting again next week.'

He sat on the bed, heavily, bouncing it enough

to make me gasp with pain. 'All right, how much did you make?'

'What?'

He laid his hand along the unbroken side of my jaw. 'Don't jerk me around, Bobby,' he said, 'or I'll screw the bottom half of your face off. How much did you make?'

'From the fight?' I couldn't understand why he should care, why he should be so downright hostile. 'I don't know. Not a lot. By the time I've paid taxes, expenses, I'll be lucky to clear 20,000 quid.'

'And the rest,' he said softly.

With a painful effort I jerked my face away from his hand. 'What rest? There isn't any rest. I got the short end of the purse, the very short end.'

Donovan took out a fat cigar and lit it. The smoke made me cough and the coughing made my ribs and jaw hurt. He didn't care. 'You know what the odds were on that fight?'

'Yes. Nine to one against me. Made me feel good, knowing how much confidence everyone had in me.'

He shook his head. 'Not those odds. I mean the odds against you going the distance. Know what they were? Five to one – five to one you couldn't go the fifteen rounds. Nobody had ever done that against Slate, nobody thought anyone could. But you did, didn't you? Because he carried you, didn't he? And you knew he was going to carry you, didn't you? So how much did you make at five to one?'

I felt sick. Losing had been hard enough to take, even if it wasn't entirely unexpected, but at least I had derived some consolation from the fact that I was still there, on my feet, at the end of the fight.

To be told now that this had only happened because it wasn't in Willie Slate's financial interests to beat me senseless hurt even more than the physical injuries he had inflicted on me. And I suppose the shock of all this must have shown in my face because Donovan said, 'Bloody hell! Are you telling me you didn't know? You weren't in on it? They let you go through all that and they didn't put a penny on for you? You poor sod.'

'If he was carrying me, nobody told me. I just thought he was beating the shit out of me.' I could feel tears starting. Anger? Frustration? I don't know. I was simply aware that my eyes were wet and smarting.

'Right,' Donovan said thoughtfully. 'Right. I'm sorry, son, I should have known. You're too honest to be on a scam like that, you stupid prick. But your little manager now . . .' he waved a forefinger at me, 'your little Morrie Abrams, he was in on it. So was Slate's manager. And so was Slate. You know how much they've taken me for, the thieving bastards – 200,000 nicker. And that's just me. God knows how much the other bookies have lost.' He got up abruptly from the bed. 'All right. I'm glad I've sorted this out. I'm glad you weren't involved. Take care of yourself, okay? Take it easy. I'll be in again.' And then he swept out with his minders tagging along behind him and giving me a parting scowl. I got the impression they were disappointed that Donovan hadn't asked them to smash up the rest of my jaw.

He came in again the next day, friendlier this time and even bringing grapes, which he ate in an absent-minded way while he told me about Morrie's betting coup. Donovan and the other bookies had realised that something much to their disadvantage was going on but Morrie and Slate's manager had covered their tracks pretty well. Neither of them had, personally, made a bet and quite likely they would have got away with it if it hadn't been for what they might reasonably have regarded as sheer bad luck. One of the people who had spread the money around the betting shops on their behalf was Morrie's brother-in-law and it was his misfortune that someone behind the counter in one of Donovan's establishments knew who he was. He also knew that Morrie's brother-in-law, being the sort of loafer who gave the word 'work-shy' a bad name, could not possibly have amassed the kind of money he was putting down. So the word was passed to Donovan.

'And,' Donovan said, 'I sent a couple of the lads around to have a quiet chat with him. Matter of fact, funny thing, he's in the ward downstairs right this minute.'

'One of life's little ironies,' I said.

'Right. Anyway, the brother-in-law told us what had been going on. Even gave us the names of a couple of other blokes who'd been spreading the bets. I don't think any of 'em will do it again.'

'Have you paid out?'

'Have I what? Paid out? I'll pay him out, that little shit Morrie. Never did trust him, evil little bastard.' He turned back from the grapes he was demolishing to look at me again. 'How do you feel about him now, knowing what he did to you?'

'Not exactly full of brotherly love,' I said. My jaw and ribs were giving me particular pain that afternoon.

Donovan nodded. 'Really turned you over, didn't

he? I'll tell you something, young Bobby: there's some bets I've got to pay out on but I'm not paying a penny on them I reckon are down to Morrie.'

I said, 'Could be tricky, you know. Unless you've got proof, if it comes down to your word against his, you could end up looking like a welsher. Not good for your reputation, Donovan.'

'I know.' He lit one of his fat cigars. There were notices all over the room saying that smoking was forbidden but he didn't seem to think that rules like that applied to him. 'Worries me a bit, that does. That's why it's worth 25,000 quid to me something nasty happens to Morrie. I mean, something sort of terminal, right?' He looked at his watch, clucked in surprise at how late it was and got up. 'You've been listening to what I'm saying, have you? Worth 25,000 quid, no questions asked. Nice little thought, isn't it?'

When he had gone I phoned Morrie's home. If Donovan was going around saying things like that it wouldn't be long before he put out a definite contract and though I didn't think I would ever forgive Morrie for what he had done to me I did at least feel he ought to be warned. There was no Mrs Abrams at Morrie's house; there had been once but she had bolted years ago, unable any longer to live with boxers and the smell of embrocation and old jockstraps that Morrie carried around with him. In her place Morrie had installed an elderly house-keeper and it was she who gave me the number of his hotel in Madrid. I called him there but he was out, getting Jackie Breslin ready for the title bout. I left a message with the cuts man Morrie always took with him to the big fights.

'Tell him to call me,' I said. 'It's very urgent. Tell

him it's about the bets on the Slate fight. Have you got that?' I said it slowly because the cuts man wasn't exactly a Rhodes scholar and even though he claimed to be writing it all down I wasn't convinced that anyone, including him, would ever be able to read it back. 'Tell him it's vital that he calls me. He could be in big trouble.'

After that I lay back and waited but Morrie didn't return my call that day so the next morning I phoned again. Morrie was still out, or anyway the cuts man insisted he was. 'I give him that there message,' he said, 'and he reckoned he didn't know nothing about any bets.'

I started again. 'Look, tell him this: it's nothing personal. I know about the bets and I'm not exactly thrilled but he's not in trouble with me. Tell him Donovan knows about the bets, too, and tell him to fucking well call me.'

But he didn't. Maybe he thought I was bluffing, I don't know. I listened to the fight on the radio and Breslin won it well. The referee called it off in the fifth after the Spaniard had been down three times. The following day I phoned again and this time I was told that Mr Abrams and all his party had left the hotel. The rest of them were on their way back to London but Morrie had gone off to Almería or somewhere for a couple of days in the sun. I tried his home number but the housekeeper had no idea where he was, so I left it and just hoped he had realised what I was trying to tell him.

Soon after that, the hospital discharged me. All the media turned up to see me hobble out because I was still a hero, the only man ever to take Willie Slate the full distance in a championship fight. Even the TV news cameras were there. I gave them as

76

brave a smile as I could manage with a cracked jaw and said there would be no return bout, despite what Morrie had told them before he went to Spain, because I was hanging up my protective cup, retiring, getting out. They were very nice to me but as I winced my way into the taxi I overheard a couple of them saying I seemed a bit subdued.

My mother was waiting for me when I got back to my flat in Chelsea. In those days she still lived in The Street but she had been keeping an eye on my place while I was in hospital. There was a big basket of flowers waiting for me as well. Donovan had sent them, which was surprising since he wasn't the type to send flowers to another man unless they concealed a time bomb. In a sense that's what these concealed, too, because the flowers were just a front for the message that came with them. 'Remember what I told you,' it said.

'What does that mean?' my mother asked.

'I don't know,' I said, though I knew very well. 'Probably something he said the other day. He said I ought to quit the fight game now, before I got my brains scrambled. But I'd decided to do that anyway. I told everyone this morning, press, telly, radio. I think they were a bit disappointed. They'd rather hoped I'd let Willie Slate put me in hospital again.'

She said, 'You sign a contract to fight him or anyone else and I'll personally come round and cut both your hands off.' A pretty tough old party, my mother, for all her slenderness and good looks. There were times when I reckoned she'd have given Willie Slate a better scrap than I did, though she'd always hated the fight game and especially my participation in it. But then I suppose the mothers of

77

most boxers feel that way. 'What are you going to do now? Now you've retired, I mean.'

'I'm not sure.' I was already in the property business in a small way with my two partners, a stockbroker and a solicitor, a couple of boxing groupies who had followed my career in the ring from day one. It was on their advice that I'd bought the flat in Chelsea as soon as I could scrape up enough to put down a deposit. It was probably the smartest thing I had ever done so far and the second smartest was going into business with them. But now they were growing ambitious. They wanted to expand what, for all of us, had simply been a sideline into something bigger; they wanted to buy not just one house at a time but two or three, convert them into flats and put the profits into buying another two or three or maybe four. To keep up with them and in with them I had to invest more money in the company and I didn't quite have enough.

'You're not going in with Donovan, are you?' my mother said.

I shook my head. 'Absolutely not. I'll just have to see what comes up.'

And what came up was £25,000. After I'd been home two days I read in the *Guardian* that Morrie Abrams had been knocked down and killed by a hit-and-run driver the previous night while he was crossing the Fulham Road. It was a hell of a shock. My feelings towards Morrie were not precisely what you would call warm at that time, but I didn't wish him dead. Donovan, on the other hand, not only believed that I had wished him dead but was convinced that I had rendered him dead because he turned up unexpectedly late in the morning with a briefcase under his arm.

'Well done, old son,' he said. 'Lovely job, quick, clean, no mess. Except Morrie, of course. They had to scrape him off the road. This is yours.' He threw the briefcase across to me. It was full of money. 'It's all there, just like I said – 25K, all right?'

'Donovan,' I said, 'I can't . . .'

He glared at me belligerently. 'What's the matter? You want to count it? You don't trust me?'

'No, no, it's not that. If you say it's all there, it's all there. It's just that I didn't –'

He held up one big hand to silence me. 'I know. You didn't do it for me, you did it for yourself, for what the little shit did to you and, by Christ, he had it coming. But a deal's a deal. I told you it was worth 25,000 to me and I meant it. Tell you the truth, Bobby, I'm still out a hell of a lot of money on your bloody fight but after what you done to Morrie nobody's going to try pulling a caper like that with me again. You done me a big favour, son, and I'm grateful. So take the money; you earned it.'

And then he got up and left. It was always like that with Donovan. He led such a busy life fixing up one crooked deal after another that he rarely spent more than a few minutes at a time in any one place. On the whole this may have been good business but there were occasions, and this was one, when his own haste stopped him finding out the true facts.

At the door he stopped for a moment. 'Now you've elbowed the fight game,' he said, 'you don't fancy working for me, do you?'

'No,' I said. 'Thanks but no. And, Donovan, listen to me. I have to tell you –'

He held up the hand again. 'Say no more. The money's yours, enjoy it.' And then he went and after that I never bothered to tell him that I hadn't killed Morrie. In fact, nobody ever found out who killed him. Eventually, the police discovered the car that had knocked him down but that didn't help them much because it had been reported stolen earlier on the day Morrie died. Quite possibly it was some joyrider, a kid, who had splattered him across the Fulham Road. Who knows? All I am sure about is that it wasn't me. But I had the money and I kept it. For a time after Donovan left I thought seriously about giving it back to him but then I thought again and what I decided was that, one way or another, Morrie certainly owed me at least £25,000 and in an indirect way I was simply collecting from his estate. Furthermore, Donovan was happy because everyone would believe that he had had Morrie terminated and that would act as a powerful deterrent to anyone else who might have been contemplating a similar betting scam. The way I saw it, the money needed a home and I was in the best position to offer it one.

So I took it and added it to whatever other savings I had and re-established myself as an equal partner in the property business. The only problem was that Arnie continued to believe that Morrie's death was down to me when the job should have been contracted out to him and therefore that was a second favour I owed him.

5

I DIDN'T GO BACK to my flat immediately that
evening I met Jinks. Instead, I picked up someone
I was seeing at the time and took her to dinner.
Then we went back to her place and what with one
thing and another it was after two before I got
home. There was a message from Donovan waiting
impatiently on my answering machine. 'Call me,' it
said and it didn't sound pleased. 'I can't find you
and I can't find bloody Arnie. What the fuck's going
on?' I ignored it and went to bed and it was nearly
ten when I woke up. There was another, later, even
angrier message from Donovan on the machine. It
said, 'You know who this is. It's eight o-bleeding-
clock in the morning and I want to talk to you
NOW.'

I showered, shaved, dressed, drank about a pint
of coffee and then I phoned Donovan at his office,
the headquarters of his bookmaking business, in
Mayfair. I didn't get him but one of his gofers, a
fellow I knew well, a big, nasty musclebrain called
Reg. He used to lead the others in beating me up
when we were all kids together in The Street. It

81

creates a bond between people, that sort of shared experience. I felt I owed him something – not a lot, just a couple of black eyes and maybe a few missing teeth – and he knew how I felt and seemed anxious not to collect.

That morning, though, he was perkier than usual, probably because I was out of favour with Donovan, a fact that Reg was more than happy to point out.

'You're right up shit creek, you are, Bob,' he said cheerfully.

'Yeah, well I'll get out of it, won't I, even if I have to come round there and use you as a paddle. Put me onto Donovan.'

'Not here, is he. Gone abroad for a bit and he didn't tell me where he was going neither.'

'I'm not surprised. Why should he confide in the office boy? Look, just get me somebody who does know where he is. Get me somebody important.'

He stopped sounding cheerful. 'He didn't tell anyone where he was going. He's like that sometimes. Left for Heathrow about nine-thirty and what he was saying about you don't bear repeating. Do you want to hear it?'

I hung up, which probably made him feel better. I wasn't too worried about Donovan because I knew I hadn't seriously upset him: I hadn't cost him money. But I should have liked to talk to him to find out what he knew about Jinks and the contract Jinks had put out on Bev and the unknown man who seemed to be linked with her. But with Donovan not available it struck me that, just possibly, Arnie might know more than he had told me, so I drove round to the hospital he had said he was checking into.

When I asked for him at reception the girl on the desk consulted a list, glanced up, gave me an odd look, said, 'Excuse me, sir', and started talking softly and urgently on the house phone. When she had finished she said, 'Would you mind waiting a minute?' So I sat down with a two-day-old copy of the *Sun*, which I found lying about on a chair, and spent a little time looking for words of more than one syllable. I had got as far as page three and 'bosoms', 'buttocks' and 'bonking' when I was summoned back to the reception desk and introduced to a middle-aged woman in hospital uniform who said she was Matron Somebody-or-other.

'Are you a relative of Mr Longbow?' she asked.

'No, just a friend. Is this a bad time? I mean, I can come back later if he's in the operating theatre or something.'

'I'm afraid it's not as simple as that, Mr Lennox. You see, and I'm deeply sorry to have to tell you this, Mr Longbow passed away last night.'

'What?'

'He died last night, Mr Lennox.'

'On the operating table, you mean?' I couldn't quite take it in.

'No, in the ward. Cardiac arrest. It was very sudden and there was nothing we could do.'

'What are you telling me? He died, right here, in the hospital before anybody had even laid a glove on him? Is that what the National Health Service is coming to? A bloke walks in under his own steam for a simple check-up and next day you carry him out in a box?'

She said coldly, 'He was a very sick man, Mr Lennox.'

'Yes, well, he's a bloody sight sicker now than

when he came in, isn't he?' I shook my head angrily, though God knows what I was angry at. Not her anyway. 'Does his wife know?'

The receptionist chipped in. 'Yes. She was here earlier. She came in to collect his belongings and . . . make the arrangements.'

It was all so hard to believe. Arnie might have looked like a corpse when I saw him a couple of nights ago but it had never occurred to me that he was imminently about to become one. I left the hospital, got back into my car and drove out to Arnie's home in Edgware, a big detached house with a high wall around it, burglar alarm notices all over the place and Rottweilers roaming the garden. For a man in Arnie's line of business these were perhaps only sensible precautions although I suppose it could have been argued that he didn't really need them. I mean, he probably didn't have an enemy in the world; he'd killed them all.

I pressed the bell push on the gate and Arnie's sister-in-law came out of the house to let me in, scattering the dogs with a series of vigorous kicks. 'Sod off out of it, you bastards!' She was wearing a black dress and a mournful expression. She'd probably bought them both at the same shop.

'Nice of you to come, Bobby, really nice,' she said, leading me into the house. 'Vera will be pleased. You've no idea how upset she is, poor cow. I mean, it was so sudden, wasn't it? One minute there he was large as life – well, large as life as he ever was considering his ulcers and his hernia and his haemorrhoids – and the next minute he's gone. Makes you think, doesn't it?'

It did. It made me think about Arnie's haemorrhoids. He hadn't mentioned them. I found Vera in the sitting-room. She had the curtains drawn to denote mourning, a bottle of Bristol Cream at her elbow and a full glass in her hand and she was watching a video nasty on the television. She looked up as I came in and waved a feeble hand at me – not the hand with the glass in it, the one holding a little lace handkerchief.

'Bobby,' she said, 'oh, Bobby, how good of you to come on this terrible, terrible day.' She put the handkerchief to her eyes and the glass to her lips. 'Poor Arnie, oh, my poor, poor Arnie.' To be fair to her, all this was not as cringe-making as it sounds. I think she really was grieving but it wasn't in her nature to show emotion. She could feel it but she could not genuinely show it. All she could do was act it. 'Do you fancy a sherry, dear?' she asked. 'Scotch? Anything?'

I said I didn't and sat in one of her pink velvet armchairs and she turned her attention back to the video nasty.

'This was one of Arnie's favourites,' she said. 'That's why I've got it on now. It reminds me of him. He watched it, oh, ever so many times. *Return of the Killer Zombies* it's called.' On the screen a young and pretty girl was about to be stripped and raped by a mob of killer zombies. They moaned and salivated a lot and they looked about as healthy as Arnie when I had last seen him.

'Anything I can do, Vera,' I said. 'You only have to ask.'

'I know, dear, bless you.' She was still looking at the screen where the screaming girl, naked now, was just disappearing under a heaving mass of zombies, leaving only a final flash of her pubic hair for us to remember her by.

'Can we turn this off?' I said. 'I want to talk to you.'

'Of course, dear.' She touched the off switch and the whole mess of yelling girl and panting zombies vanished. For a moment it was blissfully quiet in the darkened room, the only sound that of Bristol Cream gurgling into her glass.

I said, 'Arnie was in for a job when he, er, well, you know, when he, er . . .'

'Snuffed it,' she said, nodding sombrely. 'I know – a big one, too. He told me.'

'Did he tell you anything else about it?'

'No. He didn't know anything else. He just knew the money would be good. That's why he asked you to go along to the meeting for him.' She looked at me over the sherry glass. 'Are you going to do the job, Bobby?'

'What, as a last tribute to Arnie? A sort of "Lest We Forget", that kind of thing?'

'It would be nice,' she said wistfully. 'Only I was thinking, if you did you ought to give me a commission. Arnie would have liked that. Please him that would, wherever he is.' She glanced upwards, presumably towards some hitman's heaven where even now Arnie was probably waiting in the queue to collect his standard-issue machine gun. 'Besides, you'd owe it really, wouldn't you? I mean, you wouldn't even know about the job if it wasn't for Arnie.'

'That's true. I'll tell you what, Vera, if I do the job – and I'm not saying I will, I'm only saying if – I'll give you the whole fee in memory of Arnie. I can't say fairer than that, can I?'

She sniffed a bit and wiped her eyes and drank some more sherry. 'No, dear, it's very generous and I do appreciate it. Of course, there's some as would say it's no more than we deserve, Arnie and me.'

'What do you mean?'

'Well, you owed him for a long time, didn't you? That probation officer and your boxing manager. You owed him for them.'

I was rather surprised. 'You knew about all that?'

'Well, certainly I did. We had no secrets, Arnie and me. I'll tell you something now, Bobby, I expect this'll amuse you . . .' She chuckled reminiscently. It obviously amused her. 'There was a time Arnie was thinking of killing you.'

'What?'

'Oh yes, he was. He was so upset you did that probation officer. But I talked him out of it. I says to him, "Why, dear?" I says, "Bobby's a nice boy. He wouldn't do it deliberate, not to offend you. Besides," I says, "what's in it for us? Nobody's going to pay you to shoot Bobby. No, Arnie," I says, "you put that idea right out of your head. Just think of it this way – Bobby owes you now and one day," I says, "you'll be able to collect." And I was right, wasn't I?'

It was a very curious sensation to sit there hearing this stout, powdered, coiffed and hennaed house-wife telling such a story. I wasn't sure whether to be grateful or appalled. I said, 'Right, well, I suppose, you know, Arnie not being in a pensionable trade, you'd need the money, would you? If I do the job, I mean.'

'Well, I have to say it would come in handy but I can't say I really *need* it, dear. He was ever such a good provider, my Arnie. Well, you know what a conscientious worker he was, always worrying about doing the job right and wondering where the next one was coming from. Couldn't sit still for five minutes. I used to tell him, "You know what you are, Arnie Longbow? You're a workaholic, that's what you are," I used to say. But, bless him, he really took care of me. So I shall be all right, what with this house all paid for and the Swiss bank account and the villa in Minorca. Matter of fact, I think that's where I'll go, Minorca. Sell this house and spend my declining years in the sunshine. Nothing here for me now, Bobby. Just memories of happier times.'

I wondered what those memories might have been – she and Arnie sitting up in bed together, perhaps, watching rape and mayhem on a video nasty and planning his next hit.

'Sherry's a lot cheaper in Spain, too,' I said and soon afterwards I left her there, dreaming about her declining years in the sunshine. She'd turned the video back on and, the last I saw of them, the killer zombies had torn the girl to pieces and seemed to be eating the remains. I didn't wait to see who had got which bit.

6

As ARRANGED, Jinks phoned me at the wine bar a little after midday on Saturday. His call came just in time to rescue me. I'd been sitting at the bar with the *Guardian* and a glass of Sancerre, bothering nobody, when a matched set of what turned out to be American air hostesses in mufti came in on the lookout for somebody to buy them lunch and since I was the only unattached male in the place I was elected. American women have no trouble starting conversations because God forgot to give them any inhibitions. These two just breezed up to the bar, ordered a designer water each and one of them said, 'Hi, I'm Cindy, this is Kate.' They were the long-stemmed Texas rose type, both brunettes, both nearly as tall as me and each with the full American complement of sixty-four teeth. Within a couple of minutes they were sitting on either side of me, touching my arms a lot, making plenty of eye contact and wanting to know who I was, what I did for a living, was I meeting a friend and what could I recommend as the best way for a couple of single, fun-loving girls to spend a little time in London.

All right, I was tempted. I admit that. In fact, I very nearly succumbed and I was just wondering whom I could call to make up a foursome when one of them, no doubt thinking this would be the clincher to overcome my British reticence, announced that she had a crazy sense of humour and so did her friend, and then all the alarm bells rang. It's my experience that people who tell you they have a crazy sense of humour turn out to be about as much fun as legionnaire's disease because what it means is that either they have no sense of humour at all or, even worse, they enjoy practical jokes. And what that means is that not only do they have no sense of humour at all but they're vicious with it.

At that moment, fortunately, the barman said, 'Is there a Mr Longbaugh here? Arnie Longbaugh? There's a call for him.'

I said, 'I'll take it,' and went to the phone booth at the far end of the bar.

Jinks said, 'Longbaugh?'

'Longbow, yes.'

'Yeah, right. You still want the job?'

'I still want the job.'

'Okay. So be in Hollywood Wednesday evening.' He was using his brisk, rich man's don't-mess-with-me voice. I said Wednesday was fine and he asked what name I wanted on my air ticket. I told him Robert Lennox.

'You got papers in that name?'

'I got papers,' I said. 'And, listen, I want to fly British Airways. I don't want any American airlines.' I had no idea which line Cindy and Kate worked for or where they flew and when but I wasn't about to run the risk of spending eleven hours in the air with them and their crazy sense of humour.

'What's the matter? You anti-American or something?'

'On the contrary. It's just that there are two particular Americans I wish to avoid. They have a crazy sense of humour and too many teeth.'

'Jesus,' he said. That note of disapproval was in his voice again. I wondered whether it was always there or whether it was just me who caused it. 'All the other arrangements stand, right? The money we agreed will be waiting at the hotel and then I'll contact you Thur –'

'No,' I said. 'I've changed my mind. I think we should meet. I think it'll be safer. Phones can be tapped, letters can get lost, messages can be read by the wrong people.' Now that I had made up my mind to go in Arnie's place I thought it essential that I should see Jinks again, somehow persuade him to tell me why he wanted Bev and the unknown man killed. 'Name any place you like, a crowded place preferably where nobody's going to take any notice of us.'

He paused, thinking about it. 'Okay. Noon, Thursday at the Beverly Center on La Cienega Boulevard. It's a shopping mall, huge. You can't miss it. I'll be outside the See's candy store. Don't be late.' He hesitated, then said, 'Listen, there could be another job, I'm not sure yet. Are you interested?'

I said, 'Do you mean a different job or an extra job?'

'Extra.'

'It'll mean another fee, of course.'

'Yeah.'

'And it's connected with the job I'm already going to do?'

'If it happens, yes. Look, I don't want to discuss it now. Like I said, I'm not sure yet. When I am sure . . .' There was a long pause. 'When I am sure I'll really want the guy hurt.'

'You're really big on making people suffer, aren't you?' I said. 'Are you sure you wouldn't be better off hiring the Spanish Inquisition? You'll probably find them in the yellow pages.'

He ignored that. 'I'll know by the time we meet,' he said. Then he gave me the name and address of the hotel he would book me into and hung up. He didn't say goodbye.

I loitered by the phone booth for a while, wondering what excuse I could give to Cindy and Kate for ducking out on them but I needn't have worried. By the time I got back to the bar they'd hooked a couple of yuppies who were buying them dry martinis. I went up to retrieve my *Guardian* and Cindy said, or maybe it was Kate, 'Oh, are you leaving? Nice talking to you.' The yuppies, fellows in their mid-thirties who looked as if they were still hanging in there despite the Crash and the high interest rates, smirked at me with a mixture of pity and triumph. I was out; they were in. As I left one of them was saying, 'Now, where would you lovely girls like to lunch?'

I felt sorry for them. It was a fair bet that before lunch was over one of them would find a plastic black widow spider in his wine and the other an artificial dog turd in his *coq au vin*. That's what a crazy sense of humour does to you.

*

On the Tuesday I went to have tea with my mother. Donovan had given up his grocery store and retired her on a generous pension some years ago and I'd moved her out of The Street to a little terraced house in Clapham. I usually saw her about once a week and we talked quite often on the phone.

'I'm going to the States tomorrow,' I said. 'Hollywood. A business trip.'

'You buying property out there now?'

'No. Different kind of business.'

'It's not for Donovan, is it?' she asked. 'You're not doing something for him?'

'Of course not. Why would I work for Donovan?'

She looked doubtful. 'I don't like to think, but I know he's always wanted you in his firm and he's not a man to give up easy. Don't you ever listen to him, son.'

'I won't,' I said. 'Does he still visit you?'

She carried on buttering bread. I'd already told her I didn't want any bread and butter but as usual she hadn't taken any notice. To mothers their sons are always about eight years old and in need of feeding up. 'Yes. About as often as you do. Drops in for a cup of tea or a Scotch and tells me his troubles.'

'He's always fancied you, hasn't he?'

'Asked me to marry him once,' she said. 'But I married your father instead.'

'Bad move, Mother.'

'Oh, I don't know,' she said. 'Being married to Donovan wouldn't have been any better, what with all his women. Just as well he never married, really. His poor wife would have had a terrible time.' Donovan had always had a huge appetite for women and always the same type – young, tall, leggy and very pretty and every one a bimbo. If their brains had been light bulbs they wouldn't have generated enough wattage to illuminate a toilet bowl. He would keep each of them around the house for a couple of months then, feeling the need for change, would pay her off handsomely and buy another one.

My mother said, 'Do you have women, Bobby?'

'Do I wha . . . ?' I was astonished. She'd never asked me anything like that before. 'Certainly I do, not that it's any of your business. I don't have as many as Donovan, I must admit, but I do all right.'

'That's good,' she said. 'Only, you know, you not being married at your age I sometimes wonder . . .'

'Oh, that's nice,' I said. 'You thought I was queer, did you?'

'No, nothing like that. It's just that, well, it sometimes crosses my mind that maybe you're not interested in sex.'

'I'm interested,' I said. 'You don't have to worry on that score.'

'I'll tell you what it is, Bobby. I want grand-children. Haven't you ever thought of marriage?'

'Yes, a couple of times. But, I don't know, maybe I've left it too late. All those years I was boxing I didn't want to get involved with a woman, not to the point of marrying one anyway. I had enough on my mind without a wife sitting around worrying about whether I was going to be carried home with my brains coming out of my ears. And then, by the time I retired, I suppose I was kind of set in my ways. There's a lot to be said for the bachelor life – female company when you want it and not when you don't want it, nobody to please but yourself –'

'No responsibilities, you mean,' she said bitterly.

Like most women she seemed to believe that a man who refused to take on a wife and children was somehow cheating, getting away with something he had no right to get away with. And the fact that she herself had been married to a man who wouldn't have recognised a responsibility if it had sneaked up and goosed him didn't seem to make any difference. 'You know what I wonder, Bobby? I wonder whether you ever really got over that Bev.'

It's strange, isn't it? Someone can go out of your life and practically out of your mind for years and there's never a mention of her and then, suddenly, everywhere you turn she's the sole topic of conversation. 'I've got over her,' I said. 'I got over her ages ago.' But even as I said it I wasn't sure it was the truth.

The girl at the British Airways desk at Heathrow had my ticket ready for me, a first-class open return as instructed.

I said, 'I wonder if you can help me. I'm not sure which of my business associates I have to thank for this. I wonder if it's possible to check the name. It might have been Mr Jinks or possibly someone else.'

She did a little checking on the phone but, as I had suspected, without result. The man who bought the ticket had given no name and had paid in cash. It didn't really matter but if Jinks had been absent-minded enough to use his Amex card or whatever, it would have been useful to know his true identity when I met him the next day.

The flight was uneventful, the wine as usual a lot better than the food, which, in the invariable way

95

of airline meals, tasted as if it had been first cooked three weeks ago and then reheated every twenty-four hours ever since. At LAX airport I spent the inevitable forty minutes queueing up to face the implacable xenophobia of the immigration officials, collected my luggage and took it through the green channel. There, like everybody else, I was grilled by a customs man. America is the only country I know where the green channel doesn't mean that most people can walk through unchallenged; all it seems to mean is that you run slightly less risk of being body-searched and having rubber-gloved fingers stuck into your behind in case you'd secreted a pound of heroin up there.

The weather in California, even in the late afternoon, was gloriously hot. I got a cab without any trouble and made the journey to my hotel on Sunset Boulevard in silence on account of the fact that the driver was a recently arrived immigrant from Armenia who hardly knew a word of English. God knows how he made out as a cabby in a place like Los Angeles. The route he took was along La Cienega Boulevard and, just before we approached the steep little hill that leads to Sunset, I spotted on my left the Beverly Center, the scene of my impending rendezvous with Jinks.

And after that there was little more I could do until the next day. The hotel was expecting me and had a thick, heavily sealed envelope waiting for me to collect. But, just like British Airways, they had no idea who had made the reservation on my behalf. I went up to my room, showered, shaved and changed my clothes, counted the 10,000 dollars in C-notes that the envelope contained, put the money along with any other valuables into the room safe and went down to the restaurant to kill what was left of the evening. After I'd eaten I lay on my bed and spent about an hour flicking through the channels watching the kind of television that seemed to have been devised specifically for jet-lagged people who had left their minds at 35,000 feet. At ten o'clock I took a couple of sleeping pills and crashed out.

7

By nine the next morning I was in the coffee shop, still a little tired but not too bad, eating the breakfast I always order in American hotels: fresh grapefruit juice, two eggs over easy, bacon, hold the home fries, hold the cottage cheese, rye toast and coffee. I had the *Los Angeles Times* for company. There was a lot of foreign news from places in which the United States had a powerful interest – South America, Asia, the Middle East – but, as usual, it appeared to have been early closing day in Europe. If the *LA Times* was to be believed, nothing of any interest whatsoever had happened in the whole of Europe all day yesterday.

After a while I turned to the local news. There was the inevitable catalogue of violent crime: a man had been blown away by an off-duty policeman while ripping off a liquor store at gunpoint; a black girl had been found raped and murdered on a piece of wasteland; two chicano gangs had had a rumble in which one kid was killed and four had been taken to hospital with stab wounds; an Iranian immigrant had been battered to death with a beer bottle in a barroom brawl; a couple of white teenagers had overdosed on heroin; two cops had been arrested for burglary; and Mr Jinks had been shot dead at his home in Westwood.

Only his name wasn't Mr Jinks at all: it was Philippe Pascal, and he was fifty-six years old and he was a millionaire who owned three trendy and expensive boutiques much frequented by the movie set around the Rodeo Drive area. I only knew that Philippe Pascal was also Mr Jinks because of the photograph that went with the story. He was, the newspaper said, the latest victim of a serial killer who had been operating in the area for several months and had already murdered five other people. In every case, according to the report, the victims – three men, three women – had been rich, middle-aged and living alone, and the motive was always robbery. In the case of Pascal/Jinks as in every other case, a police spokesman said, the killer had presumably picked him out because of his wealth, made a careful study of his movements and life style and then, when he judged the time was right, had waited for him when he returned home from work, had probably stuck a gun in his back as he got out of his car, taken him into his own home and there shot him after forcing him to reveal the whereabouts of whatever valuables he had around the place. The wall safe in Pascal/Jinks's den was open and empty and had not been forced and the same applied to a strong box sunk in the floor under the dining-room carpet.

I couldn't believe it. I'd come all this way and the man had got himself terminally mugged before I could even talk to him. All right, maybe I should have felt sorry for him but I didn't. I hadn't liked him; I found it hard to like somebody who was putting out a contract on the only woman I had ever really loved. And that, I realised now even as I read the newspaper report, was the truth of how I felt about Bev.

But what was I to do? Take the 10,000 dollars and go home? Hardly. The fact that Jinks, or rather Pascal, was himself dead did not mean that Bev was out of danger. For all I knew he could simply have been the front man for a whole group, a consortium, of people who wanted her killed. She had to be warned but how? I didn't know where she lived; I didn't know what she did; I didn't even know what she was calling herself these days. What I did know, because I had checked, was that she wasn't listed under her own name in any of the local telephone directories. All I had that might be of any help was a copy of the last photograph she had had taken before she walked out of my life. It was a professional studio portrait and she had planned to send it off to casting directors, choreographers and the like. I had kept it for obvious sentimental reasons, though I had never liked it much because, while she certainly looked beautiful in it, she was so gravely posed and heavily made-up that she appeared years older than she was. Now I was glad of the fact. The Bev of my photograph, much more than the Bev of my memory, was very like the Bev of the picture Pascal had shown me.

So now I got it out and showed it around the staff of the hotel. 'Do you know this woman? Her hair's a lot lighter now, ash blonde, and she looks maybe ten years older. But this is still very much like her.'

They looked at her and admired her but they

weren't much help. 'Beautiful girl. What is she – an actress?'

'I don't know. I'm pretty sure she's not a movie actress but she could be on TV. A dancer perhaps. Does that ring a bell?' They all shook their heads. 'No, gee, sorry. I only wish I did know her, girl like that. What do you want her for?'

'She's somebody I used to know a long time ago in London. I lost track of her but I know she's living here now and I'd like to contact her again.'

'Who wouldn't? But, no . . .' More shaking of heads. 'I just can't help you. She's not anybody I've ever seen.' Since practically everybody in the hotel was not really a waiter or waitress or bellhop but an out-of-work actor or actress waiting for a break, this was particularly discouraging. If Bev was in show business these were the kind of people I would have expected to know her.

But one of them, the bell captain, a tall, lean fellow in his forties, with hair dyed jet black and the out-of-date looks of a 1930s matinée idol, did at least have a helpful suggestion. 'Try the talent agencies,' he said. 'She's in the business, she's got to be on somebody's books. Only I don't envy you the job. There's one hell of a lot of those vultures around in this town.'

He was right. I checked the yellow pages and every other directory I could find and there were more vultures listed there than picked carcasses in Africa. But I couldn't think of any other way to find Bev so I hired a car from the Hertz desk at the hotel and set off on my rounds. First, I drove to Pascal's house at Westwood, near the university, UCLA. The house was a well-tended, biggish, one-storey Spanish-style building which, like most of the million-dollar-plus homes in the area, was nice enough but disappointing. I could have bought a Tudor mansion in Norfolk for less than half the money this place must have cost. I was rather hoping that Pascal would have had a maid or housekeeper I could talk to, somebody who might at least have given me some idea who his friends or associates were. But if such a person existed I was not about to get close to her. There was an awful lot of police activity going on around the house and I had no wish to bring myself to the attention of the cops.

So then I hit the talent agencies. I lost count of the number of them I called on but it didn't matter because I drew blank everywhere. Nobody knew Bev's name and nobody recognised her picture. It was the same story the next day. I covered Hollywood, Beverly Hills and the San Fernando Valley from Encino to Burbank. Everywhere the response was much the same, suspicious and vaguely hostile. 'What do you want with her? Who are you? Even if we knew her we couldn't possibly give you her address.' I explained wearily, time after time, that I was an old friend trying to re-establish contact, that I didn't expect them to give me her address or even her name if she'd changed it. All I wanted, if they knew her, was that they should give her my name and Hollywood phone number and ask her to ring me as a matter of urgency. They sniffed all around that, looking for booby traps, then said grudgingly that they guessed it would be okay if they knew her only they didn't know her, so they couldn't help. Sooorreee.

Back at the hotel about eight o'clock on Friday night I got out of my car, handed it over to the valet to park, and was in the middle of an exhausted stretch when a voice said, 'You Lennox? Robert Lennox?' He was a big man, both muscular and fat, in a crumpled blue suit. His breath smelt of Scotch and garlic and I knew he was a cop.

I said, 'Yes, I'm Lennox. Who are you?'

'Santa Claus,' he said. 'Assume the position. Come on, up against the wall.'

I leant against the wall the way I had seen people do it in the movies, arms wide above my head, legs straddled, and he frisked me.

'Come with me,' he said.

'Where to?'

'Don't ask damn fool questions, just come.' He grabbed me fiercely by the arm and began to drag me towards an unmarked car parked illegally in the road outside the hotel.

'You don't act like Santa Claus,' I said. But he just tugged me a little harder.

As we approached the car, the front passenger door was opened and the cop threw me in. I found myself bouncing against a slightly, but only slightly, smaller man in a grey suit who was sitting behind the steering wheel. 'Get the fuck off me,' he said and shoved me back against blue suit who had climbed in after me.

Blue suit hit me across the chest with a stiff forearm. 'Stop bouncing around in here, goddammit,' he said irritably.

'If you're the police,' I said, 'prove it.'

Grey suit said, 'We're the police and this proves it.' He opened his jacket just enough to show me the gun holstered under his arm.

'I want to see shields,' I said.

'Fuck you,' said blue suit and punched me in the stomach. It's difficult to hit anybody very hard when you're crushed up beside him in the front seat of a car but he did well in the circumstances. The blow knocked the breath out of me, not so much because of its power but because I wasn't prepared for it.

As I doubled up, trying to get some air back into my lungs, I leaned forward into the light thrown by a streetlamp. Grey suit said, 'I seen you before someplace.'

'Michael Caine,' I said, gasping.

'What?'

'People say I look like Michael Caine before he got rich and put on the weight.'

'Bullshit,' said grey suit. 'He look like Michael Caine to you?'

'No way,' said blue suit. 'To me he looks like a horse's ass.'

I said, 'Let me out of here. You can't do this. I know my rights.'

'Rights?' said grey suit. 'This minute you got all the rights we say you got and we say you got no rights.' He reached inside my jacket, took out my wallet and riffled through the credit cards, business cards, driver's licence and all the other stuff people keep in wallets. 'Guess he's Lennox okay,' he said.

Blue suit laid a big hand along my jaw, turned my face towards him and held me there. 'So what's it about, huh? We don't like creepy guys sneaking around town asking questions. Especially we don't like creepy guys sneaking around town asking questions about women. We figure these creepy guys could be perverts and we don't like perverts. We got all the perverts we can use around here. So what do you want with this woman?' He tightened his grip on my face, wrenching my lower jaw sideways. 'You notice I'm asking you nice. I don't have to ask you nice. I could ask you nasty and I don't think you'd like that.'

I tried to answer his questions but it was difficult with my face all twisted up. 'Waal, shee, I wash jusht . . .' It sounded like a lousy impersonation of Jimmy Stewart.

There was a sharp rap on the driver's window. Both cops looked up and blue suit let go of my face. 'Shit!' he said.

Grey suit wound the window down. 'Hi, Loot,' he said.

A tall, lean black man whose receding hair gave him a brainy-looking forehead peered into the car. 'How you doing, boys?' he asked courteously.

'This is him, Loot,' said grey suit. 'This is the guy. We found him.'

'That must have been hard, seeing he left his name and address all over town.' He looked at me, frowning. 'I know you.'

'Unh-unh.' Blue suit shook his head, chuckling. 'You just think you know him on account of he figures he looks like Michael Caine.'

'No,' said the black man. 'I look like Michael Caine. God knows who he looks like.' He studied me some more. 'What's your name again? Lennox?'

'Robert Lennox,' I said. 'My friends call me Bobby but I don't seem to have any around here.'

He nodded. 'Get out of the car.'

'But, Loot,' blue suit said protestingly, 'he's our collar.'

'He's nobody's collar. Yet. Let him out of the car.' Blue suit got out first and I followed him. The black man said, 'That's all, boys. I'll take it from here. Go on about your business. Hassle a few hookers or whatever it is you do to pass the time.' He slammed the door shut as blue suit got back into the car and he watched, hands in pockets, while the two grumbling cops drove away. Then he said: 'My name's Brown. Lieutenant Harry Brown, homicide division.'

'Homicide?' I said. 'I'm wanted for murder? Whose? I only got here the day before yesterday.'

He grinned. He had a pleasant, amused grin. 'Relax. We're short-handed around here. I'm helping out, is all. You want a drink?'

'More than anything else in the world. But I'd have thought a homicide cop had better things to do than chase around town looking for me. Isn't there a serial killer on the loose? Didn't he kill somebody only the other night? Man named Pascal or something?'

Brown shrugged. 'Not my case. Besides, I'm off duty, putting in a little extra time just to prove what a good conscientious cop I am. So let's go get that drink.' He led the way towards the hotel entrance and briefly laid a hand on my shoulder. 'Bobby Lennox, huh? The only guy ever went the distance with Willie Slate.'

'You know about that?'

'Saw the fight. Only on television, of course. I still have a tape of it.' We went into the bar and he chose a table in a far corner and ordered Scotch for both of us. 'Every time I'm feeling real low I get that tape out and have another look at it and then I feel better. Because however bad a time I've been having it isn't half as bad as the time Willie gave you.'

I said, 'You know what really pisses me off? I had a good career as a fighter – bronze medal in the

Olympics, thirty bouts as a pro. I only lost three, I was never stopped and when I retired I was still the middleweight champion of Britain, the Commonwealth and Europe. But all anybody ever remembers is that Willie Slate beat the shit out of me one night.'

'Beat the shit out of you,' Brown said, '*and* carried you.'

I was quiet for a moment. 'What gives you that idea?'

'Willie's an old friend. He told me about it. He made a lot of money that night.'

'I know. Everybody made a lot of money except me.'

He nodded. 'That's what Willie said. It's any interest to you, he also said he only really carried you the last three rounds. Up to then you were giving him as tough a fight as he'd ever had. You feel bad about it, you should look at the tape sometime. You'll see what he meant. Of course, he was beating you all the way but he only carried you the last three.'

'Thanks,' I said. It did make me feel better. I had a tape of the fight at home, too, but I had never had the heart to watch it, not even once.

Brown ran his finger down the side of his whisky glass. 'So what's with Mrs Bergdorf?'

'Who?'

'Mrs Bergdorf? Beverley Bergdorf? The lady you've been trying so hard to find these last two days?'

'So that's her name now. And Mrs, too.'

'Right. Her husband's a movie producer. Pretty big time at that. So what do you want with her?'

I had a story ready. Some of it – though not much – was even true. I told him how I'd known Bev when we were very young, how she had gone away and I had tried for a long time to find her again. And up to this point what I was telling him was indeed the truth – not the whole truth, perhaps, because I didn't actually tell him I'd killed somebody for Bev's sake. It didn't seem to be any of his business. Fiction crept in during the next bit. I said an old mutual acquaintance of hers and mine had been in LA on holiday a few months back, had bumped into Bev in the street, had gathered she was somehow connected with show business but, because they were both in a hurry at the time, hadn't got her new name or address or phone number. And as, by chance, I was already planning to come here myself I thought I'd spend a couple of days trying to find her. Just to say hello. Just for old times' sake.

Brown listened attentively and then said, 'That's a nice story. Boy and girl sweethearts, huh? Star-crossed lovers? Why is it that I very nearly believe you but not quite?'

'Because you're a cop,' I said. 'You have a nasty, suspicious nature.'

He grinned. 'Could be.'

'I have a nasty, suspicious nature, too, and what I don't understand is why you're interested and how you know who it is I'm looking for.'

'A girl at one of the talent agencies recognised the lady from the picture you were showing around. The same agency that looks after her husband's business. So she called him and he called us.'

'That answers one half of my question but what

about the other half? Why do you care what I'm doing?'

He looked at me carefully. 'On account of the blackmail,' he said. 'Somebody's trying to put the bite on the Bergdorf family and we figured there might be a connection.'

'Oh, great,' I said. 'Some blackmailer I am. I don't even know my victim's name or address.' Blackmail? Who could be trying to blackmail Bev and why? Or maybe Bev wasn't the victim, maybe it was her husband, the hot-shot film producer.

'I thought about that,' he said, 'and maybe it's just a coincidence that you should happen along at a time like this, but you mind proving to me how long you've been in town? You want to show me your passport?'

I went up to my room to get it and by the time I came back he had ordered another round of drinks. 'I charged them to you,' he said. 'I figured you wouldn't mind.'

'Nice of you to tell me. It's good to find an honest cop.'

He grinned that amiable, pleasant grin again, took the passport from me and looked through it. 'Seems okay. Unless you're working with some crazy accomplice in town here who refuses to tell you who you're both blackmailing, I reckon you're clean.'

'Good. So now we've settled that, how do I get in touch with Mrs Bergdorf?'

'You don't,' he said. 'She doesn't want to see you.' Again he was watching me carefully. I had the feeling that the way I reacted could be rather important. So I looked as crestfallen as I could, stared at my beer mat for a few seconds, then

glanced up at him and sighed. It was a disappointed but resigned sigh, not a great sigh
perhaps but a good one. 'That's terrific,' I said. 'I
waste two days of my holiday looking for a
woman who won't even give me the time of day.
Well, to hell with her. I mean, Christ, maybe
she's right. It's been a lot of years. She'd probably
forgotten me. I can't say I feel very flattered
but . . .' I shrugged and stared at the beer mat
again. By way of variation I also picked it up and
twisted it around in my fingers.

Brown said, 'That's a good attitude. I like that
attitude.'

'Well, what the heck. I'm free, white, over
twenty-one, good-looking, I've got money. I don't
have to force myself on a woman who doesn't want
to know me.'

'It must be nice to be white,' Brown said.

'Sorry.'

'It's okay. Some of my best friends are white.'
This time there was a gently ironic twist to the grin.
He called the waiter over and ordered two more
drinks.

'Is this your round or mine?' I asked.

'Still yours,' he said. 'Seeing you're free, white,
over twenty-one and got money, I figure you can
afford it.'

'You forgot good-looking.'

'I'm not so sure about good-looking. And what's
all this Michael Caine bullshit?'

'A lot of people say I look like Michael Caine,' I
said earnestly. 'An awful lot of people.' Well, Arnie
did anyway; he was the first person who had ever
spotted the resemblance.

Brown said, 'They must want to borrow money

or something. So tell me – how do you plan to spend the rest of your time here?'

I shrugged. 'Do the tourist bit, I suppose. Disneyland, Universal Studios. Then maybe I'll go to somewhere like Santa Barbara, get a bit of sun and sea air.'

He nodded approvingly. 'That's good. Just so long as you keep away from the Bergdorfs.'

'Who needs the Bergdorfs?' I said.

He showed more approval. 'Nice thinking. Keep thinking that way because then you and I can stay friends and I'd like us to be friends.' He finished his drink. 'You want to eat something? The restaurant here's okay.'

'My treat, I suppose.'

'What else? You're free, white –'

'Okay, okay,' I said. 'Just so long as you don't spend the whole meal reminding me of the beating I took from Willie Slate.' So we went next door to the restaurant and we talked fights and the fight game and I don't suppose he mentioned Willie Slate and the beating he gave me more than half a dozen times. We had a nice evening. He was good company; I liked him; I even trusted him. I almost trusted him enough to tell him the real reason I was in LA. Almost, not quite. It's hard to trust a cop that much.

8

I WAS UP EARLY the next morning, looking through the telephone books again. The area was not short of Bergdorfs but there were no Beverley Bergdorfs and since I didn't know her husband's first name there was no way of telling which, if any, of the male Bergdorfs he might be. I could have phoned every number in the books, of course, but I didn't really think that would be helpful. It didn't seem terribly likely that a big-time film producer would have a listed number anyway.

Over breakfast I read the *LA Times* again. There was still no word from Europe but against that there was a fresh catalogue of violent crimes: a taxi driver had been bludgeoned and robbed in the Hollywood Hills; another black girl had been found raped and murdered on a piece of wasteland, which indicated that LA could now boast a homicidal serial rapist as well as a homicidal serial robber; an off-duty policeman had been shot dead by a man he had disturbed ripping off a liquor store, which seemed to even the score between off-duty policemen and liquor store raiders; a private detective had been shot equally dead at his home; a quantity of cocaine worth half a million dollars had mysteriously disappeared from a police station; and a couple more teenagers had overdosed on heroin. Another quiet day in sleepy old LA.

When I'd finished with the *Times* I turned to the trade papers, *Variety* and the *Hollywood Reporter*, and here I struck lucky. In the *Hollywood Reporter* there was a five-paragraph story which said that producer Freddie Bergdorf and his beautiful blonde wife, Beverley, were throwing a party that very afternoon at their home just off Coldwater Canyon to celebrate the start of production of Mr Bergdorf's new, megabucks movie, *Space Fiends: The Sequel*. There followed a list of some of the people who were expected to turn up. Most of the names meant nothing to me, though I imagined they were pretty big in the movie world, but there were a few British producers, directors and actors whom I had heard of. The actual address of the house was not given but the general location was identified closely enough to convince me that I wouldn't have too much trouble finding it. Serendipity, I thought, but not all that remarkable bearing in mind that the film industry hereabouts consisted more or less of a village community. If Bev's husband was only a halfway important part of that community, the chances were that he would be mentioned pretty often in the trades.

That afternoon, therefore, I put on my smartest California casuals, the chinos, the sneakers, the silk shirt, the light cashmere sweater draped casually and imperatively – although in this heat quite unnecessarily – around my shoulders and studied the effect in the bedroom mirror. All the designer labels were prominently on view and, as usual, they were far more impressive than the clothes themselves. Did I look like a gatecrasher? No, I did not. I looked quite as phoney as anybody else in Hollywood. I readjusted the sweater slightly and I knew I would do.

The house was indeed not difficult to find. There was so much activity outside that it was obvious a party was in progress. A sign on the sidewalk said 'Valet Parking', though I never thought of it as that: I always thought of it as 'varlet parking', which, in my experience, was a great deal closer to the truth. The varlets, Hispanics mostly, hung about in red jackets, white shirts, black ties and black slacks to take people's cars away, crash the gears and park them wherever they could find a spot.

'Name, sir?' said the varlet who opened my door for me.

'Puttnam,' I said, plucking one of the English names from the list I'd read that morning. 'David Puttnam.'

'Puttnam? Jesus, din' you useta be head of Columbia Studios?' He looked more closely at the medium-sized rented hack I was driving. 'Theengs have change, huh?'

'Well, that's show business,' I said. 'But don't worry, I'll be back. Between you and me, Paramount have made an offer.' I gave him the keys and a conspiratorial wink. For good measure I also gave him five dollars and he drove the car away, looking happy.

A man at the gate wearing a white tuxedo and holding a clipboard said, 'May I see your invitation, sir?'

114

I said, 'Oh dear, I am sorry. I gave it to that man who took my car. I thought –'

'No, sir. You're supposed to show the invitation to me. What name is it?'

'Puttnam,' I said. 'David Puttnam.' I was using my very best, most clipped English accent, not a bit like Michael Caine. I had no idea how David Puttnam spoke but I was sure he would not have been offended.

The man at the gate consulted his clipboard and nodded. 'Mrs Puttnam not with you, sir?'

'No. She's, er, she's not feeling too well.'

'I'm sorry to hear that, sir.' He opened the gate and ushered me through. 'There you go, sir. Only next time if you could just remember to keep the invitation . . .'

'If there is a next time,' I said, 'I'll certainly remember.'

A man who had been standing just inside the gate, idly swinging a golf club on the luxuriant lawn, came up to me, smiling. He looked to be in his early to mid-sixties with a good tan, thick grey hair, smooth skin and tinted aviator glasses. He was dressed all in white and his clothes proclaimed their designer origins as loudly as mine did. 'So you're David Puttnam?' he said, holding out his hand. He had a soft, pleasing voice with a slight, indefinable European accent.

'That's me,' I said.

'I'm a great admirer of your films, Mr Puttnam. And I'd just like to say how sorry I am that things didn't work out at Columbia.'

'Way it goes,' I said. What on earth was all this about Columbia? I had never followed the ins and outs of the film industry very closely but I was beginning to get the idea that something not too good had happened to David Puttnam at Columbia Studios.

'Perhaps we'll have a chance to talk later,' he said and went away to practise his golf swing some more. I walked up the short drive, with lawns and flowerbeds full of huge, multicoloured shrubs on either side, to the house. It was a big, white, two-storey building with columns and an enormous front door, and it gave a strong impression that the architect had been overinfluenced by *Gone With The Wind*. The impression was heightened by the elderly black butler who stood at the door. 'Miss Scarlett in?' I asked.

He gave me the small, resigned grin of a man who wished he had a dollar for every time he had heard this kind of stuff. 'Round the back,' he said. 'Everybody's round the back.'

So I walked around the house and into the garden. It was long, wide, dominated by an extensive patio and a swimming pool shaped like a heart. At the far end of the lawn was an expensive summerhouse built of logs. Inside it a number of elegantly casual people were hanging around a bar and there were more people, many more people, just as elegantly and casually attired lounging about on the patio and alongside the pool. I accepted a glass of champagne from a waiter in white shirt and black pants and when I had taken a sip and looked up I found I was standing beside Michael Caine.

'Oh, hi,' I said.

'Hello,' he said, hitting the aspirate carefully. I'd rather expected a look of amazement, of astonished recognition, to cross his features as he looked at me but nothing like that happened. He just blinked through his sunglasses and said, 'How are you these days?' He spoke as if he knew me but I suppose that's the way you have to carry on in the movie industry. You can never be sure that the stranger you're talking to is not, in fact, somebody to whom you were introduced briefly at a charity dinner five months ago and who is also the brother-in-law of the producer who, you hope, is going to offer you your next starring role. You have to pretend you know him or he might be so offended that he'll persuade his brother-in-law not to come through. A woman in a pink silk trouser suit rushed up and greeted Michael Caine effusively. 'Michael!' she said and kissed him on both cheeks.

'Hello,' he said. 'How are you these days?'

She looked across at me, frowning slightly. 'Have we met?' she asked. 'You look kind of familiar.'

I inclined my head slightly towards Michael Caine but no look of astonished recognition crossed her features either. It was very disappointing. She linked her arm in Michael Caine's and led him away, talking animatedly to him.

I wandered slowly through the shifting crowds, smiling and nodding at people I didn't know. They smiled and nodded back but none of them engaged me in conversation. None of them seemed to mistake me for Michael Caine and presumably I didn't resemble a producer or a director or a studio head or anyone else important either. Perhaps I just looked like a brother-in-law and therefore, unless I took the initiative and went up and talked to them, a nod and a smile were all I was due. Waiters rushed to and fro bearing trays of canapés, or hors d'oeuvres as the Americans call them, and other waiters plied the guests with every imaginable kind of drink. The unmistakable smell of marijuana smoke drifted up from behind a bush. I went into the summerhouse where a man whose eyes glittered and shone was licking something off a fifty-dollar bill, while a group stood around him chuckling, their eyes as shiny and glittery as his, saying things like, 'Feeling no pain, hey, Joe?'

I went out again and strolled back up the garden and I was just beginning to wonder whether I had gatecrashed the wrong party and this wasn't the Bergdorfs' place at all when Bev came out of the house. She looked fantastic in a dress that was both gold and simple with high-heeled golden slippers to match. Like most women she had acquired beauty after the age of thirty; until thirty no woman can truly be called beautiful – pretty, yes, sexy, yes, desirable, yes, but not beautiful. Beauty comes with age, experience and a lot of expensive care and Bev had all that going for her.

She saw and knew me in the same instant that I saw and knew her. 'Hello, Bev,' I said. There didn't seem to be much else to say really.

'Bobby!' Her mouth fell open slightly, revealing perfect, gleaming teeth that owed more to an expensive dentist than to careless nature. 'What are you doing here?' The south London accent had gone to be replaced by a California drawl. 'I don't want you here. Get out, please.'

'Bev.' I caught her by the arm and felt the same old thrill as my fingers touched the firm, silky skin. 'Bev, I must talk to you. I . . .'

The elderly party with the aviator glasses and the white outfit drifted up. He seemed to have left his golf club somewhere. He smiled warmly at me and said, 'Beverley, perhaps I should warn you that this gentleman suffers under the delusion that he is David Puttnam. I thought he was harmless enough but if he is bothering you I can easily have him escorted out.'

I said, 'Please, Bev.'

She hesitated for a moment, then: 'It's okay, Tommy. Really. He's just . . . an old friend, somebody I haven't seen for more years than I like to remember.'

I said to the elderly party, 'Look, perhaps I should introduce myself properly. My real name is Bobby Lennox –'

'Ah, yes!' he said. 'I thought you looked familiar. Bobby Lennox. A fighter, I think. I saw you once –'

'Against Willie Slate,' I said, nodding resignedly. 'Everyone saw that fight.'

'No, I'm sorry, but I didn't. Should I have? The fight I saw was at Caesar's Palace in Las Vegas. The main bout, I believe, featured Muhammad Ali against . . .' He shook his head. 'Someone whose name I cannot now recall. You were on the undercard that night against a very good New York middleweight whose name I also cannot recall. What I do recall, however, is that you were most impressive. I think I'm right in saying that you won by a knockout in the fourth round.'

I remembered the occasion and unlike him I could also remember my opponent's name. I didn't mention it, though. I simply beamed at the old fellow, liking him instantly because he was one of the few people in the world who remembered me for something other than being thrashed by Willie Slate.

'Well, if you're sure, my dear, I'll leave you,' he said to Beverley. 'Good day, Mr Lennox.'

'Who was that?' I asked when he had gone.

'My father-in-law. Bobby, what the hell do you want?'

'Is your husband here?'

She frowned. 'Yes, of course. He's . . .' She looked about her and then pointed. 'He's over there, talking to Steven Spielberg.' I glanced over at the two men she was pointing to. I didn't recognise Steven Spielberg, but I did recognise the other man: he was the one in the second photograph that Jinks/Pascal had shown me.

I said, 'Go and get him. I have to talk to both of you, somewhere quiet, somewhere private. It's very important.'

She stepped a little closer, staring into my face as if seeking hidden motives and I stared back at her. This caused me no pain; she was lovely, she was serene, she was sophisticated in a way she had never been when I had known her. And yet . . . there was something missing: a spark, an optimistic glow that she used to have. If you had never known it was there, you would never know it had gone. She didn't look defeated, disappointed, embittered; she didn't look as if life had treated her badly. There was nothing negative about her; she looked simply great. But at the same time there was nothing positive about her either. What had vanished was the glorious, touching eagerness that I remembered, a quality that had made her both exciting and vulnerable. I was looking at a beautiful, assured young Hollywood matron, a woman who knew what life had given her so far and what it had to offer in the future and who had settled for that. It was obviously by no means bad, what she had settled for, but equally it was less than she had really wanted.

She said, 'Bobby, you're not going to make trouble for me, are you?'

I shook my head impatiently. 'I'm trying to save you from trouble. For Chrissake, do you think I'd come barging in here, pretending to be David Puttnam, if it wasn't really urgent? Look, go get your husband.'

'All right.' She led me into the house, into a high, book-lined room that opened off a wide, cool passage. The room had a desk and a lot of leather armchairs; a word processor; a huge TV screen and a video recorder; a mass of framed photographs on every surface. 'Wait here,' she said.

I spent the next five minutes examining the photographs. Most of them showed her husband, Freddie, in various stages of development: Freddie as a little boy with his parents, Freddie as a teenager with his parents, Freddie as a young man with his parents. Then there was Freddie just with his father, Freddie with his father and Bev, Freddie and Bev together. The mother seemed to have vanished when Freddie was in his early twenties. He didn't look very much like either of his parents. The father's hair was thick and white, Freddie's was black and receding fast; the father was stocky, Freddie was slim and a good three inches taller. The mother had been plump and fair and about medium height. For the most part, the pictures of Bev dated back only a few years although there were one or two of her as a young girl that must have been taken when she lived in The Street but the backgrounds were strictly neutral and could have been anywhere.

When she came back Freddie was with her, looking irritable. She said, 'Freddie, I'd like you to meet

121

Bobby Lennox, an old friend. We grew up together in London.'

'Oh yeah, the guy who's been asking after you.' He held out his hand. 'Nice to see you,' though it was clear that he didn't think it was nice to see me at all. His handshake was too firm, the shake of a man who wanted to establish immediate superiority. For several seconds we went through the ridiculous macho business of trying to crush each other's fingers. He was about my height and as free of surplus fat as I was but he was more slender, less muscular, about ten pounds lighter. Where I worked out hard in the gym he looked, as I had suspected from his photograph, as if he kept fit in the pool and on the tennis court. It didn't matter to me but it mattered to him. He seemed to feel threatened by me, almost as if he felt that we were rival cavemen and I had come to drag his woman away from him.

He said, 'What's this all about – ah, Bobbie, is it?' It was a childish gambit to pretend he hadn't caught my name and, just as childishly, I went along with it.

'Well, er, Freddie, is it?' I said, 'it's simply that somebody wants you dead. Not just you but Beverley as well.'

He said, 'Ah, fuck, what is this? Some scene from a crappy movie you've written? Jesus, honey, how could you let this clown talk you into –'

'Shut up,' I said. 'Just shut up and listen. Unlike you I know that life is possible outside the cinema and, also unlike you, I know that bad things happen outside the cinema. Somebody wanted to pay me 50,000 pounds to kill the pair of you and I want to know why.'

He looked at Bev, who looked scared, and then he looked back at me and he didn't look scared; he lóoked sceptical. 'Then why the hell don't you ask the guy who put out the contract?'

'Because he's dead himself,' I said. 'He was murdered the other night by your friendly neighbourhood serial killer.'

Freddie shrugged. 'Then what's the problem? He's dead, we're not, and I imagine you don't intend to kill us otherwise you'd hardly be here talking to us.'

'Ah, shit,' I said. 'Will you please drag your mind away from movies and happy endings? The fact that he's dead does not mean you two are out of danger. What if he had associates? Listen, all I want to know is why he wanted you dead. I asked him but he wouldn't tell me and I didn't get the opportunity to ask him again. If I knew what his motive was I'd know whether the danger died with him. For God's sake, that's why I'm here – I'm trying to protect you.'

Freddie was silent for a moment. I don't think he liked me any better, despite what I'd said. In fact I think he liked me less. 'What was this guy's name?'

'Pascal. Philippe Pascal.'

'Never heard of him,' Freddie said firmly.

Bev said, 'I have. At least, I think I have. Did he own dress shops around Rodeo Drive?'

I nodded.

'I've bought clothes from him. I mean, not from him personally but from his stores.'

'Well, maybe that's it,' Freddie said, throwing in a light laugh that convinced nobody. 'Maybe you forgot to pay him and that's why he put out a contract.' Both Bev and I ignored this rubbish and just stared at him impassively.

'Jesus Christ!' Freddie said. 'I can't believe this. A guy neither of us knows hires a hitman – I guess that's what you are, right? A hitman? – he hires a hitman to kill us? And you come here asking us why? Jesus Christ!' He shook his head.

'Let's get something straight,' I said. 'I am *not* a hitman but for reasons I don't want to go into now that's what Pascal thought I was. Now, okay, the fact that he himself has subsequently been murdered is a nice touch of dramatic irony. But, I repeat, it does not necessarily mean that the pair of you are home and dry. Other people could have been involved and those other people might still want to see you both blown away. Look, please, I'm here to save your lives not to take them. Won't you, for God's sake, try to help me?'

Freddie held up both hands in front of him as if warding off an attack. 'Okay, okay. But I can't handle this right now. Jesus, I got guests out there, important people – Spielberg's there, George Lucas, Coppola, Bobby De Niro's expected. This party will be over at, I don't know, six-thirty, seven o'clock. Do you want to come back at seven-thirty. We can talk about it then? I mean, shit, you're the hitman, you're not going to kill me before seven-thirty, are you?'

'I don't intend to kill you at all,' I said wearily. 'That's what this whole conversation has been about. All right. I'll come back at seven-thirty but, please, the one thing I ask is that you take the matter seriously.'

'I will,' he said. 'Sure I will.' Then he sneered at me and left. Bev, on the other hand, was not sneering. She looked pale and frightened. 'You really mean it, Bobby, don't you?' she said.

'Of course I do! Look, this wouldn't mean anything to your husband but I think it'll mean something to you – the contract was really put out to Arnie. All right? You remember Arnie?'

'God, how could anyone forget Arnie?'

'Right,' I said. 'So I'll come back at half-past seven and in the meantime try to persuade that idiot you're married to that I'm not pulling his leg.'

'He's not an idiot,' she said stoutly. Then she led me out along the wide, cool corridor to the front door and left me there.

The butler said, 'Did you find Miss Scarlett?'

'No,' I said. 'I think she's in Atlanta, tending the wounded.'

He chuckled and said, 'Right on!' I think we'd suddenly become friends.

I went back to the gate and was just about to ask for Mr Puttnam's car when I overheard the same varlet who had greeted me in loud altercation with a latecomer, a man in a crumpled, dark suit and, despite the heat, a knitted waistcoat. 'What do you mean, David Puttnam's here already?' this man was saying. '*I* am David Puttnam!'

'Bullsheet,' the varlet said. 'I seen Meester Puttnam come een.'

'Here's my invitation,' the man in the waistcoat said. 'I *am* David Puttnam.'

Another varlet approached me. 'Name, sir?'

'Parker,' I said, summoning up another British name from the list in the *Hollywood Reporter*. 'Alan Parker. This is the registration number of my car.' He trotted off to get it while I hid behind a bush. The man in the waistcoat finally managed to get in, along with a tall, pretty blonde whom I took to be his wife. I imagined he must be the genuine article, but if he wasn't this party was going to have David Puttnams the way other people had mice.

The second varlet came back with my car. I drove a few yards down the street and made a U-turn. As I went back past the gates another man with an English accent was arguing furiously with the fellow with the clipboard and the white tuxedo. 'What are you talking about, Alan Parker's just left?' he was shouting. '*I'm* Alan Parker!'

I drove away from there with a sense of relief. The way things were going, it looked as if it might turn into a very quarrelsome party.

9

I SPENT THE REST OF THE AFTERNOON lying on my
bed watching something called *The Wide World of
Sport* on TV. There was an athletics meeting from
Florida, a reprise of the previous day's play at
Wimbledon and a fight for one of the numerous
versions of the world middleweight championship
that plodded the full course and left me thinking
that if I were still active I could have beaten both
men. Instead of just being a contender – and Marlon
Brando can take my word for it, being a contender
is no big deal – I could have been the champion.
It's easy these days. If you don't fancy the holder
of the WBA title, you can go for the man who has
the WBC title, or the IBF title, or the WBO title and
the beauty of this is that there's no logical end to it.
Now that boxing has been turned into alphabet
soup why not have the ABC world champion or the
OPQ world champion or the XYZ world champion?
Better still why shouldn't every country have its
own world champion? Or every city? Or every
suburb? How about being the Cricklewood world
middleweight champion? And if that's still too

tough a target you could have world champions at every weight in every street or house or flat. One day anybody who ever puts on a pair of boxing gloves will automatically be a world champion even if his domain doesn't extend beyond his own bathroom. I was born before my time, that's my trouble – but then wasn't every athlete who never quite made it to the very top?

Just before 7.30 I set off for Beverly Hills again. The party was over, the cars and the varlets had gone.

The black butler opened the door to me, grinned and said, 'De white folks am down in de screenin'-room, massa.'

'Then lead me to them, Pork,' I said, like Rhett Butler breezing into Tara.

He chuckled. 'Strictly speaking,' he said, 'Pork was a valet, not a butler but I guess it'll do.'

As we walked through the house I said, 'What are these particular white folks like to work for?'

'Pretty good. Well, she's better than pretty good. Considerate, you know? Like she's not all that accustomed to having servants and still figures they might be human beings, too. And he, well I guess he's okay. I've worked for worse.'

'What about the old man? Tommy, is it? Does he live here?'

'Hell, no. He's got his own place up in Bel Air.'

'One way and another,' I said, 'I'm beginning to get the idea that this is a family that's not short of a few dollars.'

He chuckled again. 'You could say that. Man, you sure could say that.'

Out in the back a small mob of menials was clearing away the detritus of the afternoon's party. Bits of food, paper napkins and plastic glasses littered the patio and something that looked at first like a large turd, but turned out on closer inspection to be a species of vol-au-vent, was floating on the surface of the swimming pool. The Bergdorfs, father, son and daughter-in-law were in the summerhouse, reclining in chintzy armchairs and drinking spritzers.

As I went in Freddie said, 'Oh, Jeeze, run for your lives – here comes Murder Incorporated.' I think he must have been tucking away something rather more powerful than spritzers that day.

Tommy Bergdorf said, 'Freddie, be nice. Mr Lennox is here to help us.' Freddie grunted something that could have been an apology, Bev poured me a glass of wine and I joined the cosy family circle. Bev was sitting between the two other men and not looking very happy.

Tommy said, 'Beverley has told me about your conversation this afternoon but I should rather like to know more.'

So I told them more. I told them about Arnie and Jinks who was really Pascal and I told them, too, that I knew somebody was trying to blackmail them and when I had finished, Bev said, 'Poor old Arnie.'

Freddie said: 'Honey, you mean you knew this guy, this killer? He was a *friend* of yours?'

'He wasn't a bad sort of bloke,' I said, 'unless, of course, you happened to stand between him and his fee. I'd have to admit that he wasn't a man to let friendship get in the way of business but otherwise he could be kindness itself. However, let's not get sidetracked here. Arnie's gone and RIP, but the whole point of my being here is that I don't want to be saying RIP over you two. If Pascal was in this alone then the danger's probably passed. But what if he wasn't alone? What if . . .'

And at this point a door beside the bar opened and my old friend and fellow boxing enthusiast Lieutenant Harry Brown joined the company.

I said, 'Christ, you people are unbelievable. I come here as an act of goodwill and you call the police in.'

Brown said, 'Hey, Bobby, it's cool. Don't worry.' He poured himself a bourbon and ice at the bar and pulled up a chair beside me, grinned amiably and said, 'How you doin'?'

I said, 'I'm not very happy', and that made two of us – Bev and me – who weren't very happy.

She said, 'Bobby, I'm really sorry –'

Tommy Bergdorf chipped in, 'Mr Lennox, we all owe you an apology but I do assure you that Lieutenant Brown was right when he said you were not to worry. He is here ex-officio. We simply felt that his advice might be helpful in these circumstances. If, after your revelations this afternoon, we had called in the police officially – and that, perhaps, is what we should have done – your position would have been extremely awkward. I'm sure you realise that. But this way we have police advice without, as it were, police interference. Lieutenant Brown's discretion can be relied upon. He and I are old friends.'

'Knew each other in Vegas,' Brown said. 'We go back a good few years, Tommy and I. But', he tapped me reprovingly on the knee, 'my nasty, suspicious nature was right last night, huh? You were lying to me.'

'No. I was simply being economical with the truth. It's a well-established British tradition, especially in diplomatic circles.' I was beginning to feel a little easier. I had trusted Harry Brown last night and I trusted him now, though still not completely. I had the feeling that this could be a very dangerous man.

He said, 'Something I want to get straight. If you're not a hitman why were you helping this guy, Arnie, to set up a hit?'

'He was calling in a favour.'

'Boy, that must have been some favour. What the hell did he do for you?'

'Nothing. I didn't really owe him at all; he just thought I did. It's too complicated to go into now.'

Tommy Bergdorf interrupted again. His tone was mild but he was watching me carefully. 'What I find hard to understand is why you agreed to help this man at all. To me it seems, to say the very least, morally reprehensible.' He may have intended this ironically but it didn't sound like it.

'Yes,' I said. 'Of course it was. But . . . Look, I don't know where any of you people come from but in the neighbourhood where Bev and I grew up most people were crooked and some of them were killers. We didn't necessarily approve of what they did, maybe we even disapproved, but at the same time it was possible to divorce the person from the occupation. Arnie was a friend, I'd known him since I was a kid; he wanted help, I gave it to him; because we both came from the same place. You probably don't understand.'

'I do,' Brown said. 'I understand. I grew up in Watts. I'm not saying I'd have done what you did but I can understand why you did it.'

And then we moved away from my relationship with Arnie, which was history anyway, while Harry

Brown told us what he had discovered about Pascal. It wasn't much. Brown had spent the latter part of the afternoon sifting through the LA police department files on the man and Pascal had come up clean. He had arrived in the Beverly Hills area from New York twenty years previously, had started his business in a small way and then swiftly thrived and expanded. His clients included the wives of movie stars, producers, directors, television people, record industry people and many others, some of them shady. But there was no evidence to suggest that he knew the shady people any better than, or even as well as, he knew the show business people. Brown had put in a request to the NYPD for anything they had on Pascal's earlier life there but nothing had come through yet and he didn't expect much of any interest.

'I mean,' he said, 'what can have happened back East more than twenty years ago to make him put out a contract on Fred and Beverley now? Freddie, you were what, twenty-five, something like that? What the hell can you have done then to piss him off for more than twenty years? And Beverley wasn't even in the USA at that time. I can't figure it.'

So then we talked about the blackmail attempt to see if there could be any connection. A man had phoned Bev a week ago and told her he had something on a video tape that he was sure she wouldn't want anyone else to see, especially not her husband. But, he said, he was not a greedy or vindictive person – for 100,000 dollars the tape was hers and she was getting a bargain because this was the mastertape and there were no copies. He had, not surprisingly, left no name but had promised to get in touch with her again within a few days. So far he had not done so, and apart from the fact that she was sure it had been a local call that was all she could tell us.

'Pascal?' Brown asked. 'Could it have been Pascal?'

'No,' I said. 'Pascal was still in London last Saturday. An accomplice maybe, that's certainly possible. Bev, did he say what was on that tape?'

She looked across at Harry Brown, who grinned his pleasant grin, finished his drink and stood up. 'Well, folks, I guess it's time for me to go,' he said. 'You want me, you know where to find me. See you around, Bobby.'

'Is that a threat or a promise?'

'Whichever.' He gave us all a casual wave of the hand and went out.

We watched him go up the lawn and round the side of the house and out of sight and then Bev said, 'I didn't want to talk in front of him. He doesn't know what was on the tape or what that man said was there.'

I glanced at Tommy and Freddie. 'But they do?'

She nodded. 'Yes. I told them. It's okay, Bobby, they know all about me. Look, a few years ago I was stranded in Las Vegas. I'd been with a dance troupe, we were playing a hotel there and it wasn't Caesar's Palace, believe me: this place was the absolute pits. Anyway, the owners went bust and refused to pay us and the troupe broke up. So there I was, out of work and with about ten dollars in my pocket and a man I'd met came along and said he knew how I could earn some money.' She shrugged. 'I'd never been much of a dancer and besides I was getting too old for it so I went back on the game. I was part of a small stable of girls this guy looked after. We serviced the high rollers who came into town. And, well, the man on the phone last week said that this video he has shows me at work. You want details?'

I shook my head. 'No, I can imagine. And you told all this to your husband and father-in-law?'

'They already knew. I mean, they knew how I'd earned my living in Vegas.'

'So where's the problem? If the only people who matter know already why didn't you just tell the man on the phone to sod off?'

Freddie said, 'It's not that simple. So far as I'm aware nobody else around here knows about Beverley's past. We all want to keep it that way.'

'But if that's so, was it really such a good idea to call in the police?'

Freddie looked at his father, who smiled deprecatingly at me. 'In this country, Mr Lennox, it's not impossible to, ah, control the police.' He looked at his watch and got up. 'Children, I have to leave you. I'm due for supper with Senator Rubens at the Beverly Wilshire.' He came across and shook my hand. 'I hope we shall meet again, Mr Lennox. In fact I'm sure we will. In the meantime, I want to thank you for what you have tried to do for Freddie and Beverley. I do appreciate it.'

We all stood to say goodbye and when the old man had left the three of us refilled our glasses and sat down again and I said, 'Which of you, ah, controls Lieutenant Brown – you, Freddie, or your father? And, as a matter of interest, how much does it cost?'

He said angrily, 'I don't have to answer that kind of question.'

'True. But the answer's not very important

anyway. It's pretty obvious somebody's paying Harry Brown. I mean, why should those two clowns have picked me up last night if someone wasn't using a little muscle behind the scenes in the LAPD? In a town with the crime rate this one has, even a couple of boozy time-servers wouldn't normally be detached to go looking for a bloke who was simply asking questions the way I was. Good old Harry was responsible for that. And a homicide lieutenant doesn't go to that much trouble out of public-spiritedness; there's got to be something pretty substantial in it for him.'

Bev said, 'You're overlooking one thing, Bobby. Freddie and his father have got a lot of clout around here, so the police would look after them anyway. Tommy's very big in the Republican Party and Freddie's just about to make the hottest picture in town.' She smiled fondly at her husband and stroked his cheek with an index finger. He took hold of her hand and sucked the finger that had stroked him.

'The hottest picture in town? *Space Fiends: The Sequel*?' I'd seen the original in London a year ago – it was dreadful; as one of the British critics had said, it was by Steven Spielberg out of John Carpenter; it was ET with a chainsaw; it was *Halloween* with a touch of the cutes. 'You must be joking.'

'The first movie,' Freddie said with cold dignity, 'the original *Space Fiends* cost 15 million and it's already grossed close to 300 domestically. It was the biggest smash since *Total Recall*. There's no telling how much it will earn worldwide. And *The Sequel* will probably make twice as much. When Beverley tells you it's going to be the hottest picture in town you better believe it. Every company, every studio wanted *The Sequel* and we had them over a barrel because it's all ours – our idea, our script. And around here that gives us power. We want the police to do something, the police do it. In this town money talks and the more money you got the harder people listen.'

Which really brought us back to what I'd been saying in the first place: either Freddie or his father was making voluntary contributions to Harry Brown's pension, pocket money or fuck-you fund. 'Were you using the royal "we" there,' I said, 'or do you have a partner?'

Freddie nodded. 'Sure, I have a partner.'

'What happens to this property, this picture of yours, if you should die?'

'What?' He looked surprised, puzzled. 'Well, my share goes to Beverley, of course. But the control of the movie passes to Karl. If I was dead he'd be the only one who could make decisions.'

'Decisions like taking the film away from the studio you're at now and moving it to another one that had possibly made a better offer? Is that what you mean?'

Freddie turned in amused disbelief to Bev. 'You listening to this, honey? Do you hear what he's suggesting – that Karl, Karl Strauss for Chrissake, might have put out a hit on me so he could make a lousy couple of million on a new deal? Is this guy for real?'

I said, 'This may come as a shock to you, Freddie, but people have had other people killed for a lot less than a lousy couple of million.'

'Forget it,' he said and he was angry again now. 'I don't even want to hear you talk this way.'

'Okay. So let's go back to the blackmailer. He

136

didn't say exactly when he was going to call again, right? He said a few days. Well, a week's a few days. Could he have called today, while you were busy looking after your guests perhaps?'

Bev said, 'I suppose – well, I suppose it's possible. I had the answering machine on all afternoon, so the household staff could just concentrate on the party. We could go check it.'

So we did. There were quite a few calls on the machine: one or two from people apologising for the fact that they couldn't make it to the party; a couple from women friends of Bev's suggesting lunch; one from somebody who had hung up without leaving any kind of message at all. ('That's our guy,' Freddie said. 'That's got to be our guy.') I told him to shut up and listened to the rest of it. A garage had rung to say Bev could take her car in on Monday and a girl's voice apologised for the fact that Mr Kaplan would not be calling after all. That was the lot.

'Who the hell's Kaplan?' Freddie said.

Bev shrugged. 'I don't know. I don't know anybody called Kaplan.'

Freddie said, 'Well, you ask me, our guy was the one who hung up, the guy who didn't leave a message. And if it was him, you can bet your life he'll call back.'

I said, 'Are you sure about Kaplan, Bev? Think hard.'

She thought hard, frowning, and then shook her head. 'I told you – I don't know anybody of that name.'

But I did. Or at least I knew of somebody who used to be called Kaplan. Because that was the name of the private detective who had been murdered at his home the previous night.

10

BACK AT THE HOTEL I looked through the *LA Times* again. The late private eye's full name was Roger Kaplan, aged fifty-four, divorced, no children. He had an office on Hollywood Boulevard and a small house in the Hollywood Hills. Both had been ransacked, presumably after the killing, which had taken place not actually in Kaplan's house but in his driveway. He had been shot twice in the back while apparently running away. The police, and the paper's headline, claimed another victim for the serial killer, while an LAPD spokesman interpreted the fact that, unlike his predecessors, Kaplan was not a rich man as a grim suggestion that the killer was no longer simply out for money – he was now killing for the fun of it. The background story said that Kaplan had been in a modest way of business along with a junior partner and a secretary. Neither the police nor the newspaper had been able to contact either of them.

It wasn't an awful lot to go on but I was interested by the coincidence of one Mr Kaplan being unable to make a call the day after another Mr Kaplan was shot dead. The way I saw it, things would be much neater all round if both Mr Kaplans were the same Mr Kaplan. I got to work with the phone books again. Unlike the Bergdorfs, Roger Kaplan was listed both at home and at work and I was just about to start calling when my phone rang and it was Harry Brown in the bar.

'Come down and have a drink,' he said. 'I have to talk to you.'

'I'm not sure my bar bill can stand all this socialising with you,' I said.

'Hey, don't be a tightwad. Listen, if it makes you feel better, I'll buy. How about that?' I went down to the bar and found he'd ordered drinks for both of us and put them on my bill. 'So I'm a liar,' he said. 'I'm also a cop. Cops never pay for drinks, you should know that. Cops are poor men.'

'Even cops who are, let's say, close friends of Tommy Bergdorf?'

He didn't like that too much and for a moment the nice, easy-going grin disappeared. 'Don't crack wise, my friend.'

There was a brief, cool silence. Then he said, 'I told you to stay away from those Bergdorfs.'

'Yes, well, in the circumstances I decided not to take any notice.'

He nodded. 'Maybe you were right. What do you make of this business?'

'I just don't know. I suppose it would help if I knew more about all these people.'

He shrugged. 'Well, Pascal you heard about this evening. Freddie, he's been in the movie business since he left college. He's always done pretty good and now, after that last picture, he's got to be one of the richest men in the industry. Did you ever see it, *Space Fiends*?'

'Yes.'

'Piece of pure shit but the kids loved it. Okay, so Freddie never needs to work again. Tommy made a fortune in real estate in New Jersey in the forties, fifties, then moved out to Vegas and made even more money. Very shrewd guy, very powerful in the Republican Party.'

'Crooked?'

Another shrug. 'Probably. Just a little. You ever hear of a multimillionaire who hadn't at least cut a few corners in his time? But I don't think serious crooked; I don't think he has mob connections, or anyway no more than anybody else in politics and big business. Tommy sold up in Vegas – oh, six months ago maybe – and that's about when he moved to Bel Air. As for the beautiful Mrs Bergdorf, I guess you know more about her than I do.'

'Her past, yes, I know about that. I don't know much about her present. When did she marry Freddie?'

'Five years ago? About then. He was married before, in his late twenties. It didn't take. They were divorced within a couple of years. No kids, not from either marriage.' He took a sip of his drink. 'What was on that video?'

'None of your business.'

He grinned. 'Okay, so don't tell me. I can guess. The beautiful Mrs Bergdorf turning tricks in some cat house in Vegas, right?' I suppose I must have shown my astonishment because he laughed and said, 'I know about Beverley. I'm a cop, remember? And besides I used to work in Vegas. Has she told Freddie and Tommy what's on the tape?'

'Yes.'

He looked impressed. 'A real open marriage, huh? Well, I guess that negates the blackmail if she's got nothing to hide. Unless the guy was threatening to show the stuff around among their friends.'

'I don't think it's got that far but I reckon that's what they're all scared might happen.'

'Right. You go to dinner at somebody's house it kind of alters your view of the hostess if you've seen her on tape with something other than chicken à la king in her mouth.'

'Crudely put,' I said coldly, 'but I take the point.'

He finished his drink and pushed the glass away. 'No, no,' he said, 'it's kind of you to offer but I won't have another one. I gotta go. I imagine you've abandoned your plans to go to Disneyland and Magic Mountain and all those other wild places?'

I said I had. He didn't seem displeased. 'You want to stick around awhile, see what you can find out about Pascal and the blackmail business, that's okay with me just so long as you don't get in the way of police work. Might be useful to have someone close to the family, time like this. I shouldn't like anything bad to happen to the Bergdorfs. It could spoil my relationship with Tommy.'

'I can imagine,' I said. 'By the way, where did Tommy come from originally? That's not exactly a New Jersey accent he has there.'

'Switzerland. Came over here right after the Second World War. Thanks for the drink. I'll be in touch.' He went out, walking with that slight, confident swagger that all policemen have, especially plain-clothes policemen who carry guns. I swallowed the rest of my drink and went upstairs to bed.

The next morning immediately after breakfast I got to work on the phone. There was no reply from Kaplan's house and for a moment it looked as if there was nobody at his office either. Well, it was a Sunday after all. The phone had rung several times before the receiver was lifted and a female voice said, 'Kaplan Detective Agency. Linda Kelly speaking. Who is this?'

'Miss Kelly,' I said, 'I wonder if you could . . .' And then I hung up as if we'd been cut off and raced downstairs to get my car. Because I knew that female voice; it was the same one that had left the message yesterday on Bev's answering machine.

Kaplan's office was on that part of Hollywood Boulevard a few blocks east of the junction with Highland. This was a rundown area of town, an area of sleazy fast-food joints, porno cinemas and cheap dress shops with a line in tacky underwear for hookers. The detective agency was one flight up, above a weary-looking secondhand bookstore, with a street level entrance that was locked. I pushed the bell a few times and the same female voice coming through the intercom beside the door said, rather irritably, 'What?'

'Miss Kelly, I'd like to talk to you. My name's Lennox, Robert Lennox and I – '

'What do you want?'

'Please, can I come in? It's rather difficult shouting messages through this thing.'

'Wait.' The intercom was switched off and a few minutes later I heard footsteps coming down uncarpeted stairs. The door was opened on the safety chain and a tall, dark-haired young woman peered out. 'You're the guy who called just now, right?'

'Yes. I'm afraid we were cut off.'

'No, we weren't. You hung up. Why did you do that?'

'Because I want to talk to you personally.' She studied me suspiciously for a few moments, then said, 'Okay' and let me in. She was late twenties, about five-nine with a good figure and long legs and she had that peculiarly Irish colouring of black hair, pale skin and startlingly blue eyes. She wore a light blue shirt, faded jeans and trainers. She said, 'Go ahead up.'

I stood aside with my old-fashioned English courtesy. 'After you.'

'Nope. After you. I don't want you walking behind me.' She followed me up the worn and wooden stairs to a glass door that had 'Kaplan Detective Agency' painted on it. Beyond the door was a tiny reception area with just enough room for a desk and a couple of chairs. Two other doors led off it. We went through the one to the left and into a small office. It was bigger than the reception area but not much, and it was just as urgently in need of redecoration. The printed sign on the desk in here read 'Linda Kelly'. Around the room were filing cabinets and a small bookcase that contained legal volumes and works on police procedure. There were a phone, a cheap word processor and a mass of files and loose bits of paper, some of them crumpled and torn. Linda Kelly sat down in the worn leather armchair behind the desk and invited me to take the equally worn but non-matching leather chair in front of it.

She put her feet on the desk and said, 'Okay, what do you want?'

'You phoned a family called Bergdorf in Beverly Hills yesterday.'

'I did?'

'Yes. You left a message on their machine to say that Mr Kaplan wouldn't be calling after all.'

She lost the rather puzzled frown she'd been wearing. 'Ah, Bergdorf. Was that the name? I didn't know who I was calling. It was just a number in Roger's diary. Here.' She handed a page-a-day desk diary across to me. Against yesterday's date was scrawled what I now knew to be the Bergdorfs' telephone number with the letters NB against it. 'It looked like it must be something important, so I called and left the message. It could have maybe been a client and we don't have so many we can risk losing one for want of a phone call. Are they clients, these Bergdorfs?'

'Not exactly. I have an idea that Mr Kaplan may have been trying to blackmail them.'

'Was he now?' She nodded slowly as if the idea made sense. Certainly she didn't seem at all surprised. 'I guess you know what happened to Roger?' I said I did. 'You don't think these Bergdorfs had him killed?'

'No. They had no idea who he was.'

She took her feet down off the desk and leaned her elbows on it instead. 'Before we go any further,' she said, 'who exactly are you? You look kind of familiar.'

I didn't have the heart to go through the Michael Caine routine again. I seemed to be encountering nothing but remarkably unperceptive people who almost wilfully failed to spot the resemblance. I told her I was a friend of the Bergdorf family, over here on holiday, had found them very concerned about

144

the blackmail attempt and had offered to help them out, specifically by trying to discover whether it was indeed Kaplan who had been putting the bite on them.

'Isn't this the kind of thing the police are supposed to do?' she asked. 'Or haven't they called the police in?'

'Not officially. They have a friend in the police force and he's advising them.'

'But he doesn't know about Roger, does he? Because if he did he'd have been round here. Why do you suppose it is that I get this strong feeling there's an awful lot you're not telling me?'

As a personal favour and at no extra charge I gave her my most charming smile. 'Probably because there's an awful lot I'm not telling you. Look, I don't even know for sure that Roger Kaplan was the blackmailer. What I do know is that he certainly wasn't working for the Bergdorfs. They'd never even heard of him.' I tried another line. 'Do you know of anyone called Pascal – Philippe Pascal?'

She shook her head and the glossy black hair, cut in a page-boy bob just above shoulder length, swung prettily. 'Nope. And that's all the information you get for free. I have this business to run all by myself now if I can just sort out the mess of paperwork Roger's left behind. I was doing that when you arrived and I'd kind of like to get on with it. I've already spent three hours here clearing up all the shit from the break-in the night Roger was killed.' She gestured towards the papers on her desk. 'That's as far as I've got. Now I have to file it all away again.'

'You're the junior partner they mentioned in the newspaper?'

'That's me. Only I'm the senior partner now. Put it another way, I'm the only partner now. Or I am unless some long-lost relative of Roger's turns up to claim his share. Not that that's worth much. You may have noticed this is not exactly the Pinkertons.'

I had noticed that. I said, 'Let me put a proposition to you. Your late partner is still my best bet for the blackmail job. So what if I give you a retainer – let's say 500 dollars – to see if you can come up with any evidence one way or the other. I mean, you're going through his stuff in any case so why not get paid for it?'

'A retainer against what?'

'I don't know. Let's haggle over that when the time comes.'

She thought about it but not for long. 'Okay. And what about this other guy, Philippe Pascal?'

'Well, if his name crops up in the mess of paperwork I'd like to know about that, too.' I didn't really think it was likely but since she was going to be working for me anyway it was worth a try.

'Right,' she said and held out her hand. 'I'll take the retainer now.'

'Ah, well, I don't actually have that much on me.' I saw the ironic lift of one nicely shaped eyebrow. 'But I can bring it here later on. No, I've got an even better idea. Why don't you meet me for lunch? Then you can report on progress so far and I can pay you and I don't have to have another meal by myself.'

Another ironic lift of the eyebrow. 'Ah, poor lonely man, all by himself in the big, bad town. What about your friends up in Beverly Hills?'

'Well, I'll tell you,' I said. 'I used to know the wife a long time ago when we were both kids. But

I only met the husband yesterday and I don't think he likes me.'

'Is she pretty?'

'Very.'

'Then if I was her husband I wouldn't like you either. You're in good shape, aren't you?'

'Well, you know, I work out. It's become a habit. I used to be a fighter. Maybe that's why you thought I looked familiar.'

'No. I don't follow the fight game. It's strictly for mugs.'

'Thanks a lot.' I got up. 'I'll see you at one o'clock. Butterfields on Sunset. You know it?'

'Yeah. And don't forget the 500 bucks.'

At the door I stopped and said, 'What do you suppose he was looking for, whoever broke in here?'

She shrugged. 'Money, I guess. Fat chance. And he didn't break in – he had the keys. Must have taken them from Roger after he shot him. You have to ask yourself whether it was worth it. I doubt if he found anything much in Roger's office and all he got from my desk was five dollars and change. Can you believe somebody would kill for as little at that?'

I said I couldn't and indeed I didn't believe it.

I left her to her clearing up and went back to my hotel to get the money from the room safe. There was a message from Bev: would I have lunch with her the next day? I called her number and got the butler. The Bergdorfs were out, having lunch at somebody else's home. Steven Spielberg's maybe. Sylvester Stallone's. Harrison Ford's. Who knew? The butler probably but he didn't think it necessary to tell me. What he did tell me, after he'd agreed to

147

pass on my acceptance of the lunch invitation, was the name of the studio where Freddie was about to make his film. I took a note of the address and the phone number of Freddie's office there and just before one set off for Butterfields.

It was on the south side of Sunset and to get to it you had to walk down a flight of steep steps. I asked for a table in the garden and a bottle of Frascati and read the sports section of the *Sunday Times* until Linda Kelly arrived about a quarter of an hour later.

I poured her wine and ordered food, and said, 'Well?'

She rested her chin on her left hand and stretched her right hand across the table. 'The money first.'

I sighed. 'Ah, shucks, there's no romance any more. Time was a girl didn't expect to get paid till after she'd delivered and then the fellow just left the cash on the mantelpiece.'

She grinned; not the ironic smile I'd seen a couple of times before but a genuine, amused grin. It made her look younger, softer. 'Sweet talk like that will get you nowhere. Give.' I gave. She opened the envelope, made sure the five 100-dollar bills were there and tucked it away in her handbag. 'Okay, which do you want first – the bad news or the really bad news?'

'Gimme the bad news,' I said.

'Right, well, the bad news is that there's no mention of Philippe Pascal anywhere in Roger's papers.'

'Terrific. And the really bad news?'

'There's no mention of any Bergdorfs either, apart from the phone number in his diary.'

I thought about it. 'And you reckon that's worth 500 dollars?'

'Well, at least now you know for sure. You aren't wondering any more.'

'Not good enough. I want my money back.'

Another grin. Like most Americans she had very good teeth but unlike most Americans she seemed to have only the regular number. That was another plus point in her favour, along with the eyes, the hair and the general shape. 'Well, you're not getting it. Besides, I haven't told you the good news yet, or anyway the sort of good news.'

'And that is?'

'The cops have given me permission to go to Roger's house tomorrow and look through his papers there. Could be interesting, yes? I mean, if he was up to something, like blackmail, he'd be more likely to do it from home than the office.'

She had a point but I wasn't very hopeful. The killer had already ransacked Kaplan's house along with his office and if he'd been looking for the video tape there was a fair chance he had found it in one place or the other. Assuming, of course, that the tape was what he was after.

'If I find anything I'll call you,' she said. 'Won't cost you a penny extra. Special offer.' She fluttered her eyelashes at me. They were long eyelashes, dark and all her own.

'Oh, very generous,' I said. 'Listen, you're robbing me blind already. Five hundred bucks, a few hours' work. I bet the Kaplan Detective Agency has never earned 500 dollars in less than a day in its whole existence.'

'Watch it,' she said, indignantly. 'Five hundred bucks is hardly more than a small fortune to us.' And then the food came and we ate and had another bottle of wine and talked about London, which she had never visited but was very interested in, and I told her how I'd fought for the world middleweight championship, which she wasn't remotely interested in, and eventually the conversation moved around to her.

I asked the obvious question, the one I had been wanting to ask ever since I set eyes on her: 'What's a nice girl like you –'

'Yeah, yeah, I know.' She brushed away the lock of glossy black hair that kept falling over her right eye. 'You want the short answer or the long answer? The short answer is that it's better than hooking.'

'And the long answer? No, don't tell me – you're not really a detective at all; you're really an actress.'

She nodded wryly. 'You got it. I came out here from New York City, oh, a hundred years ago, looking for the big break that was going to make my name. But, unfortunately, I got kind of typecast.'

'What as?'

'A waitress, what else? I was so great, so believable as a waitress they wanted me to reprise the role everywhere. So I played hotel coffee shops, fast-food joints, lunch counters and eventually I worked my way up to real restaurants. I even played the Polo Lounge. Gee, that was exciting. There they were, the producers, the directors, the writers, the stars, all those guys my agent could never get me in to see, sitting right there at my mercy. This was it, my big chance. All I had to do was wiggle up to – I don't know – Hyram C. Whoosis, head of Megalomania Productions, flash my eyes, shake my fanny, lower my voice an octave and ask him how he liked his Bloody Mary and I just knew I'd be discovered.' She dug her fork moodily into her Caesar salad.

'And what happened?'

'What do you think happened? Hyram C. Whoosis stuck his hand up my skirt, copped a feel and asked if I'd care to go to his room when I got off duty.'

There was a long silence. I said, 'And did you?'

She looked up angrily. 'No, I did not. Jesus, what kind of a question is that?' There was more than anger in her look; there was hurt as well as if, even on such short acquaintance, she had expected better of me. And indeed she had every right to do so. I expected better of me.

'Sorry. You're right, it was a lousy question.'

'Well . . .' She gave me a rueful little smile. 'Actually, I have to admit I thought about it. Once or twice. And then one day I thought, what am I doing even considering offers like that? I go up to someone's room, I'm no better than a hooker. Not that I've got anything against hookers. I mean, they earn a lot more than waitresses. But I didn't want to be a hooker. At the same time it was obvious I wasn't going to make it as an actress and so, one night at a party, I met Roger Kaplan and he said he was looking for someone, a girl, to help out at the agency. He thought it would be a great gimmick, real good for business, to have a pretty girl detective around. I think he must have had fantasies about *Charlie's Angels* or something. Anyway, I was bored with waitressing and wanted a change so I went in as his junior partner. It seemed like it might be fun for a while and besides, I thought it would look good on my résumé next time I sent it in to some casting director if I could say I was a detective as well as a waitress. It might intrigue people, you know?'

'And did it?'

She laughed. 'Not so you'd notice. So here I am, an actress who was never an actress, who became a waitress, who became a detective. And you're my only client. Some success story, huh?'

There was a note of self-mockery, a kind of gentle bitterness, in her voice. I couldn't think of anything much to say except, 'Well, not so great up to now perhaps but some day . . .'

'. . . my prince will come?' she asked, ironically.

'That, too, perhaps. But what I was going to say was that some day, instead of copping a feel, Hyram C. Whoosis will have the sense to look at your face and then he'll react like David O. Selznick did the first time he saw Vivien Leigh and then . . .'

'. . . in return for a blow job he'll give me a walk-on part in some lousy daytime soap? Yeah, that's about as good as fairytales get in modern Hollywood.' The wary, tough look that she seemed to assume as a kind of shield had come back just for a moment but then she relaxed again and, briefly, laid her hand on mine, her fingers slim and cool against my wrist. 'Sorry. I don't like to be hard. Really. But sometimes, in this town . . . Well, it's not an easy town for a girl, especially if she wants to be an actress and nobody will let her act.'

She had removed her hand from mine some moments before but I could still feel the soft touch of her fingers. I said, 'Yes, I can imagine. At least, I think I can. I . . . Look, tell me, what was Roger Kaplan like?'

'Neat change of subject.' She gave the question brief consideration as she flicked the lock of hair away from her forehead again. 'Well, he was a slea-zeball. He was a man, you could say, who lived lamented by all. You tell me he was into blackmail, I believe you. If you tell me he was into kiddie porn, pushing crack or mugging old ladies, I'll still believe you. So the next question is, if he was that bad, why did I stay with him? And the answer is, we came to an arrangement. After he made his first pass, I told him that if he tried anything like that again I'd cut his pecker off and stick it in his ear and he took the point. Aside from that I stayed around because I liked the work. If he was really blackmailing these Birddogs –'

'Bergdorfs.'

'Whatever. What did he have on them?'

'I can't tell you that. But it wasn't anything crimi-nal. So far as I know.'

'Great.' She got up a little unsteadily, the result I suppose of drinking the best part of a bottle of wine in the midday sun. 'I find out anything at Roger's house tomorrow, I'll call you. No, I'll call you anyway. Meanwhile, thanks for lunch – and the retainer.'

I took hold of both her wrists and pulled her back down into her chair. 'Stick around, have some coffee. You need it. We both need it. And you especially need it because you don't even know where to call me.'

'Sure, I do,' she said. 'The name of your hotel's on the envelope with the money in it.'

'Hey, you really are a detective.'

'You better believe it. They don't call me Shirley Holmes for nothing.'

So she stayed for coffee and when, a little later, she looked at her watch and got ready to leave again, I said, 'Don't go. It's a beautiful day. Let's drive down to Malibu or Santa Monica or somewhere. We could swim, have dinner . . .'

'And?' she said, watching me carefully, her chin cupped in her hands.

'I hadn't begun to think about "and",' I said.

'Liar.'

'All right, yes, I did have some plans – well, not plans exactly, more like wistful fantasies – for "and".'

'Forget them. I never sleep with the clients.'

'Who said anything about sleeping?' I said, indignantly. 'The thought of sleep never crossed my mind. My fantasies had nothing whatsoever to do with sleep.'

She laughed with what sounded like real amusement. 'Nice try,' she said. 'Nice thought, too. But somehow I don't think the man in my life would like it too much if I went swimming and had dinner with you. And I just know he'd hate "and".'

'Oh.' Macho male arrogance being the powerful, blinding factor it is, it simply hadn't occurred to me that there was a man in her life, though God knows a girl who looked like her could hardly have been short of masculine attention. After all, not every man in Hollywood is gay; most of them maybe but not all. 'Yes, well . . .' We both got up, rather awkwardly, or rather I felt awkward. 'Um, well, thank you for the company and for helping me out. About Kaplan, I mean.'

'Don't mention it. You're paying for everything, remember.' She leaned across the table and kissed me lightly on the cheek. There was a look about her that suggested she was enjoying some deeply private joke.

154

I said, 'Hold on. I'll come with you, get you a cab.'

'Uhuh. You have to stay and pay the check. I'll call you tomorrow. Bye.' And she left me, running effortlessly up the steep steps.

I watched her go and thought violent thoughts about Hyram C. Whoosis sticking his hand up her skirt. I wanted to do to Hyram C. Whoosis what Willie Slate had done to me.

11

THE REST OF SUNDAY PASSED SLOWLY. When you're
on your own it's as easy to be bored in Hollywood
as anywhere else, perhaps easier because there's
very little to do there. Once you've done Disneyland – which is not in Hollywood anyway but a
long, dull drive away at Anaheim – and the Universal Studios tour, there's not a lot left. And I had
done both of those in a past that was recent enough
for me not to want to do either of them again on a
hot Sunday afternoon. The other local tourist attrac-
tion is a ride around Beverly Hills to look at the
stars' homes but you need a very high threshold of
boredom to enjoy that, since one multimillion-
dollar Spanish-style hacienda looks much like
another, especially when there's rarely a human
being in sight, a gardener maybe but certainly not
a movie star. The days when Joan Crawford knew
the timetables of the tourist buses by heart and
always made a point of being out front, wearing a
floppy hat and pruning roses when the next batch
of gawpers came by, died with her.

So I didn't go to Disneyland or Universal Studios

or Beverly Hills. I just lounged by the hotel pool all afternoon and thought how much nicer it would have been to be sitting on the beach at Malibu with Linda Kelly and never mind the man in her life, whoever he might have been. I did not, however, think a great deal about Bev, which was perhaps curious considering the part she had played if not in my life then at least in my memory over the past years. In truth, at that time I did not know myself what I felt about her; she looked marvellous, yes, but that was not unexpected. The main question, though, was, what kind of a person had she become? And to that there had been no opportunity the previous day to find an answer.

I went out for an early dinner and ate at Spago, a sort of glorified pizza parlour just off Sunset which, that year, was still the 'in' place for the film community. I got in because I was on my own, but against that, because I was a nonentity, I was given a small table in a far corner. The food was fine if you like pizza and salad. From my distant vantage point I saw four movie stars come in with their wives/girlfriends/assorted entourages and discovered that they ate pizza and salad much like anybody else, which didn't really come as any great revelation. Three of them had reasonable table manners; the fourth was a pig, who splashed his silk shirt with French dressing and spent most of the meal with a strand of melted mozzarella hanging from the designer stubble on his face. Since none of the other four people at his table, one of whom I knew to be his wife, bothered to tell him he had cheese on his chin I assumed that none of them liked him very much. On the other hand, none of them demurred when he picked up the bill.

There were no messages waiting for me back a the hotel, which was a disappointment. The very least I had expected was to find Linda Kelly sitting on her suitcase outside my room, declaring that the man in her life was no longer in her life because she wanted me and only me. In her absence I went to bed alone and slept surprisingly well.

The next morning I went back into action. Immediately after breakfast I phoned the studios where *Space Fiends: The Sequel* was in pre-production, asked to speak to Karl Strauss and was put through to him at once.

He said, 'Mr Lennox, I've been expecting your call.'

'Really?'

'But of course. Freddie told me about you.' He chuckled. It was the plump, confident chuckle of a man who knew he could buy anything he wanted. 'He says you think I put out a contract on him.'

'Well, no, I didn't exactly say –'

'Please, Mr Lennox, don't spoil it. Putting out contracts is good for my image. You want to talk? Fine. You know where I am?' I said I did. He said, 'Then come on over. I look forward to meeting you.'

I went on over. The studio was south of Sunset in a predominantly industrial area. Once it and its back lot had dominated the entire neighbourhood but after the collapse of the Hollywood studio system in the 1950s, acres of ground had been sold off and now all that remained were office buildings, half a dozen sound stages, the commissary and cutting rooms and the like. Straudorf Productions were on the third floor of the main office block where Karl Strauss occupied a suite that consisted of a small kitchen, a bathroom, a reception area and a main office – his – that was about the size of half my entire flat in London. Strauss himself sat behind an oak desk and a long Havana cigar and welcomed me in with another of his plump, rich chuckles. He seemed to have me marked down as some kind of comedian.

'Sit down, Mr Lennox,' he said. 'I'll get the bimbo to fetch some coffee.' He shouted commands into the intercom on his desk and almost immediately the bimbo, a long-legged, astonishingly pretty young blonde with huge baby-blue eyes and a blank face, brought the coffee.

'She gives great coffee,' Strauss said when she'd gone away again.

'And other things, too, I expect.'

He did some more chuckling. 'Possibly. Very possibly. But I guess that's something you'll never know, Mr Lennox, unless you're a very rich man. Are you a very rich man, Mr Lennox?'

'By your standards, I sincerely doubt it.'

'Ah, well, that's a shame. There's a lot to be said for being rich, Mr Lennox. Apart from anything else you can buy bimbos like that by the dozen.' He was an elderly man, around Tommy Bergdorf's age rather than Freddie's, quite tall, well covered but not fat, with a year-round tan and whitish grey hair carefully arranged to conceal the fact that there used to be a lot more of it than there now was. He spoke English English rather than American English, with an accent similar to Tommy Bergdorf's. 'So,' he said, 'you think I want young Freddie terminated, do you?'

'No,' I said. 'I don't think anything much. But what I know is that a man named Philippe Pascal

159

wanted him terminated and I'm rather curious to find out why.'

He nodded. 'Philippe Pascal. He was murdered a few days ago, yes? By the so-called serial killer? I read about that. As a matter of fact I knew Pascal. Oh, not personally. I maybe spoke to him two or three times on the phone. But I knew him well enough to pay him a great deal of money.'

'You mean he was blackmailing you?'

Another rich man's chuckle. 'Certainly not, Mr Lennox. It was more like extortion. He provided clothes for my wife and I paid for them. The price was exorbitant. Not that I'm complaining, mind. *Space Fiends* made even more money than my wife knows how to spend, and if *The Sequel* turns out half as well as Freddie and I expect I'll have more than enough to trade her in for a younger model and buy another dozen bimbos as well.'

Around the walls of the office were framed posters for ten, maybe fifteen old movies. They had all been produced by Strauss. Many of them I had seen; most of them were good, serious films by good, serious directors and good, serious writers, and starred good, serious actors; some of them had won Oscars for such things as screenplay, design and cinematography.

I said, 'Tell me something – why does a man like you lend his name to crap like *Space Fiends*?'

He spent quite a long time relighting the Havana, looking at me down the length of it as if it were a gun barrel. He said, 'Thirty-eight years ago I married my first wife. She divorced me ten years later. I'm still paying for her. Three years after that I married my second wife. That lasted six years. I'm still paying for her, too. Women have no morality, Mr

Lennox. They marry a man who's making money, then they divorce him and take him for alimony and he never stops paying until they marry again. But the point is, they don't marry again. They have affairs but they don't get married and they keep taking the alimony. Ten years ago I married my present wife. She costs me more than both the others put together. So work it out, Mr Lennox. You're looking at a man who is seventy years old but already has seventy-three expensive wife years behind him. Now do you wonder why I lend my name to lucrative crap like *Space Fiends*?'

'My heart bleeds,' I said.

'Don't let it. I'm not asking for sympathy, I'm merely proffering an explanation. Before Freddie and I teamed up to make *Space Fiends* I was up to here in debt. Oh, yes, I had a fine reputation as a film maker but I was being bled white by the three most voracious women it has ever been my misfortune to meet. Today they're still bleeding me but at least my corpuscles are healthy enough to take the strain.'

'If they're all that terrible, why on earth did you marry them?'

'Because each in her own way was sensational. Women are my hobby, Mr Lennox. Some men collect stamps; I collect women. They're a lot more expensive than stamps and they don't keep their value but for a little while, when they're at their peak, they are considerably more rewarding. Don't you agree?'

'I don't know,' I said. 'I've never owned any. How did you get into partnership with Freddie Bergdorf?'

'Ah. Down to business, I see.' He nodded

161

approvingly. 'Quite right. There's no percentage in idle chit-chat. Through Tommy, Freddie's father. You've met him, I imagine? Yes. Well, we knew each other years ago in New Jersey. We were both in the property business at that time and then, when I moved into films, we kept in touch. Tommy's a good friend and also a useful man to know. Very big in politics in this country. Anyway, Freddie had been earning a dollar here, a dollar there, churning out low-budget movies for the teen-age trade but then he came up with this idea for *Space Fiends* and, naturally, the studios tried to rip him off. What he needed was somebody with a name and know-how and a little influence, so Tommy brought him to me and we both got rich.'

I said, 'After *Space Fiends: The Sequel*, when you've made another multimillion dollar fortune, will you go back to producing worthwhile pictures again?'

He shook his head. 'I doubt it. What I've dis-covered is that kudos and good reviews are no sub-stitute for money in this town. The richer I am, the more respect I'm shown. Wouldn't matter if I'd made the money from snuff movies or the drug trade – the important thing is that I made it some-how. This is a town that loves a winner, Mr Lennox, and the only way they judge a winner is by how much money he has. In the past I was nearly a winner, close but not quite there. Today I'm the fellow on the rostrum getting the gold medal and, to tell you the truth, I like it. I really like it.'

The bimbo put her head round the door and announced in a breathless, rather excited voice, 'Your next visitor is on her way up, Mr Strauss.' She didn't actually say who this next visitor was but when the bimbo had gone, Strauss volunteered the name – the name of one of the currently hottest, sultriest sexpots in Hollywood.

'Is she going to be in *The Sequel*?' I asked.

He laughed. 'Are you crazy? Why would she need to appear in garbage like that?'

'Oh, I see. The next Mrs Strauss perhaps?'

He laughed again. 'Who knows, Mr Lennox? Who knows?' He looked at his watch, one of those thin, platinum Cartier numbers. 'Now is there anything else I can tell you?'

I said yes, there was. Did he know anything about the attempt to blackmail Freddie and Bev? Or about Pascal and why he should have wanted them both dead? He shook his head. 'I do know about the blackmail. That surprises you? It shouldn't. As I said, Tommy and I are very old friends. But where the tape came from or who has it or where it is now, that I don't know, of course. As for Pascal, all I can say is, I'm astonished. I spoke to him briefly and I didn't like him. He wasn't my kind of fellow. But why he should put out a contract on Freddie or Beverley I simply cannot imagine. They're very nice young people, don't you think?'

I grunted something that probably sounded like agreement. I was prepared to believe that Bev was still a very nice young person but I couldn't swear to Freddie. Strauss looked at his watch again and stood up. He said, 'It's been interesting to meet you, Mr Lennox. I'm sorry I have to cut our interview short but, as you know, I do have another appointment . . .' His smile was conspiratorial, one man of the world to another, which rather ignored the fact that his world and mine hardly existed within the same solar system.

At the door, I said, 'One last thing: where did you come from originally?'

He blinked in surprise. 'Switzerland,' he said. 'I came to the States in late 1945. Why do you ask?'

'Just curious. Were you in the movie business there?'

'In Switzerland? The movie business? What movie business? Besides, I was little more than a boy when I left.'

I nodded; he chuckled; we both said goodbye.

The sexpot, all golden hair and full-lipped pout, was sitting in the reception area showing a lot of leg and bust and reading *Cosmopolitan* with her lips moving. I had to admit she looked a great deal more fun than a Penny Black.

Bev had booked a table for lunch at the Dome on Sunset, one of Hollywood's more elegant restaurants. It was the kind of place where you didn't feel conspicuously over-dressed if you were wearing a jacket and tie. You didn't have to wear a jacket and tie but I did and so did quite a few men at the other tables. It made a nice change, Hollywood being a town where, generally speaking, formal dress means you wear socks. The Dome was obviously a cut above that. Bev arrived ten minutes late in something dark blue and linen of a classical cut. Her legs and arms were bare and nicely tanned. People looked at her as she crossed the room towards me with the maitre d' and a couple of waiters prancing along in her wake. They were asking – or rather the maitre d' was asking – how she was and how Mr Bergdorf was and how Mr Bergdorf's father was and doubtless they'd have got around to the state of health of the kitchen cat if they'd had much further to walk. The overall impression given was that Mrs Bergdorf was a regular and welcome customer at the Dome.

I said, 'You're looking good, Bev.'

She nodded and smiled a little, though not much. 'It's strange to hear you call me Bev. I haven't thought of myself as Bev for a long time. People don't call me that any more. They call me Beverley now.'

'I'd noticed.'

'I prefer it,' she said.

'Ah.'

The wine and the first course came and when we'd chomped our way through some of the avocado and smoked salmon she said, 'I can't believe we've met again like this. You know? I've often thought what it would be like if we ever did bump into each other, what we'd say, how we'd feel, how we'd interact.'

'How we'd what?'

She put her fork down and leaned a little towards me. 'Don't make fun of me, Bobby. I live here now. I'm an American citizen. I think American and I talk American. If you've come here looking to find little Bev Timkins, the friendly neighbourhood tart, forget it. I'm Mrs Beverley Bergdorf. You may think it's a funny name but it means something in this town and I'm proud of it. Bev, the teenage dancing hooker, doesn't exist any more. She hasn't existed for a long time.'

I stuffed some more food into my mouth and stared across at her while I gave it a thorough mashing. When I'd done that and swallowed it I said, 'I believe you.' She still looked like Bev, more mature, of course, and possibly more beautiful than even I had imagined she would become, but there was nothing else about her to remind me of the girl I used to know. I'd killed a man for that girl but I was not at all sure whether I would kill a man for this woman, this elegant Hollywood matron, this stranger.

'I liked Bev, the teenage dancing hooker,' I said. 'As a matter of fact I was in love with her.'

'She was in love with you, too.'

'But Mrs Beverley Bergdorf isn't?'

She smiled, a big smile this time. 'Are you in love with Mrs Beverley Bergdorf?'

For a moment, seeing that smile and the brief, mischievous glint in her eyes, I could imagine how it might be possible: not right then, perhaps, but given time and the chance to get to know her in this new guise . . .

'No,' I said.

'Just as well. Mr Bergdorf wouldn't approve and I don't suppose Mrs Bobby Lennox would either.'

'There is no Mrs Bobby Lennox. There never has been.'

'Oh.' If there had been any indication in that 'Oh' that it pleased her to think of me going unmarried through life, carrying a flickering torch for the girl I used to know, then quite possibly I might have started to fall in love with her all over again. But there wasn't. Well, it's a lot to ask of an 'Oh', I suppose, and this was just an ordinary 'Oh', non-committal and no more than politely interested.

I said, 'Why did you run away, Bev?'

'Do we have to go into that?'

'Damn right, we do. We were in love with each other, remember? Christ, we've only just been talking about it. You can't have forgotten already. We had plans. We were going to get married when I'd finished at university, I was going to take care of you, support you until you got your break as a dancer. We used to talk about that for bloody hours. And then suddenly you were gone, out of my life, out of everybody's life without a single word and it's been bothering me ever since. I want to know why.'

She sighed, ran her hand through her hair, pushed her plate away from her.

I pointed towards the expensive food she was about to reject untasted. 'Eat that,' I said sternly. 'This is real life, not a Hollywood movie where nobody ever finishes their meals. That's going to cost one of us a lot of money and it's good stuff. So you eat it and enjoy it.'

And she did. Or anyway she picked at it and maybe that helped because the food gave her something other than me to look at while she talked and she didn't seem too keen to look at me. She said: 'Do you remember that man, that probation officer, who . . . who raped me?'

'Yes.'

'Well, you know he was murdered and the police thought he'd been shot by a jealous husband or something?'

'Yes.'

'Well, he wasn't. I mean, of course he was shot but not by a jealous husband. Donovan killed him.'

I sat very still for a moment, absolutely shocked. 'Donovan?' I said.

She nodded. 'A little while afterwards when the fuss had died down a bit – you were back at university – Donovan told me all about it. He said he'd killed the man for me, so that he could never bother me again.'

'Donovan said that he, personally, had shot him? He hadn't bought it done? He hadn't hired anybody? He'd gone out with a gun and killed the man himself?'

Another nod. 'He said it was because . . . because he loved me. He couldn't bear the thought of anybody hurting me and . . . I was grateful. You've no idea how that man hurt me and frightened me and the thought that somebody had cared enough to make sure he never hurt me again . . .' She was silent for a moment, staring over my shoulder, staring back into the past. 'What could I do, Bobby?'

'You slept with him, right? Donovan, I mean. You had an affair with him?'

'Yes. Because I owed him, you see. But, I didn't love him. I loved you then. Sleeping with Donovan was . . . was like sleeping with another john. But I knew you wouldn't see it like that. I couldn't bear the thought of you finding out. So I went away.'

I felt sick, with rage and shock and a kind of despair. So we both sat there not eating and it *was* like a fucking Hollywood movie. I said, 'Oh, Jesus. Why didn't you trust me enough to tell me? I could have –'

Gently, she said, 'You could have what, Bobby? Gone and beaten up Donovan? What good would that have done? The way it turned out, that was the best way. If I'd stayed around you'd have been bound to find out what was going on, sooner or later. And that would have been the finish for us. You know it would.'

And I think she was right. Even back then it might have been too late to tell her it wasn't

Donovan who had done the killing and it was certainly too late now. 'Got a lot to thank Donovan for, haven't we?' I said, bitterly. 'Good old Donovan. If it hadn't been for him we'd –'

'We'd what?' she said. 'We'd have got married? Yes, probably. And you'd still be a teacher. And I'd have tried to be a dancer and failed and right now we'd be living in some tacky little house in The Street, or somewhere just like it and we'd have a bunch of kids and no money and . . .'

'Kids? So it's not you who can't have kids – it's Freddie.'

'So what? Who needs kids? I've got a good life, Bobby, and I figure you have, too. If we'd got married we'd never have been able to afford to eat in a place like this or even come to this country on a lousy package holiday. You'd never have become a fighter, I wouldn't have anything close to the life-style I have now. It's better this way, don't you see that? Donovan did us a favour. Oh, sure, he didn't mean to but that's what he did. I'll tell you something, Bobby, when I left The Street I decided to put you right out of my mind and I did it. It took a long time but I did it. Love is great but you can't live on it, you can't pay the bills with it. What I have now is better than just love. I have a nice house, nice clothes, a nice car, a good social life, more money than I can spend . . .'

'I've got a lot of that, too,' I said. 'And I'm not particularly happy either.'

'Damn you,' she said angrily.

One of the prancing waiters brought the coffee and when he had gone away again I said, 'Tell me about Freddie.' And then, seeing the antagonistic gleam in her eyes, I added quickly, 'No, no, hang

169

on. I'm not trying to goad you and this isn't morbid curiosity. May I remind you that because of Arnie's untimely demise I am officially the hitman hired to kill you and I'm still trying to find out why. So anything you can tell me . . .'

'I met him in Vegas,' she said. 'I told you, I'd had to go back to hooking there and because I was a few years older than most of the other girls and had an English accent they thought I was classy. So I got on the party circuit, the political party circuit and particularly the Republican Party party circuit. They used to hire us, me and some of the other girls, to go to fundraisers and things like that and sweet talk the high rollers into giving bigger donations than they'd intended. That's how I met Tommy Bergdorf.' She gazed defiantly across at me, shaking her head. 'I know what you're thinking but you're wrong. I didn't sleep with him. At the beginning, before I met Freddie, maybe I would have done but he never asked. He treated me like a daughter.'

'I see. He paid you to fuck the socks off his friends and shake them down for bigger and better donations to the good old party funds but he treated you like a daughter. That's a nice way to treat a daughter.'

Wearily, she said, 'I knew you wouldn't understand. Tommy didn't hire me. Other people did that. I just met him at one of those fundraisers. He knew why I was there, of course he did, he knew it was my job. But he never tried to take advantage, he made sure I was treated well and we became friends. You don't understand that either, do you – a whore and a rich widower and all we were was friends? Well, it's the truth. We used to have lunch or dinner together and he'd take me to the shows at Caesar's and the other places. And he never, never once tried to get me into bed. He's a wonderful man and a very important and powerful man, too. If he'd been born in America he could have become President.'

'Ah, heck,' I said. 'Who are we talking about – Abraham Lincoln reincarnated? No, all right, all right. I'm sorry. Go on.'

And in the resigned manner of one talking to the terminally cynical she did. 'At one of these functions he introduced me to Freddie, who'd flown down from LA. And Freddie fell in love with me. He knew who I was, what I was. I told him; Tommy told him, but it didn't make any difference. Freddie wanted me, wanted to marry me and in the end I said yes.'

'And Tommy didn't mind – his son marrying a hooker, I mean?'

'I don't know whether he minded or not. He never said that he did, never showed that he did. Freddie was married before, you know, and it was very unhappy. I think that hurt Tommy a lot. What he wants above all is for Freddie to be happy. I suppose it's the Jewish thing, or the fact that Freddie's adopted, but when it became obvious that the only thing Freddie wanted was me –'

'Hold on,' I said, 'Freddie's adopted? And the Bergdorfs are Jewish?'

She seemed surprised. 'Well, it's a Jewish name, isn't it? And anyway what difference does it make? What have we got here – anti-Semitism?'

'No, of course not. It's just that . . . well, yes, come to think of it, I suppose it is a Jewish name.'

'Well, they're not Orthodox. They don't eat

kosher food or observe the holidays. I think they're agnostic more than anything else but I guess if you're born Jewish you're always Jewish. It's not something you can shake off. Anyway, it's never been a problem for me. I don't know what I believe in. As for the adoption, well, Tommy's wife couldn't have any kids so they adopted Freddie back in New Jersey when he was little.'

'And the wife – Mrs Tommy? What happened to her?'

'She died a long time ago. I never met her. It was way before my time.' She summoned the waiter over with one flick of an index finger and told him to charge the meal to her account. 'Does any of that help?'

'Not much,' I said. 'I suppose there's no chance that you slept with Philippe Pascal at one of those Republican Party parties is there?'

'Absolutely none. I have to tell you, Bobby, I can't really take this death threat seriously. It's just too weird.'

'Yeah, I know what you mean. But what about the other business? You haven't heard from the blackmailer, of course.'

She gazed at me suspiciously. 'No, we haven't. But how do you know that?'

'Because', I lied, 'you'd have told me if you had.' I escorted her out of the restaurant and back to the varlet parking. When she had got into her car – a tasty little Mercedes sports job – I said, 'Well, we've met again. How did we interact?'

She smiled, leaned across and kissed me in a sisterly sort of way. 'In the end better than I'd expected. I feel as if I've laid a ghost.'

'Thanks a bunch, Bev.'

'Beverley,' she said and drove away.

I watched her go and was still standing there, staring westward along Sunset and thinking, when I became aware of someone running out of the parking lot, of a voice saying, 'Was that my wife? Was that my wife?' and of a hand grabbing me by the shoulder and wrenching me around. It was Freddie, of course.

'Was that my wife?' he said again, yelling.

'Yes, Freddie,' I said, 'that was your wife. We just had lunch.'

'You bastard. You goddamn bastard. Jesus, I've had it with you. You go round to my partner. You . . . you ask him questions. You . . . You meet my wife in secret –'

'In secret? Here? At this place? Are you kidding? She walks in there, it's like a royal visit. Everybody knows her.'

I didn't seem to be placating him. His face was still red and angry. 'Keep away from us. Do you understand? I don't want you near me, my wife, my partner. Just keep away.'

'Freddie.' I laid a brotherly hand on his shoulder. 'Remember me? I'm the fellow who's trying to help you. Just cling on to that thought.'

He let out a bellow of rage and frustration. 'Leave my wife alone, goddamn you!' And then he threw a punch at me. It was a tennis player's punch, a big overhand right that looked as if he was trying to serve an ace. I moved slightly, watched it go over my shoulder and without thinking popped him on the nose with a left jab. Blood spurted down his lips and onto his Ralph Lauren shirt. 'Ah, Freddie, Freddie,' I said. 'I'm sorry. I shouldn't have done that.'

173

He glared down at himself, licking blood off his mouth. 'Jesus, look at my shirt. Look what you've done to my shirt, you bastard. You know how much this shirt cost?' And then he launched another punch at me, a big swinging left this time. I stepped inside that, too, and popped him again – a good straight right into the stomach. 'Hurnh,' he said and sat down on the pavement. A couple of varlets who had been watching moved forward uncertainly. I think they'd been hesitant about interceding before then because they weren't sure which of us would give them the larger tip. Now they had decided that Freddie was in the bigger trouble and therefore more likely to show his gratitude. I turned to face them, holding up my hands palms outward. 'Okay, fight's over. Thanks for your interest.' I reached into my pocket and gave them a couple of five-dollar bills. 'Usually when I fight, people pay me. I've never had to pay the audience before. Only in America, I suppose . . .'

Freddie got up, holding his stomach with one hand and dabbing a handkerchief to his nose with the other. 'You're finished,' he said. 'You know that? You're a dead man. I'm talking to a corpse here.'

'Freddie,' I said, 'the movies have softened your brain. Are you listening to yourself? Do you really believe that dialogue? I don't. I don't even believe what's happened here. I had lunch with your wife, yes. And do you know what we talked about? We talked about you. She's not interested in me. She was once but that was a long time ago. I'm no threat to you, Freddie. I'm not going to try and take her away. I couldn't afford it.'

But he wasn't listening. He'd gone back, escorted

by one of the varlets, to retrieve his car. And maybe it was just as well. I think that if he had heard my last remark and if he was half as macho as he seemed to believe himself to be, he'd have come back and tried to hit me again. And maybe this time I'd have let him because it was a cheap crack. The fact that it was also true, that Beverley – my Bev, as was – had become an expensive lady in a money-mad town, someone beyond my financial reach, someone whose material priorities I could not understand, someone I no longer wanted and who no longer wanted me, made no real difference. It was still a cheap crack.

12

WE WERE IN THE BATHROOM, standing shoulder to shoulder and staring into the open cabinet above the wash basin. The shelves were empty, stained in places with red here, yellow there, green some-where else – stuff that had dripped down the sides of medicine bottles and left their indelible marks on the cheap woodwork. There was no back to the cabinet; that had been unscrewed to reveal not just the plaster wall but a high, shallow, brick-lined hole in the wall. The hole was empty.

'How did you find this?' I asked.

Linda Kelly smirked. She'd been a clever girl; she had a right to smirk. 'When I joined Kaplan and the agency he'd just moved into this place. He was having things done to it – new kitchen, new bath-room suite, that kind of stuff. Well, one night I came over to talk about the job and the deal and like that. Now I think of it, that was the night he made his pass. It seems years ago. Anyway, after I told him what I'd do if he tried anything like that again I came in here to fix my face. So naturally I opened the cabinet to see what kind of stuff he kept in here.'

'What do you mean, "naturally"?' I said. 'I don't look in other people's medicine cabinets.'

'Well, that's because you're English and weird. Normal people always look in other people's medicine cabinets. So I looked in this one and it was just as you see it now, only the hole in the wall was new then. I thought it was kind of strange but I guess I forgot about it until today.'

It was late in the afternoon. Linda had called me at the hotel about thirty minutes earlier with a message to get on over to Kaplan's house and take a look at what she'd found there. What she had found she was holding in her left hand. Right now she was explaining how she had found it.

'When I got here today I looked everywhere but – nothing. There was a safe in the den but whoever killed Roger had opened that – a boy scout could have opened it with a paper clip. If there'd ever been anything important in there it had gone now. So I hunted around among all the mess and then I decided to take a leak and it was while I was sitting there . . .' She gestured towards the lavatory. '. . . that I suddenly remembered this cabinet. So I took a look inside.'

'You pulled your pants up first, right?'

She frowned. 'What? Yeah. I guess. What a crazy question. Why do you ask?'

'Just wanted to get the picture clear in my mind.'

She was looking particularly pretty in a short, pale shirtwaister dress and matching high-heeled sandals that made her almost my height. The dress had probably not cost much but on her it looked expensive and the long, tanned legs seemed to go on for ever.

She glanced at me suspiciously. 'Whether I'd

pulled my pants up then or not I've got them pulled up now, okay? They're made of bulletproof metal, they're padlocked and I've swallowed the key so don't get any strange ideas. Right. We okay now? Good. So I looked in this cabinet and it had a back, like you'd expect, screwed to the wall. So I got out my pocket knife and unscrewed it and there was this hole and in the hole . . . ta-ra!' She held up the video tape in her hand. 'Just this. Nothing else. So I called you because I figure this is probably what you're looking for and if it is you owe me at least another five hundred.'

'We'll see,' I said, all businesslike. I'd just remembered that there was a man in her life and for the moment I didn't care whether her knickers were padlocked or programmed to self-destruct, taking all their contents with them, at the slightest touch of some other masculine hand. 'Let's see what's on the tape first.'

We went into the den of the untidy, slightly scruffy masculine pad that the late Roger Kaplan had called home. Linda put the tape into the video machine and we sat together, a respectable distance between us, on a brown moquette sofa to watch. What we were looking at was a silent home movie, one that appeared to have been shot on a concealed camera operated by somebody who didn't really understand the equipment. The focus switched from sharp to fuzzy and sometimes the action was missed altogether so that where, presumably, we should have got a set of pumping buttocks all we saw was a pair of feet. But one thing at least was clear: the heroine of the action was Bev, energetically plying her hooker's trade. The tape lasted for an hour and, allowing for breaks in the action, covered the arrival, the coming and the going of four of her clients. Who they were I doubt if their mothers or even their wives could have told with any certainty, the camera being more interested in their family jewels than their faces. Three of them, to judge from their shape, deportment and skin texture, were middle-aged to elderly; the fourth, whom we never saw at all from the front, looked fairly young and fit and was otherwise distinguished from the rest by a large, jagged, roughly Z-shaped scar on his back. The tape ended just as the scarred man had finished the agony stroke and rolled away to complete his pleasure by sniffing coke through a rolled-up dollar bill. The final shot was of Bev horizontal with her feet towards us and her legs apart.

'I guess that's the blackmail tape, huh?' Linda said.

'Yes, I guess it is.'

She nodded. 'How much did Kaplan want from the Birddogs?'

'A hundred thousand dollars.'

She stretched her legs out in front of her and raised her feet from the floor. 'You can have it for fifty.'

I laughed. 'I haven't got that kind of money. Go ask the Bergdorfs.'

'Okay. What's your offer? How much will you give me for it?'

I considered the question. I had Pascal's 10,000 dollars but that was dribbling away fast and I didn't know how much longer I would have to stay around until the matter of the death threat was resolved. If I wasn't to end up funding the enterprise myself I would have to go carefully, since I could hardly ask Freddie to pay the expenses, especially after today's encounter. I said, 'I could let you have a couple of thousand, top whack. Maybe a bit more later, maybe not.'

She said, 'Gee, thanks. I'd rather hold onto it myself.'

I shrugged. 'It's up to you. Do as you please. Remember one thing, though – there's no blackmail percentage in it any more because I know you have it.'

'I wasn't thinking of blackmail. What do you take me for? I was thinking of going to the house, all upfront, knocking on the door like a polite little girl and saying, "Hey, folks, I have this strange tape for sale. What's it worth to you?" What do you think?'

'Could work. Unless they call in their tame cop to take it away from you and work you over with his night stick.' I got up and started ejecting the tape from the video machine.

'Leave that.' There was a sharp note of command in her voice and when I turned towards her I could understand why. She was holding a .38, a police special, in her hand. It was pointing roughly in the direction of my navel.

I said, 'Hey, come on. What did you think – I was going to snatch the tape and run?'

'Yep. Something like that.' She was watching me almost pleadingly, her lower lip caught between her teeth. 'I'm sorry to do this, believe me. I like you, I really do. But, hey, that little piece of pornography is worth a fortune to somebody and I'd rather that somebody was me than you. I mean, a girl has to look out for herself, doesn't she? So, okay, take the tape out and toss it – gently – on the floor by my feet.'

I took it out and tossed it. She picked it up, still keeping her eyes and the gun on me. 'Now put your hands on top of your head and move, slowly, towards the door.' I did that and she followed me. She said, 'Quite a lady, your girlfriend, isn't she? How could anybody do those things for money with fat old men like that?'

'Not everybody can be a detective,' I said.

She laughed mirthlessly, and ushered me at gunpoint into the little driveway in front of the house. 'Give me your car keys,' she said. I gave them to her. 'Right. Now walk across the street and stand under the light. Not the first light, the second one.' I crossed the street and took up my position under the lamppost, about fifty yards away from her. 'Keep your hands on your head,' she said, so I did.

She got into her car, a battered red Ford that must have been about ten years old, drove out into the street and turned left, away from me. About a hundred yards down she stopped, shouted, 'Hey!' and threw my keys onto the pavement. Then she revved up and sped away.

I felt like yelling after her: 'You didn't fool me. I know you wouldn't have shot me.' But I didn't. In the first place she was probably too far away to hear and in the second place if she had heard there was just a chance she might have come back and shot me.

I drove round to the Kaplan office on Hollywood. Linda wasn't there. Surprise, surprise. But she had obviously been in touch because the receptionist, a girl who seemed to have modelled herself on the young Diana Ross, was expecting me and also trouble. To protect herself against the latter she had called in her boyfriend, an enormous kid about twenty-two and 210 pounds, the kind of fanatical body builder who looked as if he could benchpress 100 kilograms with his ear lobes. He propped himself against the wall behind the girl and glared at me. I gave him a wink and an amiable grin and addressed myself to his girlfriend, being just about as charming and English as I knew how. None of it worked. No, she couldn't possibly give me Miss Kelly's address or phone number. That would be quite against company policy, wouldn't it, Earl? Earl grunted and shifted and I gave him another amiable grin, just to keep him friendly or, failing that, at least docile. But I didn't risk a wink this time; I thought he might misinterpret that.

'Why you keep grinnin' at Earl that way?' asked the girlfriend.

'Just trying to be nice,' I said. 'He keeps glaring at me and it makes me nervous. I don't want him to think I'm one of the bad guys and start doing something about it. I mean, look at the size of him: if he fell on me he'd kill me.'

Earl pushed himself off the wall, growling. The girl said, 'Hush now, Earl. You be still, you hear?' Her words were more effective than my grin. He grunted something and settled back into his original pose, flexing the odd bicep at me in a menacing sort of way.

The girl said coldly, 'Is there anything more I can do for you, Mr Lennox?'

'Is there anything *more*?' I said. 'Now that's an interesting question. To ask if you can do anything *more* suggests that you've already done something. But since you've done absolutely nothing it might have been more appropriate if you'd asked if you could do *anything* for me and that would have brought us back to the one piece of information I require, namely the address and phone number of –'

'Get the fuck out of here,' said Earl. And since that seemed like a very sensible idea, I did, pausing at the door only long enough to blow him a kiss. Well, I'd tried a grin and a wink and they hadn't convinced him of my obvious charm. I didn't wait to see what effect the kiss had but as I went down the stairs I could hear him growling and cursing and moving around and the girl saying, 'No, no, Earl. It isn't worth it. You'll only get in trouble again.'

I wasn't particularly proud of myself. Teasing Earl had been much like going home and kicking the cat after a hard day at the office – a cheap and easy way of getting rid of anger and frustration. In my own defence I could argue that I'd had plenty of both that day but it was hardly Earl's fault. On the other hand I could think of one man who was at least partly responsible for my problems and since I was in the mood to give somebody a hard time I thought I might as well give it to him.

I made the call as soon as I got back to my hotel room. A familiar voice at the other end said: 'Yes? Who do you want?'

'That's not the way to answer a phone, Reg,' I said. 'You're supposed to be polite and give your number and say things like "May I help you?" I can't understand why a man like Donovan employs anybody as uncouth as you. Anyway, put Donovan on. It's Bobby Lennox here.'

'Bobby!' he said. 'Funny thing, we was talking

about you only the other day, me and some of the lads. Half of us thought you was probably dead and the other half hoped so. Nice to be popular, isn't it? Well, well. Donovan you want, is it? I'm not sure he wants to talk to you, Bobby.'

'You're not even sure where your own arse is,' I said, slipping easily into his style of witty badinage. 'Just get me Donovan, all right?'

Donovan came on the line, booming and blustering. It was understandable, I suppose. He still had no way of knowing why I had been impersonating Arnie in Pascal's room that night in London. 'Bobby! Where the bloody hell have you been? And what the hell's going on? You know Arnie's dead, I suppose –'

I said firmly, 'Donovan, I don't have time for this. This is not a social call, I want information. You put Arnie onto a certain American party who was in London recently. What I want to know is who put that American party onto you.'

He was silent for a moment. Then: 'What? I'm not going to tell you that. It's none of your bloody business.'

'Yes, it is my business and you are going to tell me because it's your business, too. The American wanted Arnie to see to two people and one of them was Bev.'

Another silence. 'Bev?' he said, as if he couldn't believe it. 'Bev?'

'Yes. Bev. You remember Bev, I imagine? She sure as hell remembers you.'

'I don't know what you mean,' he said.

I grunted impatiently at him. 'Look, I'm in California. I'm in Hollywood. I've met Bev. We had a nice long chat, talked about old times right

184

p to and including the reason she left The Street. Need I say more?'

'Hold on.' I could hear him shouting at people: 'Get out! Who asked you to come in here fucking eavesdropping? This is a private conversation.' There were muttered apologies, the sound of a door closing, then Donovan said, 'I'm sorry, Bobby. I'm really sorry. I was hoping you'd never find out.'

'That I can believe. But I have found out and you owe me one. You owe Bev, too, because she's still one of ours and we look after our own, don't we? I want to know why that American party had taken against her.'

'Why not ask him?'

'Well, I would, wouldn't I, if he was here to ask? But he's not. He met with a fatal accident. So now I want to talk to the people who put him onto you.'

'Jesus. Hang on a sec. Let me think about it.' I listened to him thinking. It seemed to necessitate quite a lot of heavy breathing and sucking of teeth. He said, 'Listen, Bob, these are very big people, know what I mean?' He sounded worried.

'I don't care how big they are,' I said. 'I don't care if they make the Harlem Globetrotters look like midgets, I still want to talk to them. There isn't anybody else who can help.'

He did some more thinking and when he'd finished he sounded more like the old, decisive Donovan. 'Right. Okay, this is what we do: I can't put you on to them, they wouldn't like that at all. What I can do, though, is ask them to contact you, as a favour to me like. That's it, Bobby, really it is. That's the best I can manage. It'd be more than my life's worth even to tell you who they are. But I will call them, I'll do that for you. What's your address over there, your phone number?' I told him. He said, 'Fine. I can't promise anything mind but I'll do what I can.'

I said, 'Okay,' and was about to hang up when Donovan said, 'About Bev and me –'

'I don't want to talk about it. Later maybe, when I get back to town, when I feel less inclined to kick both your lungs in.'

Impatiently, he said, 'Yeah, yeah, I know all that. What I was going to say, though – you won't tell your mum, will you? I wouldn't want her to think badly of me.'

'She already thinks badly of you, Donovan,' I said maliciously, and this time I did hang up. I felt a lot better. The idea of Donovan being afraid of my mum finding out about his fling with Bev made me quite cheerful and this mellow mood was not even disturbed when, five minutes later, Harry Brown called from the bar with instructions to go down at once and pour alcohol into him.

The barman charged our orders to my room number without even asking and Brown said, 'You got any news for me?' I said I hadn't. 'Well, I have news for you,' he said. 'They got the serial killer.'

'Hey, that's marvellous. What happened?'

'It was beautiful. The Revenge of the Old Farts. There's this old guy, diamond dealer, seventy, seventy-three years old, lives in Bel Air. His wife's in hospital, it's the help's day off, so he eats an early dinner somewhere in Beverly Hills, drives home and the perp's waiting for him, skulking in the bushes near the garage. He steps out and sticks a gun in the old guy's neck. Now the old guy's carrying, he's a diamond dealer, he's got a permit. The perp takes the gun away from him, marches him into the house. Give me your money, your watch, your wife's jewellery – the usual. And then they get to the safe. The old guy's pleading with him, Don't hurt me, don't hurt me, I'm an old man, I have a heart condition. The perp doesn't give a shit. He's a young guy, white, not too big but the gun makes him strong. So, Yeah, yeah, I'm crying for you inside, now open the fucking safe. The old guy opens it then suddenly he clutches his chest, moans and hollers and falls on the floor. He's had a heart attack, right? The perp says, Ah, shit, this is all I fucking need, turns away and looks into the safe. And then, and this is the really beautiful bit, the old guy pulls *another* gun out of his sock – I mean, do you believe this? A gun in his *sock*? Jesus, he must have been watching the cop shows on TV – and he blows the perp away. Three shots, two in the back, one in the head. There are pieces of him all over the wall. So the old guy gets up, dusts himself down, pours himself a brandy and calls the cops. End of story. How do you like it?'

'I like it a lot. The gun lobby will like it even better. When did all this happen?'

'Couple hours ago. Some of the boys went round to the perp's address. He was the serial killer, all right. They found enough stuff belonging to the earlier victims to establish that. Bonds, jewellery, things like that. It's the perfect ending. No more serial killer – until the next one, anyway – the State's been saved the cost of a long trial and all the old farts in town have got a hero their own age to admire.'

'Of course, you know what'll happen,' I said. 'From now on every senior citizen in America will pack a .44 Magnum and any young man who stops one of them to ask directions to the next street will get his head blown off.'

Brown waved his hand airily. 'Yeah, yeah. But that's America for you – home of the brave and land of the gun-happy.' He swallowed some more Chivas Regal. 'You sure you haven't anything to tell me?'

I shrugged. 'What would I have to tell? I had lunch today with Beverley Bergdorf, I had a talk with Freddie afterwards and neither of them had heard from the blackmailer. More to the point, nobody had tried to kill them either, so unless you've found out some more about Pascal it looks as if the whole thing's just going to fade away.'

He looked doubtful. 'Maybe. To tell you the truth, the Pascal business I never really believed in anyway. I'm not saying you lied, I just think the whole thing's crazy, a fantasy, who knows? A case of mistaken identity even. Who'd want to kill Freddie, for Chrissake? He's harmless, he's an asshole. And as for Beverley, why should anyone want to kill her, a respectable retired whore? But . . . the blackmail thing I do believe in and I don't think that's going to fade away.'

I didn't think so either. I had a nasty feeling that Linda would make the mistake of trying to sell the tape to Freddie and Freddie would call in Harry Brown and tuck some nice green notes into his pocket and suggest that good old Harry should go around to Linda's home and hurt her. The conviction that this was precisely what Harry would do if so instructed didn't change my attitude towards him, though. That was just the sort of cop he was. I still liked him and I was still prepared to trust him – so long as I knew who was paying him, of course.

13

HE WAS WAITING OUTSIDE MY ROOM when I got back from breakfast, a tall, tough-looking young man with dark, curly hair and wide shoulders.

He said, 'Mr Lennox? Bobby Lennox?'

'Yes?'

'Don Carlo would like for you to visit him at his home this p.m. at three o'clock.' It was amazing. He looked and sounded like a bit player in *The Godfather*.

I said, 'Don Carlo who?'

He shook his head, clearly unable to comprehend such ignorance. 'Don Carlo Minelli. Who else? He is a friend and business associate of Mr Donovan and he would like for you to –'

'Yes, right, got that bit. What's the address?'

He gave it to me and turned away without even saying goodbye. I don't think he was very impressed with me. But just as he got to the lift he stopped and looked back. 'I seen you before? You remind me of somebody.'

'Michael Caine perhaps? Before he made all the money and put on the –'

He shook his head. 'No. I can't even remember what Michael Caine looks like. But you . . . Some kind of athlete maybe? A ball player? A runner . . . ?'

I said eagerly, 'Right, a fighter. I was –'

He laughed. 'Don't kid yourself, friend. You're no fighter. You don't even look like no fighter.' And then with a casual wave he stepped into the lift.

I went into my room and the phone was ringing. It was Linda Kelly, sounding contrite. I wasn't really surprised to hear from her.

'About last night,' she said, 'I don't know what made me do it. I knew at the time it was a crazy stunt to pull but . . . oh, damn, what can I do except apologise?'

'Well, I should think so, too. Pulling a gun on an old friend. It's the kind of thing that makes one doubt the true strength of the relationship.'

She laughed, with relief I think to find that I wasn't furious with her. 'I hear you went to my office and blew kisses at Earl.'

'Only one kiss.'

'Yeah, well, he's a formidable-looking dude.'

'Oh, certainly. If he'd been born at the right time he'd have been the pin-up boy of every Neanderthal housewife.'

She chuckled and then there was an awkward silence before she said, 'Listen, about that tape . . .'

'Don't tell me. I thought at first you'd be stupid enough to try something on your own but then I came to the conclusion you weren't that dumb. So I imagine you've thought it over and you realise that there's nothing you can do without me, am I right? I mean, if you took it to the Bergdorfs, however openly, they wouldn't know who you were and they'd take it as a blackmail attempt. So then they'd call in their friend Lieutenant Harry Brown –'

'Who's he?'

'Their tame cop. I suspect the Bergdorfs are contributing very handsomely to his retirement fund, so he's awfully loyal to them. And I think Harry would come round to your house and take the tape away from you and, just as a hint that you shouldn't do anything like that again, he'd probably knock all your teeth out.'

'God,' she said. 'That's an even nastier scenario than I'd imagined. He sounds like a beautiful guy.'

'Oh, Harry's all right. We drink together quite often. Well, he drinks and I pay. That seems to be the way the cops like it round here. As a matter of fact I was with him last night.'

Anxiously she said, 'You didn't tell him I had the tape?'

'No. I was tempted to but then the memory of our last romantic meeting came back to me, you gazing into my eyes and me gazing into your gun barrel . . .'

'I'm really sorry about that. I – Well, it just suddenly occurred to me that for the first time in my life I was in possession of something that could be really valuable and I guess I was overcome by temptation and . . . and . . .'

'Greed.'

'Yeah. I guess that's as good a word as any.' Again she hesitated and I let the pause drag on, knowing what was coming. 'Would you set the deal up for me, Bobby? The Bergdorfs know you. If you were with me they'd know I wasn't trying to

191

blackmail them. I just want to sell it to them for whatever they think it's worth.'

'That's different from blackmail, is it? It sounds very much the same thing to me, except that it's the blackmailed rather than the blackmailer who sets the price.'

'Ah, come on, Bobby. Please. Okay, I know I should just give it to them. I know that's the decent thing. But if they're prepared to pay a little, whatever they decide, I could sure use the money. Well, my share of it anyway.'

'Not a question of shares. Whatever you negotiate from them is yours. I don't want any of it.' It sounded prissier than I meant it to but I didn't want any money, not from Bev, nor from anybody close to her.

Linda said, 'Gee, are you rich or something?'

'Put it this way: I'm London well off and Beverly Hills poor. I just don't want to take anything from the Bergdorfs.'

'No, I can understand that. But you will set the deal up for me? Will you do it today?'

I thought about it. It would be difficult. I could hardly approach Freddie and I was reluctant to go to Bev with a proposition as tacky as this. Ideally, I would have liked to hand her the tape, give it to her with instructions to dispose of it as she wished. But the tape was not mine to give. Strictly speaking it was not Linda's to sell either, but she had it in her possession and that counted for a lot. 'Not today,' I said. 'I'm busy today. Call me tomorrow, about this time. Or, if you like, we could meet for dinner and discuss a plan of campaign.'

'No,' she said and she sounded amused. 'Until we've disposed of the tape I want to keep this on a businesslike footing. I'm glad you asked, though. It shows you still like me a little bit.'

'Just a little bit,' I said and hung up.

Don Carlo Minelli lived on top of a hill in Bel Air. Let me put that another way. Don Carlo Minelli *owned* the top of a hill in Bel Air. I suppose, if asked, he would have said that what he had was an estate but to the casual observer it looked more like a four-star de luxe, maximum security prison compound. All the way round it, all the way round the hilltop, he had built a wall about ten feet high and on top of the wall was a couple of feet of wire, almost certainly electrified, and behind that wire was more wire, barbed. Unless you were invited you couldn't get in and once you were inside you probably couldn't get out unless you had a key. The place looked to be pretty well impervious to anything short of a full-scale aerial attack. The only obvious entrance was by way of a pair of enormous wrought-iron gates, electrically operated. Just inside the gates was a lodge built like a blockhouse. A wide, paved driveway curled through lawns and lush flowerbeds to a two-storey, mock Tudor house that you could only just glimpse from outside. I pulled up at the gates and hooted but nothing happened. So I got out of the car, walked up to the intercom on the gatepost, pressed the button and said, 'Hello.'

A harsh male voice said, 'Yeah?'

'Lennox,' I said. 'Bobby Lennox, here to see Mr Minelli.' No response. 'Don Carlo?' I asked. 'The Godfather? He's expecting me.' The heavy metal door of the lodge opened and two men came out, each with his right hand tucked inside his jacket and looking like Napoleon just before he started retreating from Moscow and just after he'd lost his glove.

They walked slowly up to the gate and one of them said, 'How about some ID?'

I slipped my passport through the bars and they handed it back and forth between them, comparing my features with those of the startled halfwit in the photobooth picture inside. Eventually they both grunted and one of them turned towards the lodge and nodded. The gates began to swing slowly open.

The larger of the two men, the one who looked as if he had just eaten Arnold Schwarzenegger, lightly grilled, for lunch, said, 'Drive uppa the house, switch off the engine, stay inna car. Keep your hands on toppa the wheel so everyone can see 'em and just wait.'

I did all that. The lawns and the flowerbeds, all immaculately tended, stretched around both sides of the house and off into the distance beyond. The house itself was huge and rosy pink with a flight of marble steps leading up to an enormous oak door that must once have graced a real Tudor house somewhere in England. I waited for about a minute with my hands on top of the steering wheel and then the oak door opened and the man who had brought me the invitation came out and approached my car.

'Okay,' he said, 'here's what you do: you get out slowly, turn and face the car and put your hands on the top. Then you don't move till I tell you.'

So I did all that, too, and he frisked me as expertly as the pair of Keystone Kops had done a few nights back.

I said, 'You know, I do love American hospitality. You have this incredible gift for making strangers feel welcome.'

He said, 'What do you want? This way you get to walk into the house. You hadn't done what I told you, a coupla the guys woulda had to carry you in.'

I followed him up the marble steps, through the door and into a great hall with a wide, sweeping staircase at the far end and a small fortune in Indian and Persian rugs scattered about the tiled floor. Oil paintings of ancestors – God knows whose – looked down at me sternly from the walls. We picked our way over the rugs and past the staircase, down a broad, light corridor and through French windows onto a deep, grey stone terrace, down some more steps and into the rear garden. More beautifully cropped lawn led to a swimming pool surrounded on all sides by about ten yards of pink paving stones. Beyond the pool was a changing-room-cum-bar-cum-heavens-knows-what, about the size of a four-bedroom bungalow. Around the pool, at tables shaded from the sun by colourful beach umbrellas, sat a dozen or so middle-aged men with paunches. Each man was attended by at least one tall and nubile young woman wearing high-heeled slippers and the bottom half of a bikini. Another three or four men, equally middle-aged and paunchy, splashed about in the shallow end of the pool with half a dozen more semi-naked and squealing girls. There were drinks and snacks on every table. I stopped to survey the scene and said, 'Are you sure this is Mr Minelli's house? It looks more like the Playboy mansion.'

My escort said contemptuously, 'The Playboy

mansion? Hugh Hefner could see this, he'd eat his heart out. Stay there.'

I stayed there, a dozen paces or so from what passed for the action, watching. Some of the nubile girls looked up at me with interest, not because I'm so irresistible but because I was at least twenty years younger and thirty pounds lighter than any of the men they were currently playing with. My escort approached a table where three men sat with four girls, paused behind one of the men, bent over and whispered softly to him. The man leaned back, listened, nodded, stubbed out a cigar in the ashtray and stood up. He was wearing a blue and white towelling robe, beach shoes to match and whatever brand of trendy, expensive sunglasses was in that year. He waved the escort away and came towards me.

'Mr Lennox?' he said. 'I'm Carlo Minelli. Welcome to my home.' I don't know quite what I'd expected: someone like Marlon Brando in *The Godfather* perhaps; someone who mumbled incomprehensibly because his cheeks were padded out with Kleenex. But Minelli was not at all like that. He was about forty-five and just above medium height, lean and clearly very fit, deeply tanned and handsome with thick, expensively tended chestnut hair. His accent was New York, mostly Upper East Side with just a hint of Little Italy. He gripped me firmly by the elbow and guided me to the only occupied table on the far side of the pool. When we got there he smiled courteously down at the three men and the three girls who were drinking bourbon and groping each other and said, 'Would you excuse us, gentlemen?' He seemed to take it for granted that the ladies would excuse us and he was not wrong. All six of them got up, muttering apologies, and carried their drinks to another table about twenty yards away. Minelli and I sat down and immediately a tall, leggy girl with waist-length black hair and the apparently obligatory bare breasts came over and asked us what we'd like to drink. Minelli ordered a bottle of Veuve Clicquot and when it had arrived, perfectly chilled, and he'd poured and we had toasted each other, he said, 'So you're a friend of Donovan's, huh? He speaks highly of you.'

'That's nice. Sometimes I speak highly of him, too.'

Minelli chuckled. It was an amused but guarded chuckle. He belonged to a world in which there were bosses and underlings. To him I was obviously an underling and underlings who were cheeky about their bosses went against the natural order of things. 'I take it you don't exactly work for him, right?'

'I don't work for him at all.'

'So why is he asking me to do you a favour?' I could feel the eyes boring into me behind the Rayban, or Dior or St Laurent, or whatever-the-hell sunglasses he was wearing.

'I suppose because he trusts me,' I said.

Minelli mulled that over and then nodded. 'Okay. I guess Donovan knows what he's doing.' He took a tiny sip of his champagne. 'I saw you fight a couple times. You were good.' He waggled his fingers judiciously. 'Not quite good enough but good even so.'

'That's why I got out – because I wasn't quite good enough.'

He nodded, slowly. 'I like that. That's smart. The guy who knows his limitations, who knows when to quit, that's a smart guy. I can always use a guy like that. I got guys around me now, ex-fighters, guys who in their time were probably as good as you were – contenders, not champions, know what I'm saying? – who didn't know when to quit and finished up with mashed potatoes where their brains used to be. They're no use for anything now except frightening other people.'

'I met a couple of them down at your lodge.'

He laughed. 'Right. So what do you think of my little spread?'

'Nice,' I said. 'And I love the help in their high heels and bikini pants. But who do all the paunches belong to?'

We both sat looking at the pool where an undisciplined kind of water polo game had broken out. For the male players grabbing the ball took second place to grabbing the nearest girl. It was touch and go whether the swinging guts or the wobbling tits were setting up the bigger waves.

'The paunches?' Minelli said. 'Oh, they belong to friends and business associates, people who owe me or are going to owe me, people who need me or are going to need me. Maybe you won't believe this, Mr Lennox, because you're a stranger in town, but in that pool, making total assholes of themselves, are some of the most influential men in southern California.' He took another little sip of his champagne. 'So what can I do for you?'

'To make me owe you, too, you mean? Or to make Donovan owe you?'

He took his sunglasses off. His eyes were large and brown and about as warm as frozen dung. 'Maybe one, maybe the other, maybe both. We'll see. Tell me what you want.'

So I told him everything – about Pascal and how, pretending to be Arnie, I'd gone along to meet him in London and how Pascal had put out the contract on Bev.

He listened carefully but at the end he said, 'I don't think I can help you much. I knew Pascal fairly well. Well enough, anyway. A Frenchman, came to the States as a kid near the end of World War Two and became a citizen. A few years back my family was having cash flow problems – I don't know, some politician had goosed the Feds into something that resembled action and they were clamping down on our activities. Anyway, Pascal laundered some money for me. It wasn't hard for him, he was always going to Europe, dealing with the fashion houses. But at least he did it, which showed his heart was in the right place.' He paused, chewing thoughtfully on one of the arms of his sunglasses. 'He wasn't a man I liked to have around much. Always seemed to have some kind of chip on his shoulder, a secret grievance, know what I mean? Like life had treated him dirty. Anyway, he came to me and said he wanted to put out a contract but he didn't want to use local talent so who could I recommend. When he said he was going to London I told him to get in touch with Donovan. And that's all I know. I wasn't really interested. I didn't even ask who he wanted hit but now you tell me I can see where he'd want to use out-of-town people. I mean, you say this girl Beverley is married to Freddie Bergdorf and he's the son of Tommy Bergdorf? Boy, somebody wasted Tommy's kid, believe me, some serious shit would hit the fan around here. Tommy's very big backstage in the Republican Party. He pulls a lot of strings.'

'But you can't think of anyone who would want his son dead?'

He shook his head. 'A serious movie lover, maybe, but outside that, no.'

A tall, lean, handsome man came out of the changing room, accompanied by a couple of long-haired blondes. He waved at Minelli, who waved back. The man started in our direction but Minelli shook his head slightly and the threesome changed direction and settled at a table on the other side of the pool.

'You know him?' Minelli said. 'Peter Vincent, the next Governor of California and the next-but-one President of the United States. I own him. I have his marker in my safety deposit box and his pecker in my pocket. Any time he steps out of line I put my hand in my pocket and squeeze his balls and he says, "Ouch!" and comes running. It gives me a very warm feeling.'

'Juices him up a bit, too, I should imagine,' I said. 'Nice for you, of course. You can't have too many friends in that class.'

'He's not a friend,' Minelli said contemptuously. 'He works for me. And when he's President he'll still be working for me.'

Across the pool the future President stood up and pulled off his pale blue sports shirt. He waved again to Minelli and then turned to say something amusing to his blonde playmates. A large, pale Z-shaped scar stood out against the deep tan of his back.

'See the Mark of Zorro there?' Minelli said. 'He got that as a kid down on a farm in Dropdead, Pennsylvania, or somewhere. Fell into a mess of barbed wire. He tells me women love to run their tongues along it.'

'No accounting for taste,' I said.

'Yeah. You want to meet him?'

'No, I don't think so. I'll wait till he's President. Then he can invite me to the White House.' I got up to leave. Minelli said, 'Unh-unh. When he's President *I'll* invite you to the White House. He'll be living there but I'll hold the deeds.' He walked me back to the house where the usual messenger was waiting to escort me to my car.

As we shook hands and swapped goodbyes, Minelli said, 'Sorry I couldn't be more help. I'll make a few enquiries about the Bergdorfs. If I hear anything I'll let you know.' I followed the messenger into the house and at the door I paused and glanced back. Minelli was standing there looking towards the pool, his sunglasses on top of his head, his hands in the pockets of his towelling robe, the master of everything – and everyone – he surveyed.

At 8.30 that night I pulled into the parking lot of a twelve-storey apartment block in Encino, just off Ventura Boulevard. Encino was known locally as 'the Beverly Hills of the Valley', but only if you lived south of Ventura. If you lived north, you were socially dead, goodness knows why, because the buildings and the houses looked much the same on either side. The apartment block was north of Ventura. It was where Linda lived.

She had called me at the hotel about half an hour earlier.

'Oh, thank God you're there,' she said. 'Would you come over here? Please? Now?'

'No,' I said. 'In the first place I don't know where

''here'' is and in the second place I'm just going out for dinner.'

'Please? Please? Don't let me down.' There was something desperate about her voice, a note of urgency and, more than that, of fear. 'I really need you here.'

'All right,' I said. 'What's the address?'

She told me. 'And bring the tape.'

'What? What tape?'

'The Bergdorf tape,' she said and hung up.

So there I was, outside her apartment building, baffled, wary and empty-handed, not having been able to bring her a tape she already had. I pressed the buzzer with Linda's name above it and at once the glass entrance doors opened. I took the lift to the seventh floor, found Linda's apartment and rang the bell.

A shortish, stoutish, middle-aged man with tinted glasses opened the door. 'You Lennox?' he said.

I said I was and he let me in, closed the door and chained and bolted it. We were in a small living-cum-dining room, furnished with nice, non-matching stuff that looked as if it might have been assembled by someone with a discerning eye at up-market garage sales: a couple of easy chairs and a two-seater sofa, a dining table and chairs, one or two scatter cushions, bookshelves, a TV set and VCR. Linda was over the far side with her face pressed against the wall. A very big man was leaning on her and twisting her right arm way up behind her back. She was crying, but softly, as if she was afraid to make too much noise.

'What the –'

'Shut up and sit down,' said the middle-aged

man. 'I'll tell you when you can talk.' A certain weight was added to his words by the fact that he had a gun in his hand.

I said, 'Yes, but what I –'

'Harve,' he said, 'Harve, come over here.'

'Why?' Harve said. He was holding Linda's right wrist in his own right hand and with his left hand he was massaging her buttocks. He seemed to resent being disturbed.

'Because I want you to ask this man to sit down.'

Harve looked at me and grinned. 'My pleasure,' he said. He shoved Linda away from him and she caught her knees sharply against the wooden arm of one of the chairs and half fell across it. There was a vivid red mark on the side of her face. She looked as if somebody had slapped her very hard.

Harve came slowly towards me, still grinning. He had the look of a man who was about to have himself a nice time. He was a tall, very heavy man with thick arms, big shoulders and a beer belly.

I said, 'Please, no violence. I'll do anything you want but no violence, I beg you, don't –'

Harve backhanded me across the face and knocked me down into the chair behind me. The blow really hurt. It jarred my teeth, rang bells in my head and brought tears to my eyes. 'That hurt,' I said. 'Please, no more –' Harve grabbed a handful of my hair and jerked my head up. Now there were more tears, running down my cheeks. 'No,' he said, 'that didn't hurt. That was a love tap. You really want to know hurt, just keep not doing what the man tells you.' He gave my hair another yank and shoved me down again.

I blinked the water from my eyes and looked up. Harve and the middle-aged man were smiling at me, amused, contemptuous. Linda didn't look very impressed with me either. 'This the best you can do, honey?' Harve said to her. 'This your idea of a boyfriend?' He shook his head sadly.

The middle-aged man said, 'Okay, Lennox, we got your attention now?'

I nodded.

'Right, so where's the tape? The lady asked you to bring the tape but I look around me and I don't see no tape. Do you see a tape, Harve?' Harve shook his head. No, he didn't see no tape either. 'So where is it? Huh?'

'It . . . it's in my car. In the parking lot.' I glanced at him eagerly. 'I'll go and get it for you.'

The man laughed. 'Hear that, Harve? This hero's gonna go get the tape for us. Isn't that nice? Only thing is, I have an idea that once this hero gets out of here he's gonna start running and he won't stop till he hits the ocean. I got a better idea, hero. Why don't you give your keys to Harve and he can go get the tape while me and my little friend here,' he waved the gun about casually, 'keep you and the lady entertained?'

'Yes,' I said, 'all right. Whichever you prefer.' I started fumbling around, patting my pockets. 'May I . . . may I stand up? I'm . . . I'm rather nervous and I can't remember what I did with my keys.'

'Let him up,' the middle-aged man said. Harve moved away from me a pace or two and I stood up, still fumbling.

'Hey, honey,' Harve said to Linda, 'he's really something, this faggot boyfriend of yours. Do you suppose they're all like him in England?' He half-turned towards her and that's when I hit him. I threw the left first and he swayed away from it as had expected he would, bringing up his hands to block the punch. The following right hook, with plenty of shoulder and body weight behind it, thumped sweetly into the flab under his heart. He grunted and doubled up and I got him on the nose with two fast left jabs, sank another big right in the middle of his beer belly, hooked him in the mouth with a left and pounded a beautiful one-two combination into his belly again. He went down on his knees, clutching his stomach and moaning. I swung away from him and caught the middle-aged man flush on the cheek with a roundhouse left that knocked his glasses off and sent him sprawling against the wall. He still had the gun in his hand but it wasn't pointing at anybody any more so I stepped up and took it away from him. He didn't offer any resistance.

Behind me I heard scrabbling noises as Harve tried to pick himself up but he didn't get very far, just to his hands and knees, because Linda stepped up behind him and, as beautifully balanced as a soccer player taking a penalty kick, swung her right foot between his slightly parted thighs and buried the sharp point of her high-heeled shoe into his testicles. He screamed and fell forward on his face, clutching his genitals with both hands.

'I enjoyed that,' Linda said. She was flushed and panting slightly. 'I really enjoyed that.'

I waved the gun at the middle-aged man. 'Now,' I said, 'I'll tell you what, you go over there and sit on Harve's back. That way I'll be able to keep an eye on both of you.' He did as he was told.

'Can I have my glasses?' he said. 'I don't see too well without my glasses.'

'You can have them when you leave. And you

can leave just as soon as you tell me what the hell this is all about.'

Sullenly he said, 'I just want the tape, is all. Jesus, it's my tape. I just came here to get my own property back. If she'd given it to me when I asked her nice we wouldn't have had all this unpleasantness. I think you broke my cheekbone.'

That was possible. I was lucky I hadn't broken my own hand and if I had it would have served me right for ignoring the cardinal rule that you don't hit people about the head unless you have gloves on.

'Before we go into the niceties of who owns what,' I said, 'why don't you introduce yourself? You know us but we don't know you and that doesn't seem quite fair. So take your wallet out and toss it to the lady.'

He hesitated. 'What if I don't? What are you gonna do then – shoot me? I don't think you'd shoot me.'

'And you are quite right,' I said. 'But then I don't need to shoot you, do I? You've seen what I can do with my hands. If you give me any trouble all I have to do is beat the crap out of you until my arms get tired. And while you consider that, consider this – in my time I've beaten the crap out of infinitely tougher people than you for fifteen, three-minute rounds.'

I could hardly believe myself, bragging like that. The only excuse I could offer was that it was an over-reaction to having played the wimp; a vaguely pathetic attempt to recover some self-esteem. Still, it seemed to impress him. 'You a fighter?' he asked.

'Was.'

He nodded, sighed and threw his wallet across

Linda. She looked at his driver's licence and business cards and said, 'His name is Walter Castelli. From Las Vegas. And it says here he's an entrepreneur, whatever that means.'

'Whatever Wally wants it to mean, I imagine. Isn't that right, Wally?'

He nodded again.

'Okay,' I said, 'now if you're comfortable and Harve's comfortable – well, no, I can see Harve's not comfortable but that's his problem – why don't you explain exactly what we're all doing here tonight?'

He thought for a moment, gave another sigh, glanced towards Linda and said, 'Her partner – Kaplan, right? – came to me a couple, three weeks back looking for information about a hooker called Beverley Timkins, English girl, used to work in Vegas. So I . . . Hey, you guys know what's on the tape, right?' I said we did. 'Okay, that makes it easier. Thing of it is, I knew this girl. I –'

'Why did Kaplan go to you?' I said.

'Because I know him fifteen years. He used to be a private eye in Vegas. We were not friends exactly but we got along. And, well, I run girls myself, not always but sometimes.'

'A natural part of being an entrepreneur, I suppose,' Linda said acidly.

'Right. And, well, I know all the whores in Vegas. It's my business, know what I mean? So I knew this Beverley. Better than that, I had her on tape.' He hesitated, then – 'What the hell, a few years back I was working for the guy who ran the stable she was in and I had this idea of taping some of the girls at work, putting a package together and selling the videos. Not in Vegas, Jesus no. I mean, the guy who ran the stable he'd have had both my leg broken, he'd discovered what I was doing. That's why it didn't work out. I couldn't let him know, I couldn't let the girls know. I had to use a two-way mirror they didn't know about, I had to do the camerawork myself and I'm no good with a camera. Well, you've seen the tape. Who's going to buy anything that lousy quality? Anyway, I made maybe half a dozen tapes and they were all terrible so I gave it up. But I kept the tapes. For my own amusement, you know? And I remembered the name of this Beverley. So when Kaplan asked about her, I showed him what I'd got and he got very excited, believe me he was excited. He said if I let him handle the deal he could sell it and make us fifty grand each.'

Suddenly, Castelli started bouncing up and down. Harve was stirring. I walked over and gave him a prod in the backside with my foot. 'Lie still, Harve, and keep your balls in your hands,' I said. 'Otherwise I'm going to grind them into the carpet.' He lay still. 'Did Kaplan say how he was going to make the money?'

Castelli shook his head. 'No, but I figured it was some kind of blackmail, what else?'

'And, of course, that was perfectly all right to an entrepreneur like yourself, so you gave him the tape. Why? Did you trust him that much?'

He brooded for a moment or two. 'Not really. But, see, I didn't know what the fuck it was about. I mean, this girl, she was a hooker, how can you blackmail a hooker? Obviously, I figured there was more to it than that but whatever it was Kaplan wouldn't tell me, so what am I going to do – hang on to a tape that's not doing me any good sitting

208

around my house, or take a chance on Kaplan? So I told him I'd think it over, made all the enquiries I could about the girl and came up with zilch. Kaplan came back two days later and I told him okay and gave him the tape.'

'And that was two, three weeks ago?'

'Yeah. He called a couple times, said everything was going okay, be patient, the money was coming. I wasn't worried. I needed him, I knew where to find him. Then two things happened at the same time – I see a picture of Mrs Beverley Bergdorf giving some kind of party in the *Hollywood Reporter* and Kaplan gets himself wasted. So I figure it's time to get my tape back because now I know where to sell it and now Kaplan's gone I can make a hundred grand instead of fifty. You really want to know any more? Today Harve and me went to Kaplan's home, then to his office. No tape. So we thought we'd call on his partner, have a little talk. She said her boyfriend had the tape, so we had her call you and tell you to come on over with it and that was our first mistake.'

I thought about all this while he sat quietly on Harve's back. I said, 'Mrs Bergdorf probably gets her picture in the trade papers quite a lot. Are you telling me you've never seen any of those pictures or, if you have, you've never until now associated her with the Vegas hooker on your tape?'

He nodded. 'That's what I'm telling you. Look, maybe I seen pictures of her. I don't know. I don't remember. And if I saw the pictures, so what? I don't look at pictures of some Beverly Hills movie producer's wife and say, "Hey, that's a hooker I used to know". She looks different; okay, now I know who she is, now I look at the picture and the hooker's in my mind because she's going to make me some money at last, I can see she's not all that different. But she's still different.'

All right, I accepted that; there was a logic to it. He didn't seem to be the kind of man who would study the society pages, even in the trade papers, unless there was likely to be some money in it for him. 'So now what?' he said. 'It's still my tape.'

'True. But we've got it. We also have your gun and your minder isn't looking too healthy right now. This doesn't seem to put you in much of a bargaining position, does it?'

To do him justice he was not without courage, or anyway bluster. 'You don't give me my property back, I can make a lot of trouble for you. I know people.'

'I know people, too,' I said. 'I know Don Carlo Minelli. I was at his house only this afternoon, drinking champagne.'

'Ahh,' he said, thoughtfully.

'I also know a homicide lieutenant called Harry Brown. He's a very good friend of the Bergdorfs and one of his keenest desires in life is that they shouldn't be hassled by people like you. Who do you know?'

'Never mind,' he said. He sat quietly for a moment or two, blinking myopically while he thought things over. 'Can we make a deal? Partners?'

'There's no deal to be made. The tape has no value now. The only advantage a blackmailer has is that nobody knows who he is. If I gave you the tape and you tried to put the bite on, I'd just tell the Bergdorfs and Harry Brown who you are. And if they couldn't do anything, I'd tell my friend Don

Carlo and I feel sure he'd be able to think of some way of taking you out of the game.'

He winced. 'Don't even talk about it.' There were a few more moments of thoughtful silence, then he shrugged and said, 'I guess that's it.' The side of his face where I had hit him had begun to swell and redden. It looked quite painful. 'Okay if we leave now?'

I said it was and he stood up slowly. Harve stood up, too, even more slowly, still clutching his groin. 'My balls are killing me,' he said to Linda in a tone that was both baleful and aggrieved. 'You didn't have to kick me so hard.'

'Teach you not to slap a woman in future,' she said.

I gave Wally back his glasses and his wallet and escorted the two men to the door. 'Do I get my gun?' Wally asked hopefully. I shook my head. 'Ah, well,' he said. 'Plenty more where that came from.'

I watched their slow progress down the hall to the lift and when they were about halfway there I said, 'You know your trouble, Wally? You're like everyone else around here – you watch too many movies. I've noticed lately that the bad guys in the movies are all big, fat men like old Harve. But fat doesn't mean tough; fat means slow. Next time you're looking for a minder pick someone who's lighter and faster, someone with muscle.'

'Up yours,' said Harve.

I went back into the flat and locked and bolted the door. Linda put her arms around my neck and kissed me, quite lovingly, on the mouth. 'My hero,' she said and she didn't sound altogether mocking.

I pushed her away a little. 'Talking of heroes,' I

said, 'why did you call me and not the man in you life?'

'I did call him,' she said, 'but he just stayed in the kitchen, drinking his milk.'

'He did what?'

'Well, he's a cat. What would you expect a cat to do?'

'That's it?' I said. 'The man in your life whose existence stopped you going to the beach with me is just a fucking cat?'

'He is not a fucking cat,' she said, indignantly. 'He used to be a fucking cat but I had him neutered and now he doesn't fuck any more.'

'Well, that explains it. If you had him neutered that explains why he didn't come to your assistance. He's probably still nursing a grievance and who could blame him?'

I took my car keys out of my pocket but she moved in closer and kissed me again. 'You can't leave me,' she said, breathing the words into my mouth. 'Laurel and Hardy might come back.'

'I doubt it,' I said, giving her her own breath back. 'Besides, a gentleman doesn't take advantage of a lady's gratitude.'

'Who said anything about gratitude?' she murmured. 'This is good, clean lust.' So I stayed there that night.

14

WALLY AND HARVE had been unable to find the tape in Linda's flat for the very good reason that it wasn't there. She had put it back where she found it, in the hole in the wall behind Kaplan's bathroom cabinet, on the assumption that that was the last place I would look for it. And since I was the only person apart from herself who knew it had even come to light, I was the only one she was worried about. It was good thinking, really: I knew she had the tape; I knew where she had found it; and, if I had been hunting for it as she thought I might have been, I would have spent a lot of time hunting elsewhere before it occurred to me that she might have returned it to its original hiding place.

In the morning we set off to retrieve it. The plan was that I should then call Tommy Bergdorf, not Freddie or Bev, set up a meeting and arrange a deal. We would play the tape to Tommy and ask him what he thought it was worth. Without telling him so in advance, Linda would accept whatever he decided, so long as it was at least 5,000 dollars. It took a long time and a lot of argument before she would even agree to this figure. The fact that she had no legal right to the tape whatsoever didn't seem to enter into her thinking. It was in her possession, therefore it was hers and she reckoned it was worth 5,000 dollars minimum. Feminine morality can be very hard to grasp sometimes. I pointed out to her that only the previous day she herself had suggested that she would take whatever Tommy Bergdorf offered but she said things had changed, the goal posts had been moved and now she really had something to sell. It had become a legitimate deal, nothing remotely to do with blackmail, and therefore it was madness to let the purchaser set the price. I said, trust me – do it my way and you'll probably get more than five grand. So in the end she agreed. Reluctantly.

It was an unreal sort of morning. Not the morning itself; that was all right. Blue skies, sun shining. Typical Californian day. What was strange was waking up together for the first time in the same bed. Getting up together. Pottering naked about the place. Sharing the bathroom and the shower. Jostling for mirror space while I shaved and she made up. Preparing coffee and breakfast together. Kissing, touching, talking, falling silent. Sitting, head down over the bacon and eggs, then glancing up and unexpectedly catching those new lovers' looks on each other's faces – secret, meditative, smiling looks. The knowledge that (a) nothing like this had ever happened before and (b) that exactly the same sort of thing was probably going on simultaneously in hundreds of thousands of apartments all over the world.

We drove to her office first, to check the mail and see if, by any chance, somebody wanted her to find

Maltese falcon or a rare doubloon. But it seemed to be the closed season for things like that. All that awaited us, apart from her secretary's greeting, which took the form of a smile for Linda and a scowl for me, was a message to call a Mr Perry Lance. It had to do, the girl said, with a job Mr Kaplan had been doing for somebody called . . . She scratched around among the stuff on her desk and came up with a scruffy sheet from a memo pad. 'Here,' she said. 'This is the guy Mr Kaplan was working for. At least, I guess he was but he didn't tell me. That's Mr Lance's phone number underneath.'

We looked at the message. The name written on it was Philip Paskell. 'Are you sure this is the way to spell it?' I asked. The girl gave a little toss of her head and directed her answer to Linda. I was obviously some kind of non-person as far as she was concerned. 'That's the way it sounded to me,' she said.

'Call Mr Lance,' I said to Linda.

So she did and half an hour later we were knocking at the door of the late Philippe Pascal's house in Westwood and Perry Lance let us in. A tall, balding man of about sixty, over-dressed for California in a dark blue suit with tie to match. 'Mr Kaplan?' he said to me.

'Er, no. This is Mr Kaplan's partner, Linda Kelly. My name's Robert Lennox. I'm a London associate of the Kaplan Agency.' It sounded pretty high-powered and obviously Lance thought so, too, because he gave an appreciative nod and ushered us in to a large, well-appointed living-room. The windows, and the French doors leading to the patio and the pool area were wide open.

Lance said, 'If it's too warm for you I could close

215

everything and put the air conditioning on. Only until I got here yesterday nobody had been in this place for days and you know how rooms get when nobody uses them.'

We said we did. Musty they got, we said, stale, dead. Well no, we said realising that dead might seem a little indelicate in the circumstances, not dead exactly, more like lifeless. Well no, not that either really. What we actually meant was more like not lived in.

Lance said, 'It's okay. I know what you mean.' Linda and I sat in easy chairs and he went over to a neat little Georgian desk in the corner. 'Why I called you,' he said, 'was on account of a bill here from Mr Kaplan that I'm afraid Philippe hadn't gotten around to paying before his, er, his . . .'

'Right,' we said nodding.

'There's no real problem,' he said. 'It's quite a small amount, a couple of thousand dollars or so. Well, I'm sure you must know that, Miss Kelly. Or is it Ms Kelly?'

'Miss is okay,' Linda said. 'It's easier to say.'

'Yeah. It is, you're right. But, ah, about this bill. It's maybe none of my business but all it says is "For services rendered", and I just wondered what those services were.'

I looked at Linda; Linda looked at me. I said, 'Forgive me if I seem rude, Mr Lance, but Miss Kelly and I don't know exactly who you are.'

'Oh, gee,' he said. 'I'm sorry. I should have . . . Well, I'm Philippe's executor. I'm his cousin. From New York?' That upward inflexion at the end of the sentence, as if he wasn't entirely sure that we would believe he came from New York. As though to prove it beyond doubt he gave us a business card ach. The card gave his name, office address near Madison Avenue and a phone number. It didn't say anything about being an executor.

'Thank you,' I said. 'But I'm afraid we find ourselves in a difficult position, Mr Lance. The work we do for our clients is highly confidential and even though Mr Pascal is, alas, deceased, that confidentiality remains.'

He nodded his approval. 'That's good. I like that. I wish there were more people with those kind of scruples.'

I thanked him again with the solemnity he would have expected from a man of scruples. 'The trouble is, you see, that unless we can be sure that you already have a pretty good idea of the work we were doing for Mr Pascal we're simply unable to discuss it with you.' I could feel Linda's eyes boring into me with wonder or, as I preferred to think, admiration.

'Yes,' he said. 'Absolutely. I like the way you guys do business. Okay, well, I do have a pretty good idea of Mr Kaplan's activities. I've been going through Philippe's papers and I came across this file.' He tapped his finger on a large, fat Manila envelope on the desk. 'It wasn't here, it was in his safety deposit box at the Chase Manhattan.' He shook his head sadly. 'Poor Philippe. This was his obsession, you know. All his life this, this terrible thing simply dominated him. But I guess you know all about that.'

I remembered something Carlo Minelli had said. 'His grievance, you mean? The chip on his shoulder.'

Lance didn't seem too happy with that. 'That makes it sound kind of flippant, don't you think?

217

To Philippe it was much more serious than a chip on the shoulder.'

'Of course,' I said, soothingly. 'I'm sorry.'

'Yes, well . . . This latest bill from Mr Kaplan. I just wondered if it was simply the final reckoning or whether he'd discovered anything more. Where is Mr Kaplan, by the way?'

A moment's hesitation, then Linda said, 'I'm afraid he's dead. He was shot by the serial killer, the same one who killed Mr Pascal.'

Lance shook his head in disbelief. 'The serial killer? You mean the guy who was blown away by the old man with the gun in his sock? Jesus, what a horrible coincidence.'

'Indeed,' I said, 'and it places us in an awkward situation. You see, Mr Kaplan had been dealing with Mr Pascal personally. So although Miss Kelly and I are familiar with, let's say, the broad outlines of the case, we don't know the fine detail. That may seem strange but I can only say that at the Kaplan Agency discretion is placed above all else.'

Lance bought it. He was as big on discretion as he was on scruples. He did have one query, though. 'But surely you must have Mr Kaplan's notes, the duplicate of this file, in your office?'

Linda said, 'Oh, sure, it'll be there. We're going through all his papers now but it's kind of complicated because, as I'm sure you know, the serial killer ransacked the homes and offices of his victims. He left a terrible mess and it's going to take time to sort it all out.'

'Right,' Lance said. 'Right.' He thought for a moment or two. 'See, I'm not sure how much further to go with this investigation. Strictly speaking, I guess it should have died with Philippe. But confess to a personal curiosity. I know the background, I've read the files –'

'Files?' I said. 'You mean, there's more than one?'

'Oh, sure.' He fiddled about in a drawer of the desk. 'There's this, too. From a German detective agency? The stuff goes back years. I mean, Philippe really cared about this. I didn't like him too much but, well, he was kin and for his sake I'd kind of like to see the whole thing resolved.'

I looked at Linda, took a deep breath, crossed my fingers and said: 'May I suggest something, Mr Lance? Why don't you tell us exactly what you know and then lend us the files so we can study them and decide whether we truly think there's any point in continuing? Obviously, for that there'd be no charge either to the estate or to you. We'd give you our report and then, if you wanted us to carry on, we'd come to a completely new arrangement.'

He thought about that. 'No charge?'

I nodded.

He thought some more. 'Okay.' And then he gave us the background . . .

Philippe Pascal was born in a small town in Upper Normandy in 1934. When he came along his parents, Joseph and Marie, already had a son of three and a daughter aged eighteen months. A year later Marie had a serious miscarriage and after that there could be no more children. But that was not so bad because three were about as many as Joseph Pascal could support. He had a small dairy farm roughly midway between Rouen and Dieppe and this kept the family reasonably well housed, clothed and fed. He also had an apple orchard and the cider and Calvados that this produced added a few little extras. Such luxuries as they all enjoyed were provided by Marie, who had a flair for fashion and was greatly in demand as a dressmaker.

When the war and the Nazis came along, life carried on much as before except that now Joseph was obliged to supply food to the occupying troops and Marie to make dresses for their girlfriends. Neither of them was happy about this. They were both deeply patriotic and nurtured a fervent hatred of Germany, an inheritance from their parents and the First World War. Joseph, therefore, joined the Resistance. In the interests of protecting the safety of French people, the local cell shunned the spectacular. It did not go in for planting land mines, blowing up railway lines, assassinating German officers or anything else that might have brought down reprisals on the local citizenry; instead it concentrated on smuggling information about troop movements and the like back to England and, from time to time and acting on information received from Marie Pascal, it would swoop on the home of some girl who was sleeping with a German, carry her off, shave her head and, if the necessary materials were to hand, tar and feather her. Nobody claimed that such activities ranked in achievement with starting the Second Front but they were good for local morale. Besides, by 1942 Joseph's cell had taken on other duties, too. British and Free French agents were parachuted into the area and from there smuggled out to Rouen; and because Joseph's farm was in a small and isolated hamlet it became part of the escape route for Allied airmen who had been shot down over France. Philippe and his brother and sister soon became accustomed to the fact that every now and then strange men who spoke little or no French would mysteriously turn p in the cellar, the attic or one of the barns and, a few days later, would just as mysteriously vanish, never to be seen again.

Then came D-Day and the Normandy invasion. Even at the age of ten, Philippe was aware of a new excitement and optimism in the district. The Allies were here, they had landed, they were on their way and soon the Germans would be gone, fleeing back to the Fatherland with bullets buzzing around their backsides. Soon after the invasion a British pilot officer, who had been forced to part company with his fighter plane only a few miles away, stayed briefly at the Pascal farm before being sent on his way to the coast. The news he brought with him, fresh from London that very day, cheered everyone even more.

The flyer had only been gone an hour or two and the senior Pascals were still celebrating the forth-coming Allied victory with a drop of Joseph's better Calvados, when the Germans arrived. They came down the hill into the hamlet with their vehicle lights and engines switched off and they had forced their way into the Pascals' farmhouse – a dozen of them, led by a young SS captain wearing an Iron Cross, second class – before anyone knew they were there. It was the British pilot they were after.

They charged into the living-room, knocking over tables and chairs as a matter of habit, hitting the Pascals with their rifle butts, herding them into a corner. Only Philippe escaped. A few minutes before the Germans burst in, Joseph had sent him out to the barn to fetch another bottle of Calvados and he was still outside in the yard when the uproar started in the house. For a while he was too terrified to move but then he tiptoed to the living-room

window and looked in through the gap where th
blackout curtains didn't quite reach the sill.

From where he stood he could hear little; the
sound of voices, yes; not individual words. But he
could see everything and what he saw was the basis
of the chip, the grievance, the obsession, whatever,
that dominated the rest of his life. He saw his family
shoved and kicked into the corner of the room; he
saw his father gesticulating, trying to explain something to the SS officer; he saw him reach out to
open the walk-in cupboard behind him; he saw the
young officer raise his pistol and fire bullet after
bullet into his father's body. And he saw the other
soldiers, an impromptu firing squad, slaughter his
mother, his brother and his sister. For the rest of
his life he remembered the blood spurting onto the
walls and the ceiling, the bodies bucking and
jerking as the bullets struck. And he remembered
the noise of the gunfire. *That* he could hear – a noise
so loud and brutal that it drowned his own shouts
and screams, so that it seemed to him that he was
yelling as loudly as he could and yet was making
no sound.

When the shooting stopped and the Germans
broke up into groups of two or three to search the
house and the outlying buildings, Philippe turned
and ran across the fields to the nearest farm a few
hundred yards away and the neighbours took him
in and hid him until the Germans had gone.

A few days later the Allied troops advanced into
the district. They met little resistance and swept on
through towards Rouen, leaving another liberated
town behind them. In that area Joseph Pascal, his
wife, his elder son and his daughter were the last
French casualties of the war. Except for Philippe,

though his injuries were emotional not physical. Of the next few months he remembered hardly anything except his grief. For some time he was in a state of shock, withdrawn and uncommunicative, indifferent to what was going on around him while his parents' friends cared for him and discussed what to do with him. He had nowhere to go in France, no other family but he did have an uncle, his mother's brother, in New York and eventually it was decided to send him there. So he was taken first to London, then by ship to America to live with his uncle and aunt and his three cousins.

And there he took on a new nationality and began a new life. He was an intense, quiet boy, a steady and conscientious student but not easy to know or easy to like. He seemed to reject affection or any kind of close relationship. His cousins tried dutifully to treat him as a brother but they were never comfortable with him and he had little in common with his contemporaries. At first there was a language difficulty and even when that was overcome he still kept himself apart from other people. After he graduated from high school he went into the rag trade and because he had inherited his mother's flair for designing he set up on his own as soon as he could. By then he had left his uncle's house and was living alone in a two-room apartment in Little Italy, and though his cousins kept in touch and saw him as often as possible, he seemed to them to be an acquaintance rather than family.

And all the time he remembered constantly, vividly, the night his father and mother and his brother and sister were murdered. And he remembered the young SS captain who commanded the death squad; a man who had been stationed in the Pascals' area for several months; a man who was neither more nor less popular than any other German officer; a man whose name Philippe knew to be Heinrich Müller.

Perry Lance said: 'What Philippe wanted was vengeance. He was like an Italian – it was a vendetta. He wanted that bastard dead. He told me, God knows how many times, that he had this dream that one day he would find Müller and the guy would be happy and prosperous and living with his family and Philippe would have them all wiped out. That's what he lived for. I mean, Jesus!' He laughed, though not with any merriment. It was more of a grunt than a laugh. 'He was kind of bizarre. You know? Talented – a good designer, a good businessman. Made a lot of money. He could have had a great life. But all he wanted was to find Müller and have him killed. End of story.'

'Can we borrow those files?' I said. 'I mean, there are bound to be duplicates somewhere in Mr Kaplan's office but, as we said, there's a certain amount of chaos there at the moment.'

He hesitated a second, then shrugged. 'Yeah, why not? I don't really know what's in them. I've only had a chance to look at the first couple of pages, see what they're about. But, sure, take them. It'll probably save you some time.'

I put the files in their big Manila envelopes under my arm. 'We'll get them back to you as soon as we can, Mr Lance. How long will you be in town?'

'Couple days, maybe longer. There's no big hurry.'

I thanked him prettily, said goodbye and made for the door but Linda hung back. She said, 'Mr Lance, about that bill. From Mr Kaplan?'

He frowned. 'Yes?' His tone was just a little less friendly than it had been.

Quickly I said, 'What Miss Kelly was about to say was that, of course, we're perfectly happy to wait for payment until you've got everything straightened out. Until then don't give it another thought.'

He smiled. 'You're good people. You know, I've always hated this town. The rip-off capital of the world. I've been screwed here more times than a ten-dollar whore. Figuratively speaking, you know what I mean? But you two guys are beginning to restore my faith.' He paused. 'Of course, you don't exactly come from around here, do you, Mr Lennox?'

'No, but Miss Kelly is a local resident and we have very much the same – how shall I put it? – principles in matters of business. Isn't that right, Linda?'

Linda smiled tightly and said yes, that was quite right and we said goodbye again and left and as soon as we got outside she kicked me savagely on the right calf.

'You dork! "Don't give it another thought." You . . . you . . . absolute asshole!' She aimed another kick at me but I got out of the way of this one; my footwork was still pretty good. 'I need that two grand.'

'Then I'll give you the two grand, but now is not the time to ask Lance for it. When he looks at us he sees two people dripping with scruples and integrity and I want to keep it that way.'

'He's crazy.'

'Well, of course he is.'

'And you're crazy, too.'

'Very probably. But we might need his help again

and if we do I want him to be willing – no, eager – to offer it. Hitting him for two thousand dollars right now would simply have got up his nose. And if you try to kick me again I'll kick you back.'

She was silent until we got into the car. Then she said, 'Actually, I think you ought to give me more than two grand. We could've gotten a retainer out of him as well if you hadn't gone swaggering around like Mr money's-no-object Rockefeller.' Her voice became a high, whining drawl. '"Oh no, Mr Lance, we don't want any money, Mr Lance, pay us only if you think we're worth it, Mr Lance."'

'Who's that supposed to be?'

'You, who else?'

'I don't speak in a falsetto.'

'Not yet,' she said darkly. 'But you turn down any more money on my behalf and you sure as hell will.'

We stopped at a traffic light and I looked across at her. 'I've noticed something about you when you're angry,' I said. 'The pupils of your eyes turn into bright, flashing dollar signs.'

'Huh.' She put her feet up on the dashboard and scowled at the road ahead. 'Are we going to stay here for ever? Are we going to live here? I mean, the goddamn light turned green an hour ago and we're not moving.'

'Sorry. I hadn't noticed.' I drove off into the intersection. 'And you only noticed because green is the colour of money.'

'How the hell would I know what colour money is?' she said. 'Thanks to you I never see any of it.'

I laughed.

'Why are you laughing?' she said. 'I don't want you to laugh. I'm mad at you.' But she grinned. All ight, so it was a reluctant grin but it was still a grin.

When we got to my hotel and parked she said, 'Come here,' and reached across and put her arms around my neck and kissed me. I made soft, appreciative sounds and was really enjoying myself until she pulled away slightly and murmured, 'You owe me two thousand dollars.' And that made us both laugh.

15

WE STARTED ON THE GERMAN FILES FIRST. There was
no doubt that Pascal had been very serious indeed
about finding Heinrich Müller. He had even
approached Simon Wiesenthal, though without
success. Sympathy, yes, Wiesenthal had offered
that but he was unable to offer help. No doubt he
had bigger and more spectacular game in his sights
and anyway Müller did not seem to be registered
officially as a war criminal. Wiesenthal had no
record of him.

So then Pascal turned to a detective agency in
West Berlin, sometime in the late 1950s, and at first
he had no better luck there. The devastation
wrought on Germany during the last year of the
war had played havoc with individual records. The
paperwork on hundreds of thousands, if not millions, of people had simply been wiped out by the
bombing and the task of tracing one obscure SS
captain was akin to turning up in Africa and asking
passers-by if they happened to have come across a
black man, early twenties, about this high. In the
intermittent correspondence that went on over a

long period of years, the German agency claimed to have uncovered a number of trails but all of them led down cul-de-sacs. There were reports that Müller had fled to Argentina, to Spain, to Portugal, to Peru and to Brazil and the agency dutifully followed the leads. And in each case it either turned up an entirely different Heinrich Müller or nobody at all.

All trace of the real Müller, Pascal's Müller, ended during the heavy fighting around Rouen as the Allies thrust forward towards Germany and Müller's unit was fairly comprehensively slaughtered. Of the five survivors whom the agency was able to find, four said they had no idea what had happened to him and the fifth was pretty sure he had seen Müller's body lying in a ditch. But two of the interviewees opened up a fresh trail, though a pretty impassable one. They knew where Müller's home was, they said. Dresden.

'Dresden!' I said, when we got to this bit. 'Jesus. Even the rubble was reduced to rubble at Dresden.'

'Yeah, well,' Linda said, 'nobody ever promised it was going to be easy.'

Assiduously, the German detectives went to Dresden. It took a lot more time to discover that, as far as anyone could tell, Müller had not been seen there since a brief spell of home leave late in 1944, which information came from a woman who had once lived a few houses down the street from him. The woman, who had lost her husband on the Russian front and her three children in the bombing, said that Müller had been married and had a baby son. It was her belief that the boy had been born either just before or during the period of home leave. Either way, she said, Müller never saw his son again because his house suffered a direct hit during the night of the infamous Dresden raid on 13–14 February 1945, when around 135,000 people were killed and one of the most beautiful cities in Europe was bombed to dust for no better reason, really, than to prove that the Allies could do it.

And that, more or less, was where it ended. Or where it should have ended if Pascal had not been so obsessive. For the most part the evidence indicated that Müller had almost certainly died at Rouen and his family in the bombing. It had taken years – and a great deal of money – to discover that much, but Pascal was still not satisfied. He wanted death certificates, he wanted proof. Before he settled for being deprived of his revenge, he wanted to be absolutely sure that there was nobody left to take revenge on. So the investigation continued and in the end all that persistence was rewarded.

The last report from the German agency, dated a few months ago, confirmed that Müller's wife, Frieda, had indeed been killed the night Dresden was destroyed but his son had survived. There had been no other family to look after the boy and until the war was over he had been moved from one institution to another. And then late in 1945, under the aegis of a German-American adoption agency, he had been taken to New York. The boy's name was Friedrich.

I looked across at Linda. 'Friedrich, Freddie,' I said. 'Bingo!'

She nodded thoughtfully. 'Hell of a leap, though,' she said. 'A German kid called Friedrich Müller comes to New York to be adopted; Tommy Bergdorf has an adopted son called Freddie. How many adopted kids called Freddie do you suppose there are in this country?'

'Thousands, probably. But there's got to be a connection. In his own way Pascal was certainly crazy but he wasn't crazy enough to put out a contract on every adopted child called Freddie. Ergo, he must have had reason to believe that Freddie Bergdorf was also Friedrich Müller.'

'Ergo,' she said admiringly. 'Gee, I haven't met ergo since I was in college.'

'I'm not surprised,' I said. 'Ergo has his standards, you know. He doesn't mix with everybody.'

She reached for the Kaplan file. 'You want to continue with the Latin lesson or shall we see if my late partner can throw a little light on what the hell this is all about?'

'Let's give Kaplan the old college try,' I said.

And indeed Kaplan's reports cast quite a lot of light, although initially he, too, had had his problems. Pascal had obviously asked him to chart the progress of the toddler Friedrich from his arrival in New York onwards and this had not been easy. The adoption agency which had brought the boy to America had started in business in 1935, had done a brisk trade before and for a few years after the war and had then gone into decline. In 1955 it had closed down. Kaplan's chief difficulty had been to find anybody who had ever been closely connected with it and then to persuade him/her/them to talk to him. From his reports it seemed that he had approached three or four people who had refused even to see him before he struck lucky with an elderly woman whom the agency had employed as a nurse. The others he had contacted had been pretty well-to-do but the nurse was living in ill health and poverty in the Bronx and the gift of a certain amount of money had jogged her memory to a remarkable extent.

Oh yes, she remembered Friedrich Müller, a lovely little boy with dark hair and brown eyes. But it wasn't just his cuteness that made him stick in her mind; it was the way the agency had acquired him. Most of the babies, she said, simply arrived, sent over because the agency, funded as far as she was aware by philanthropic German-Jewish immigrants, wanted to make a spectacular act of forgiveness by adopting the Christian ethic of turning the other cheek and finding American homes for German orphans, whether their parents had been Jews or Nazis or neither. But young Müller, she remembered, was different. For him there had been a specific request. The agency had been provided with the name and address of the orphanage where he was being cared for in Berlin and had been asked, as a matter of urgency, to bring him to America. The request, she said, had been made by a man named Strauss. She couldn't remember his first name but she was pretty sure it began with a K. Kurt, perhaps. Or Klaus. Or . . .

'Karl?' I said.

Linda nodded. 'Let's go with Karl.'

Kaplan's report offered no confirmation of the first name. It merely quoted the nurse as saying that this K. Strauss was a young, unmarried man in no position to adopt a child himself. But, for reasons of which she was unaware, he was very anxious that this particular child, this Friedrich Müller, should find a good home. And he did. Or at least she supposed he did. In any event, the adoption agency only took care of him for a few weeks and after that . . . well, after that she had no idea what happened to him.

But Kaplan knew. The boy, he discovered – and this must have been the easiest part of the entire investigation – had been adopted by a Mr and Mrs Thomas Bergdorf of New Jersey. Mr Bergdorf was at that time a recent immigrant from Switzerland; Mrs Bergdorf, née Schmidt, was American-born of German parents. There were copious biographical notes by Kaplan on Tommy Bergdorf: details of his business interests in New Jersey and later Las Vegas, of his recent retirement to the Los Angeles area, of his wife's death from cancer some twenty years earlier, of his involvement and influence in high-level Republican politics. The file on Karl Strauss (because Kaplan had made the same connection that Linda and I had) was also fairly comprehensive, charting his arrival in America in late 1945, his brief but in the end fairly lucrative interest in the real estate business, his American citizenship, his move to California, his subsequent career as a movie producer and his various marriages. There was a lot about Freddie, too: his education at high school and college, his entry into the film industry, his first marriage and eventual divorce, his second marriage to Bev and his partnership with Karl Strauss.

And, too, there was a file on Bev, a thin file that dated only from her arrival in America but gave pretty good coverage of her career in Las Vegas, glossing over the dancing and concentrating heavily on the hooking, and her marriage to Freddie. And that was all. Kaplan's last report was dated two weeks before I met Pascal in London.

'What does Strauss look like?' Linda said.

'What? Oh, I see what you mean.' I thought about it. 'He's about the same height as Freddie, brown eyes like Freddie. His hair's white now but it could once have been dark. He's put on a little weight but he has the same kind of build as Freddie. Yes, I suppose there is quite a resemblance.'

'Yeah,' she said. 'Interesting, isn't it? Anyway, let's see what we've got: Freddie Bergdorf is Heinrich Müller's son and that was enough for sweet little old Philippe Pascal to want him dead. And not only him but his wife as well. But . . . I don't know. After all these years? I don't believe it.'

'Revenge is a dish best eaten cold,' I said. 'You know what puzzles me? That Pascal never even mentioned Karl Strauss or, come to that, Tommy Bergdorf. Those two knew each other in Switzerland, right? They come to America – Bergdorf a month after the war ended, Strauss some time later. Strauss has this one particular kid brought over from Berlin but can't adopt him because he's not married, he's got no money and he's not even a citizen. So his mate Bergdorf, who is married to an American, takes the kid instead. If you were Pascal wouldn't that make you think a bit? Wouldn't it make you wonder why a Swiss immigrant called Karl Strauss should be so interested in the infant son of a Nazi?'

'Yep,' she said. 'I know what conclusions I might draw.'

'Then why didn't Pascal draw them? Why didn't he put out a contract on Strauss as well as Freddie and Bev?'

'How do we know he didn't? Or how do we know he wasn't just waiting awhile? Remember, he told

234

you there was somebody else he might want hit, but perhaps not yet, because this was somebody he really wanted to suffer. Kill the son first, and the son's wife, let Strauss really feel the grief and then kill him.' We both thought about it. Then she sighed and said, 'Maybe it's not as simple as we think. We're assuming that Strauss started life as Heinrich Müller but what if he didn't? What if he really is and always was Karl Strauss? I mean, maybe he and Müller knew each other before the war when they were kids. Well, it's possible. Germans can go to Switzerland on vacation, the Swiss can go to Germany. Maybe that's how they met. Maybe they even went to school together, became best friends. And maybe good old Karl, who'd spent the war yodelling on top of a Swiss Alp, heard his old buddy had been killed and decided to do something for his kid.'

I thought about that, too. 'The only thing wrong with that story,' I said, 'is that it needs a violin accompaniment. Actually, there's another thing wrong. How come Strauss found out so quickly what had happened to Müller and his kid when it took a German detective agency decades? Doesn't that indicate that Strauss and Müller were the same person?'

'It does look like it,' Linda said, 'and if so I seem to have guessed right – Pascal wanted the kids dead first so that Strauss could suffer a lot before he finally got his.'

I flicked irritably through the Kaplan file. 'Or perhaps he was still having Strauss checked out.'

Linda sighed. 'And that we'll never know because Kaplan got himself wasted by the serial killer.'

'Or by Strauss,' I said. 'Don't forget that possibility.'

As Linda reminded me, there was still the question of the tape and whether Tommy Bergdorf wanted to buy it. I told her sternly that she really should try to concentrate her mind on higher things than money but she said there were no higher things than money, especially for someone as poor as she was.

'All you rich guys are the same,' she complained. 'You keep telling poor people that money doesn't buy happiness but have you ever tried to check it out? Have you ever spread any of that money around, see if you could buy a little happiness for somebody else? Okay, maybe you're right, maybe money doesn't buy happiness but I'll tell you something – happiness sure as hell doesn't buy money.'

So I gave in. I talked nicely to Bev's butler, got Tommy's phone number and made an appointment for us to see him at his house that evening. I didn't tell him what it was about; I merely said I wanted to see him, alone if he didn't mind, about something important and he asked no questions. He even said, with what sounded like sincerity, that it didn't matter whether it was important or not; he'd be delighted to see me anyway.

Then I called Pascal's German detective agency, broke the sad news that their regular meal ticket was dead, said I was helping to clear up his estate and asked if they were currently investigating anyone or anything on his behalf. They said they weren't; they had had no instructions from him for some time. I threw in the names of Karl Strauss,

Freddie and Tommy Bergdorf and Beverley Timkins-Bergdorf but they didn't mean anything to any of the assorted Teutonic Spades and Marlowes.

'So that's it then,' Linda said. 'Pascal had obviously dropped the German end of the investigation and just had Kaplan working on it.'

'And now they're both dead,' I said. 'Convenient, isn't it?'

'Yeah, very. But at least the danger's over so far as Freddie and your old girlfriend are concerned.' An acquisitive gleam came into her eye. 'So let's go see Tommy. I have this lovely dream of him handing me a big fat cheque and I want to find out if it can ever come true.'

'Why do you dream about money? Why can't you have erotic dreams like other people?'

'Money is erotic,' she said.

Tommy Bergdorf's house in Bel Air was a few hilltops away from Don Carlo's estate and roughly the same size. I liked it better, though. For a start there wasn't a guardhouse at the gate and the walls didn't look as if they had been transported, brick by brick, from Stalag 17. Besides, Tommy's Spanish hacienda-type house looked more natural among all the tropical plants than Don Carlo's mock Tudor. It was furnished Spanish style, too, but genuine Spanish, not Mexican. I'm not particularly keen on that kind of old world Castillian décor but what he had was obviously good stuff, genuine, no reproductions.

The den he took us into was less formal, more modern, than the other rooms we saw on our way to it, the sofas and chairs in lighter, friendlier colours and the pictures on the wall, six of them, all Hockneys, had the bright and cheerful look of the artist's Californian swimming pool period. The view from the huge French windows was almost pure Hockney, too – a gleaming blue, Olympic-size pool with a wide, colourful patio all around. The only thing it lacked was a couple of beautiful young men posing in and around the water but I didn't imagine Tommy went in for that sort of thing.

I made the introductions and we all chatted about this and that while a Mexican butler poured champagne, French naturally. If you're very rich in California, French, rather than domestic, champagne is what you offer your guests to prove you're very rich. Either that or, if you're both very rich and in the entertainment industry, cocaine. Tommy didn't seem to be into cocaine, which was just as well because neither were Linda nor I. We could both think of better ways of passing an evening than sitting around burning holes in the sides of our nostrils.

Tommy said, 'I hear you had a little trouble with Freddie.'

'Ah, yes. I'm sorry about that. I hope I didn't hurt him.'

He shrugged. 'A swollen nose and injured pride. Nothing broken. In any case, from what I hear it's he who should apologise. He's very jealous, I'm afraid, particularly of you. He thinks you have come to take Beverley away from him.' The intent way he was looking at me almost turned that last sentence into a question.

'The thought had occurred,' I said. 'But that was before I met her again. I don't mean that as any reflection on Beverley. It's just that I carried the memory of somebody else, the girl she was when I knew her in London. But she's changed and so have I. I don't think we have too much in common any more.'

'That's what she told Freddie.'

I wasn't altogether surprised to hear it but it still gave me a nasty little pang. All very well for me to have got over Bev but she might at least have had the decency to feel some regret that all we had once been to each other was now history. There is no romance in women any more; or perhaps there never has been; perhaps they have always been the brisk and businesslike sex, philosophically prepared to make the best of what comes along; perhaps men are the true romantics.

Unseen by Tommy Bergdorf, Linda caught my eye and, scowling, mouthed, 'Get on with it.'

I said, 'We've got some good news for you. We've found the tape.'

'Really?' He looked pleased and excited. 'Where? How?'

'Ah, well, that's something I'd rather not go into, if you don't mind. And I don't want to tell you who had it in the first place, though I can assure you there's no danger from that source any longer. What I will say is that Linda was helping me look for the tape and it, ah, came into her possession a couple of days ago. Apart from that, what you should know is that until I approached her she had no knowledge even of its existence, let alone what was on it. Oh, and I'm just about one hundred per cent sure that there are no copies.'

'I see.' He glanced across at Linda. 'I assume that what Mr Lennox is trying to tell me is that there is now no question of blackmail?'

She nodded.

'May I have it?'

239

'Of course.' She took the tape from her bag and handed it to him.

He said, 'There should naturally be a finder's fee for this. Would you like to suggest a sum?'

Linda hesitated, a little glint of pure greed in her eyes, while she tried to reach a compromise between a comparatively modest finder's fee and a figure that would be tantamount to blackmail.

I said, 'I'd like you to watch it first.'

He tapped the videotape gently on his knee. 'I think that might be a little painful.'

'I know. But it's important that you should see it and not only because I'd like you to be satisfied that it's the genuine article.'

'Not only for that reason?' He thought for a moment. 'Very well. I wonder if you'd both mind waiting by the pool. I don't think I want to watch this in company.'

We refilled our glasses, grabbed a bowl of peanuts and went and sat outside in the late evening sunshine while Tommy Bergdorf crouched alone in front of his television set, watching his daughter-in-law turning tricks in a Las Vegas hotel room. Well over an hour had passed before he called us back in and by then the sun had gone and it was growing cool.

'Thank you,' he said and he looked like a man who had just been through a bad time. 'That was not at all a pleasant experience but . . . I suppose it was necessary. I'm grateful to you both for bringing this to me and not to Freddie or Beverley.'

'It did seem the more tactful thing to do,' I said. 'But as I said there was another reason why I thought you would be particularly interested in it.

You watched the tape carefully, all the way through?'

He nodded, unhappily. 'Yes. But what specifically should I have been looking for?'

'One of the men involved, youngish, rather fit-looking, had a Z-shaped scar on his back. You spotted him?'

Another nod, more alert this time, less unhappy. 'Yes?'

I took a deep breath. 'Well, unless there are lots of people around with identical scars, which I doubt, the man on the tape is Peter Vincent. Does that mean anything to you?'

'The politican? That Peter Vincent? It can't be.'

'Ah, but it is. I saw him stripped to the waist standing beside a swimming pool a couple of hill-tops away at Carlo Minelli's place. I don't think there's any doubt that he's the man on the tape.'

He was silent for quite a long time. Then: 'You know about this man?'

'Only that Minelli reckons he's going to be the next Governor of California and then President of the USA.'

Tommy leaned forward urgently in his chair. 'Then you know that Minelli is Mafia, important Mafia, and that Vincent belongs to him.'

I nodded. 'That's why I wanted you to see this tape. I thought you might be able to use it.'

'Yes,' he said slowly. 'Yes. But why . . . ?'

I said, 'If Minelli has the political muscle he thinks he has, it's not a question of *whether* Vincent becomes President but *when* he becomes President. And it seems to me that there are enough crooks and spivs running the world already. At least with this tape you could stop Vincent adding to their number. It wouldn't be easy because, after all, the girl in the action is rather close to home. But we're the only ones who know that. To everyone else this is just an anonymous hooker and you have moving pictures of Peter Vincent going down on her before and after snorting coke.' I stopped. 'Sorry. That was rather tactless. What I'm trying to say is that there must be some way you can use all that to destroy him without destroying your own family as well.'

'Yes,' he said, nodding again. 'Yes, I think so. I'm sure the tape could be edited to make Beverley quite unidentifiable.' A pause, then: 'Tell me, Mr Lennox, are you a Republican? No, of course not. You're not even an American citizen. Perhaps I should ask: are your sympathies with the Republican Party?'

I laughed. 'No. If I'm anything at all I'm a democrat with a small d.'

'I see. So your attitude to this Peter Vincent business is not exactly political.'

'No, I just don't like crooks much. Actually, I don't like politicians much either. I believe that, with very few exceptions, they're venal, greedy, arrogant, power-hungry and generally self-seeking. And those are just their good points. But they're not necessarily crooked. Vincent, though, is crooked and it would be nice to see him stopped.'

Tommy considered that for quite a little while. 'I imagine you know', he said, 'that I have a certain amount of influence within the Republican Party. And what with that and this,' he tapped a finger on the videotape, 'I think I can promise that Mr Vincent's political career will come to a sudden end. America will have reason to be grateful to you, Mr

Lennox. Not that it will ever know, of course. Sad, isn't it?'

'Heartbreaking,' I said. 'Now what about Miss Kelly's finder's fee?'

'Ah, yes.' He turned his attention to Linda, who sat up eagerly, smiling and batting her eyelashes, like a little girl expecting a very nice prize from teacher. 'Until I actually saw the tape and realised its significance I was going to offer, perhaps, ten thousand dollars. But now . . . Well, now I wonder whether twenty-five thousand might be acceptable.'

'Twe . . .' Linda said and her eyes were huge, gleaming with dollar signs. 'Twe . . .'

'I think she's saying yes,' I said.

He chuckled and turned away to his desk to scribble out a cheque and when he'd handed it to Linda I said, 'Do you know of a man named Heinrich Müller? A German. Used to be a captain in the SS back in the glorious days of the Third Reich.'

He became suddenly very still. He had his back towards me and he half-turned, looking at me over his shoulder, his eyes wary behind the aviator glasses. 'Why do you ask me this?'

'Just curious.'

He smiled, finished what was left of his champagne. 'I . . . ah, no I don't think I know anybody of that name. Is he a friend of yours?'

I shook my head. 'But I think he's a friend of yours.'

'Why do you say that? Tell me, what do you know of this, ah, Müller?'

'Not a great deal. I know he had a son called Friedrich who was brought from Berlin to New York by Karl Strauss and then adopted by you. But as for Heinrich, all I know is that he apparently died in the fighting in France, towards the end of the war.'

'You say apparently. What does that mean?'

'Simply that I don't think he died at all. I think he waved a magic wand and turned himself into Karl Strauss.'

Bergdorf sat down quickly in one of his nice, softly cushioned armchairs. 'Oh dear,' he said. 'Oh dear.' Linda went across to him and emptied the remains of the champagne into his glass. He drank it down fast.

She said, 'Do you feel like telling us about it?'

He made an odd little sound in his throat, a grunting, anguished sound. 'I didn't know about the SS. I mean, I'm a Jew. If I'd known . . . I thought he was simply *Wehrmacht*, a Panzer regiment . . .' His face was very drawn and the polite smile he directed towards Linda was obviously achieved only with an effort. 'In that little refrigerator in the corner,' he said, 'there is some more champagne. Would you mind? I think I need . . .' She found the bottle, opened it, poured some into his glass, hesitated and then with a shrug poured some for me and for herself as well. Linda was not a girl to pass up good champagne.

Bergdorf said, 'I met Karl in Zurich in 1945. February, March, I can't exactly remember. He came for a job at my father's bank. Well, it was not my father's bank; he was simply a director. But, anyway, I was working there, too, and we became friends. We were of an age, young men with similar interests – music, tennis, girls, that sort of thing. And we were both eager to go to America when the war was over. We thought Europe was finished and the future lay here.' He grinned ruefully. 'With hindsight I'm not so sure we were right. After all, look at Germany today. Well, anyway, I liked him immediately. He was *gemütlich*. Charming. You know? Very personable, very amusing. The only thing was he, he said he was born and raised in Berne but I knew he was lying. I knew Berne very well and he quite obviously didn't.'

'And it didn't occur to you to challenge him about that?'

'Oh, it occurred to me but . . .' He shrugged. 'It's difficult, you know, to turn to a friend and call him a liar. Besides, he was honest enough in every other way and, well, it was his business, not mine. But one night we picked up a couple of girls at a party and one of them came from Berne and when we started talking about the place Karl was so plainly out of his depth . . .' Linda went to refill his glass but he shook his head and so she refilled her own instead. 'That was the night he told me who he really was. But he didn't tell me about the SS. He said he was a deserter from the army. He said he had always hated Hitler, the Nazis and one day he decided he wasn't going to die for them. I forget now how he said he made his way to Switzerland or how he got new identity papers. I don't think it was hard in those days. It was expensive – I remember he said it cost him all he had – but it wasn't hard. That was the night, too, when he told me about Friedrich, Freddie. Karl's wife had been killed in an air raid and the boy was in Berlin, in some kind of orphanage. Karl wanted him back but there was very little chance of it then. The Germans weren't about to hand the baby over to a deserter who'd run away to Switzerland.' He got up from his chair. 'Do you mind if we go outside? It's a little warm in here.'

We went out to the poolside, Linda bringing the bottle, and there he told us the rest of it: how they had come, separately, to America at the end of the war; how he, Tommy, had met and very quickly married a girl called Beate Schmidt, the daughter of old family friends; how, with the help of those old family friends, his career had swiftly flourished.

'America, the new Promised Land,' he said. 'Well, it certainly lived up to its promise. All of a sudden I was a married man with a good business and I only seemed to have been in the country five minutes. Everything was perfect except . . . well, except that Beate couldn't have children and we both wanted them.'

Which was where Karl came in. At that time Karl was not doing as well as Tommy, not having the same kind of well-connected American friends or an American girl to marry and give him respectability. Tommy did what he could to help, but even so Karl was struggling – and worrying about his son.

Tommy said, 'He was obsessed by the boy and by the fear that he'd simply be swallowed up in the mess of post-war Germany. What scared him most was the thought that he would never see the child again. He knew where Freddie was but there was no possibility, in the position he was in then, that he could bring him to America. So Beate suggested that we should adopt him.'

'And Strauss didn't mind?' I said.

'He was overjoyed. We could offer the boy safety, a home, a decent life. And love. We wanted a child very badly.'

So it was arranged. Strauss contacted the New York adoption agency, Tommy and Beate paid the costs and Friedrich Müller, Aryan son of an SS captain, became Freddie Bergdorf, adopted son of an enterprising Jewish businessman.

'Does Freddie know about this?' I asked.

'No. He knows he was adopted, of course, but we decided right at the start that all he should be told was that he was born in Germany and his parents were killed in the war. So far as he's concerned Karl is just a kind of honorary uncle, somebody he's known all his life. They have a fine, fond relationship. You can imagine how proud Karl was when they went into partnership.'

'Turned out nicely for both of them,' I said. 'Pity about the movie, though.'

He gave a wry little grin. 'Yes. Tell me, how did you find out about all this?'

So now it was my turn, and Linda's, to take up the narrative.

When we'd finished he said, 'You mean Karl murdered these people? The Pascal family? My God. He killed them?'

'So it would seem,' Linda said.

'I had no idea. He never . . . Well, obviously, he . . . he wouldn't mention such a thing.' Tommy gazed out over his swimming pool, his lawns, but he didn't seem to be looking at anything there. Maybe he was staring at a new mental image of his old friend, at good old Karl who had just acquired the devil's horns. 'I had no idea. I simply had no idea.'

I said, 'I'd like to talk to him.'

'To Karl? What for?'

'To warn him. The last time I spoke to Pascal he

247

said there was someone else he wanted killed but not at the same time as Freddie and Bev. He wanted this man to suffer first. My assumption was that this was another contract he was going to put my way but I don't know that for sure. He could have made separate arrangements.'

'But why? Why wait?'

'Who knows? What we have to remember is that as well as his parents, Pascal's brother and sister were killed that night. Maybe in his mind Freddie stood in for the brother and Bev for the sister. And maybe he wanted them dead first so that Strauss could suffer a lot of grief before he was blown away, too. Look, Pascal was crazy – I don't mean crazy-crazy, gibbering and running up the wall – but he was as obsessed with Müller and revenge as Müller was with his son. It dominated his whole life.'

Tommy said, 'I could warn him.'

'No. I want to do it. To tell you the truth, I'm curious. I want to confront him with all this, see how he reacts. I imagine you don't like that idea but I intend to do it anyway. So if you'd just give me his home address and telephone number . . .'

'No,' Tommy shook his head firmly. 'If you must see him, very well. But I don't want you bothering him at home unless he wishes it. Whatever he has done he is still my friend. He has been my friend for a long time. And . . . and he gave me my son.' He hesitated, glanced at his watch. 'It's nearly seven o'clock. He won't be in his office now. What I will do for you, I will phone him at home, tell him you want to see him and why. Then he can decide where and when you should meet.'

I shrugged. 'Okay.'

We all trooped back indoors and Tommy made

the call. He kept his body between me and the phone so I couldn't see the number he was dialling. He said, 'Karl? Tommy. Yes, fine, thank you. Listen, Karl, I have some shocking news for you. Mr Lennox, you remember? Who came to see . . . Yes, that's right, the Englishman. Well, he's found out about . . .' He took a deep breath. 'He's found out about Heinrich Müller.'

I eased a little closer. From where I stood I could hear Strauss jabbering away at the other end of the line but I couldn't make out what he was saying.

Tommy said, 'Yes, he does. Everything. He knows about everything. He even knows things I didn't know.' He took a deep breath. 'He knows about the SS and . . . and what happened to the Pascal family.' More jabbering, then, 'Listen, Karl. He wants to see you. What? No, no, it'll be all right. I promise you. He . . . one moment.' He put his hand over the mouthpiece and turned to me. 'Do I have your word, Mr Lennox, that you won't do Karl any harm?'

I thought about it. All things considered I reckoned that *somebody* – preferably a War Crimes Tribunal – ought to do Karl a fair bit of harm but it was hardly my job.

I nodded. 'Yes. Right.'

He turned back to the phone. 'It'll be all right, Karl. I can guarantee it.' Now it was Karl's turn again, the jabbering urgent, anxious. Tommy did a lot of nodding and 'yes, yessing' and 'no, noing' and then he said, 'Very well, at your office tomorrow morning. Ten o'clock? Right, I'll tell him . . .'

'No, wait,' I said. 'Ask him if I can see him tonight, at home.' Tommy waved at me to be quiet and said, 'Yes, Karl, I can imagine how you feel. Believe me, it hasn't been pleasant for me either. I'll call you tomorrow, after you've seen Mr Lennox. I'm, I'm so sorry to be the bearer of such bad . . . Yes, of course. Goodbye, Karl.'

He put the phone down and sat silent for a moment. 'You hear that? He'll see you tomorrow in his office at ten. He can't meet you tonight because he's taking his wife to the airport and then he has a dinner appointment. Besides, he wants to keep this away from his home.' He smiled. 'It seems strange but I think I can understand. So, before you ask again, no I will not give you his address.'

I looked at Linda, said, 'I think it's time we went,' and got up. She squeezed the last drops of champagne into her mouth and I did likewise.

Tommy escorted us to the door. As we left he shook my hand and said, 'I don't quite know what to say to you, Mr Lennox, whether to thank you or . . . Well, no, of course I must thank you. For the videotape and for – for behaving so . . . so honourably in this other business.' He paused. 'Don't be too hard on Karl. Remember it was all a long time ago and he was very young and it was wartime.'

I nodded. 'And the people he killed were two unarmed civilians and a couple of children. Goodnight, Mr Bergdorf.'

16

THE WAITER BROUGHT THE PASTA and poured the
wine. Linda was still on champagne but I'd
switched to Valpolicella; I like champagne on its
own, not as an accompaniment to food, especially
Italian food, which demands something more
robust, more macho. Linda had complained at first
that ordering two bottles of wine was extravagant,
especially as she was paying. She was a frugal
soul.

'You can afford it,' I said. 'You're a lady of
substance now.'

'Yeah.' Her eyes gleamed as she thought of her
25,000-dollar cheque, which was the reason we
were celebrating. We'd had a couple of problems
with that cheque, the first being that her initial jubil-
ation at the size of it had been quickly tempered by
doubt.

'Do you think I could have gotten more from
him?' she asked.

'Probably.'

She thumped me on the arm, a fairly dangerous

thing to do since I was driving through heavy traffic on Sunset Boulevard at the time. 'Then why didn't you say something?'

'Because twenty-five grand is quite enough.'

'For saving my country from falling into the hands of the Mafia? I think we sold to the wrong guy. We could have got millions.' She took the cheque out of her purse and kissed it. 'Oh, what the heck. The country's probably been in the hands of the Mafia before.'

The next problem was what to do with the cheque. She didn't want to carry it with her in case she got mugged and robbed and she didn't want to leave it in the safe in my hotel room in case I (a) got mugged and, in her scenario, killed, which she felt would make it difficult for her to get her property back, or (b) absconded with it. In the end we compromised: we persuaded the hotel reception to give us a safety deposit box in her name and she left it in there. Then we went to dinner in an Italian restaurant on Melrose Avenue.

'You realise you'll have to stay with me tonight, don't you?' I said.

She looked at me suspiciously. 'Why?' She was wearing her normal uniform of pale and faded designer jeans, a blue shirt and trainers and she looked marvellous. There was a sparkle in the astonishing blue eyes, a general vivacity about her which, I hoped, owed more to me than to the champagne she had been drinking. On the other hand it could well have been down to the sudden acquisition of 25,000 dollars.

'Why? Because then you'll be able to sleep close to your money,' I said.

She leaned across the table and kissed me on the

mouth. 'True, but I was going to stay with you anyway.'

'Forward hussy. I hadn't even asked you.'

'Yeah, but I knew you'd get around to it. You're crazy about me.' She stuffed fettucine Alfredo into her mouth, leaving a string of pasta hanging from her lower lip. Even then she looked terrific. Well, she did to me.

'Am I indeed?'

'Of course you are. I knew that from day one, when you came to the office and asked me to lunch. That's why you're not interested in Mrs Beverley Birddog any more.' She washed the fettucine down with champagne. 'I have supplanted her in your affections.' She said this in a low but sonorous tone, as if it were a line in some Victorian melodrama. It made me laugh.

'How do women know these things?' I asked, because what she had said was true. Bev Timkins had vanished; Mrs Beverley Bergdorf was an entirely different person. I knew now that I could never be in love with Mrs Beverley Bergdorf.

Linda shrugged. 'We just do. We know the signs. A guy doesn't have to say anything, do anything. We just know.' She wolfed another huge forkful of fettucine. Like so many slim women she had a most remarkable appetite. 'You, for example, were playing the little boy lost. "Come to lunch so I won't have to eat another meal alone."' She said this in the curious falsetto she had used before when imitating me.

I said, 'I don't know how good an actress you are but you're a lousy mimic.'

She grinned. 'Gets to you, doesn't it?' She leaned across and kissed me again, leaving on my lips the taste of champagne and cream and pasta and something else, something much sweeter, much more exciting, something that was exclusively her.

'Shall we go?' I said.

'Are you crazy? I'm starving. I have this great veal dish with home fries and zucchini coming my way. We can't go now.' Another example of masculine romance and female practicality. She looked at me gravely and said, 'It's nice to have that effect, though.'

We ate the rest of the meal more or less decorously, give or take a little hand holding and cheek stroking. Just before the coffee was served I said, 'The last time I saw a couple behaving like this in a restaurant the man's wife came in and stuck a spinach soufflé on his girlfriend's head.'

'What colour was the girl's hair?'

'Red.'

She nodded, thoughtfully. 'Probably didn't look too bad then. Green wouldn't go so well with black, though. I hope you haven't got a wife who's going to come in here and try the same trick. Are you going to drink some more of that wine?'

'No, I've had enough.'

'Me, too. God, what a waste. I can't believe I'm going to walk out of here leaving two bottles half drunk. Is that what it means to be rich – you can afford to leave stuff?'

'Yes, but you don't stay rich very long if you do it too often.'

In the car and at odd moments during the meal we had talked about Tommy Bergdorf, Pascal and Strauss and at one point we had even toasted them all, linking their names with Linda's 25,000-dollar cheque. Now she said, 'Can I come with you when you go to see Karl Strauss? I'd like to see what kind of man he is. I've never met a real Nazi up close.'

'Yes, you can but I think you'll be disappointed. He looks much like any other multimillionaire.'

She ran her hand through her glossy black hair. Her fingers were long and slender. 'Before he went in for garbage he made some great movies, the movies I grew up on and made me want to be an actress. I didn't care who was in those pictures or who directed them. His name on the credits, Karl Strauss, meant quality. Now I find out he kills children and unarmed people and I want to meet him, to look at him. To see if . . . if any of it shows. Why don't we go see him now?'

'Because,' I said, patiently, 'we don't know where he lives.'

'Is that all that's bothering you? You should have said. I still have my contacts in the business. One phone call, maybe two and I'll have his address for you. Let's go see him.'

I hesitated. 'Well, yes but . . . What about you sleeping near your money?'

She gave me a slow, lascivious wink and pouted like Kim Basinger on heat. 'Time for that later. The night is young.' Then she shook her head briskly. 'Anyway, we have to warn him that he could be in danger, right? Tommy didn't get around to it.'

'Are you surprised? Tommy had too much other bad news to give him.'

She got up. 'Wait there. Two phone calls. Maybe three.' I watched her walk across the room towards the pay phone. Most of the other men in the place watched her, too, so because they were looking at my woman I looked at theirs. On the whole an attractive bunch but . . . too Hollywood, I decided;

too carefully dressed, too carefully groomed. Linda looked real; they didn't.

'You look real,' I said when she came back.

'This is a compliment?' she said, astonished. 'I look real? You can't say I look beautiful or sexy or adorable? All you can say is I look real?'

'It is a compliment. Believe me, it's a compliment.'

'Not good enough. Tell me I'm beautiful, sexy and adorable or I won't give you Karl Strauss's address.'

I gripped both her hands in mine and stared passionately into her eyes. 'You're beautiful, sexy and adorable and where does he live?'

The house was in a quiet street on the north side of Sunset Boulevard, just behind the Beverly Hills Hotel, and set back from the road with an expanse of lawn, a tarmac drive and flower beds full of hibiscus and roses stretching out in front. It was a nice enough place, two-storey, Spanish-style, maybe five beds and five baths. It was a fair bet that more lawn and a swimming pool lay beyond it and there was certainly a private cinema somewhere around. Given all those wife years the man was paying for it was a decidedly lavish pad. The road itself was quiet, dimly lit, deserted except for a black Ford sedan parked about fifty yards beyond the Strauss home. I stopped at the kerbside and switched off the engine.

'Aren't we going in?' Linda said.

'I don't know.' A light above the porch illuminated a large stretch of the lawn and the drive but otherwise the house was dark. 'Maybe he's still out. Or maybe he's gone to bed.' It was only eleven o'clock but contrary to popular belief Hollywood is not a town of late nights and wild revelry. It's an early-to-bed, early-to-rise town whose inhabitants need a good night's sleep before rising with the lark refreshed and bright-eyed and eager to screw each other rigid in yet another business deal.

'Let's go find out.' She got out of the car and began to walk up the drive. After a moment I followed her, reluctantly. An impulsive visit like this no longer seemed such a good idea. I reckoned Strauss would have every right to tell us to get the hell out of there.

Linda waited for me, frowning, on the porch. 'Well, ring the bloody bell then,' I said.

'I'm not sure that's wise,' she said. 'Look.' The front door was pulled to but not closed; a gentle push swung it open. Inside, the large, square hall was dark and no light came from any of the rooms that opened off it. 'Do you suppose he's all right?' I said.

'What am I – a clairvoyant? How do I know if he's all right?' She took another step into the hall, cleared her throat and said: 'Mr Strauss? Are you okay?' No reply. No sound at all. We tiptoed across to the foot of the stairs and gazed up into total darkness, except . . .

'Jesus!' I said, or rather whispered, 'there's somebody up there with a torch.' Just for a moment a thin beam of light had shown from one of the upstairs rooms and then vanished.

'What –'

'Shhh. Listen.' For a few seconds the silence continued and then, faintly, came the sound of a window being eased open. I ran out onto the porch with Linda close behind me. 'Get into the car,' I said, 'and stay there. Get down out of sight.' And then I ran on, round to the back of the house. A man was lowering himself by his fingertips from the window-sill of one of the upstairs back rooms. He was a very big man, not fat like Harve, the overstuffed minder of a couple of nights back, just big.

'Hey!' I yelled. He glanced towards me and let go of the windowsill, stumbling as he landed. His right hand was reaching for something inside his coat.

Before he could recover his balance I brought him down with a rugby tackle, not a great rugby tackle – the purists might have thought it was a little high – but good enough. We both landed in a flowerbed and rolled away from each other. Because I was the one who had been expecting the impact I recovered first. He was still on his knees when I caught him on the cheekbone with a left hook, not a great left hook – the purists might have thought that was a little high, too – but enough to rock him backwards. He was fit, though, as well as big and his reactions were sharp. He swayed out of the way of my follow-ing right and launched himself at me, still from a kneeling position. I brought my knee up into his face but his impetus knocked me over nevertheless. Again I was the first up but this time he was close behind me, still reaching for whatever it was he had in his coat. I moved in and caught him with three solid left jabs, splitting his right eyebrow and increasing the flow of blood that was already coming from his nose and lips. These were good punches but he just shook his head and came at me with both hands, making low grunting sounds in the back of his throat. I got him with another jab and a glancing right hook that jerked his head back but otherwise had no discernible effect because he still came towards me and now I was the one on the defensive. He was no boxer, that was clear, but he was hard and muscular and remarkably strong, and he must have outweighed me by at least thirty pounds.

I backed away across the lawn, still trying to keep him off by jabbing him with both hands. Quite a few of the punches landed on target and in the ring they would have put me way ahead on points but here there were no judges and no referee and besides the big fellow wasn't looking to win by a decision. His tactics were crude but forceful: if he couldn't grab me in a bear hug, which seemed to be his basic ambition, he kept me away from him with great, roundhouse swings calculated to knock my head into the next-door garden. I was fighting now purely for survival, though I did manage to shake him up with a jolting left hook when, once again, his right hand disappeared into his coat.

Somehow we had made our way, the big fellow going forwards, me going backwards, around the side of the house again. We were running out of lawn and coming to the area where the tarmac began and that was where he caught me. As I stepped back off the grass, my ankle turned and I lost balance – and a wild, swinging right hand landed on the side of my head. I went down hard and half-stunned on the driveway. I think I would probably have beaten the count if anybody had been around to bother about such technicalities; my opponent certainly had no interest in them because he had thoughtfully brought his own referee with him – a snub-nosed, short-barrelled revolver which, at last, he had managed to extricate from the recesses of his jacket.

I lay there, brains lightly scrambled, vision blurred, ears buzzing and blinked up at him as he moved towards me. He was still a few paces away, bringing the gun carefully into firing position, when suddenly a car jumped up the drive at about sixty miles an hour, headlights blazing, horn blaring and Linda leaning out of the driver's window and yelling at the top of her voice just in case nothing else had caught our attention. The big man and I went our separate ways. I rolled off the tarmac into a flowerbed and he leapt backwards onto the lawn. He fired once, too high, at the car and then ran back down the lawn towards the road as Linda spun the wheel and drove straight at him, missed, cursed, reversed, uprooted a couple of rose bushes and swung back after him.

He was running down the middle of the street towards the parked sedan when Linda crunched through Strauss's little wicket fence and bumped off the kerb and into the road. Her lights picked him out and he turned and fired another wild shot. By then I was up and running and lights were coming on in houses on both sides of the street. The big man stopped now, aimed, fired again. The bullet shattered the windscreen of Linda's car and the car stopped.

And then a voice from across the street said, 'Drop the gun, mister.' It seemed to be coming from behind a tree. And from another tree a few yards down another voice said, 'Yeah, drop it – NOW.'

The big man turned, startled, peering into the darkness across the road, then moved to his car and started to open the driver's door, and a two-voice chorus yelled, 'I said drop the gun!'

He pulled the door open and twisted round to

fire twice towards the trees and a fusillade of shots from two directions just about cut him in half.

I started running now towards Linda's car but the voice of one of the unseen gunmen said, 'Hey, you, hold it right there. Hands above your head where I can see 'em.' I did all of those things. I held it right there and put my hands up. There was a moment of calm and silence and then two old men with shotguns came out from behind the trees across the street and shuffled towards the still, blood-soaked body lying in the road beside the dark sedan.

'I got him,' one of the old men said. 'I got the bastard.'

'Did you fuck. *I* got him,' the other one said. 'That was my shot blew him away.'

'It was not!'

'It was so! You never could shoot worth a damn. I've seen you miss a whole goddamn elk at thirty paces . . .'

To my relief, Linda got out of the car and walked shakily towards me. She was pale and trembling and she was bleeding from a cut on her forehead where glass from the shattered windscreen had caught her. I took hold of her and held her and felt her blood running down my cheek.

One of the old men said, 'Hey, I told you to stay put.'

The other one said, 'What the fuck is going on here?'

Their eyes behind their gun barrels glared at me through designer bifocals.

'Call the police,' I said.

17

THEY FOUND KARL STRAUSS'S BODY on the floor in his living-room. A cushion had been placed over his face and he had been shot twice through that. Upstairs, the wall safe in his bedroom had been opened and papers were strewn over the floor.

The cops kept us there for an hour or more and would have detained us longer if I hadn't suggested that they ask Harry Brown to come over. He talked to the policemen who had caught the call, talked to us and then took us back to my hotel. A doctor came in, grumbling, to dress Linda's wound, stopped grumbling when he saw Harry Brown's shield, said the cut would need a few stitches and took her away to the hospital after I had stuffed quite a lot of money in his pocket.

Then room service brought us a bottle of Chivas Regal and some ice and Brown fixed himself a drink, sprawled out on my bed and said, 'Okay, you want to tell me what that was all about?'

I told him, looking him in the eye and lying, that Linda and I had arranged to go and see Strauss after dinner to find out if he had any idea why Pascal should have put out a contract on Freddie and Bev; that we had interrupted the big man as he was about to leave the house and that, one way or another, from Linda and me and the two old gunmen and the cops on the scene, he pretty well knew the rest. He listened in silence, sipping his drink and smiling sceptically, until I had finished.

'Why do you suppose it is that I don't altogether believe you?' he said.

I didn't answer that one. Instead I said, 'Who on earth were those two old men? Christ, it was like the Gunfight at the OK Corral out there.'

'Just a couple of concerned local residents.' He shrugged. 'Like we were saying, ever since the old fart shot the serial killer every senior citizen in California is going around heeled. These two heard the commotion, came out and figured they'd get themselves another serial killer. Saved your ass anyway. And your girlfriend's.'

'What about the other fellow, the one they shot?'

Another shrug. 'Not too much ID on him but it looks as if his name was Willie Viertel and he was out of New York. That's about all we know right now. We'll get more in the morning.'

'He was no burglar,' I said.

Brown considered the point. 'No, I don't think so either. It was a professional hit but I think he was after something else, too. We found 5,000 dollars in new bills, still in the wrapping from a Beverly Hills bank, in his pocket. I figure he took those from the safe but burglary wasn't what he had in mind. There was a lot of jewellery in that safe, too, and he didn't take any of it. I think he grabbed the money because it was there and it seemed a shame to just leave it lying around.'

'There were a lot of papers on the floor,' I said. 'Did he take any of those?'

'No. Nothing in his pockets but my guess is that that's what he was looking for – some kind of document. Maybe it wasn't there or maybe you interrupted him before he could find it. So tell me – who put out the hit on Strauss?'

This time I did the shrugging. 'Pascal?'

'What, from beyond the grave?'

I shook my head. 'The last time I talked to Pascal he said there could be somebody else he wanted killed. Well, you know that. It was all rather vague but he sounded quite excited.'

'Vague, how? Vague about whether there really was somebody else he wanted hit or vague about whether or not he wanted you to do it?'

'I don't know. Either. But if there was to be another hit Strauss could have been the victim and Pascal could have hired this guy Viertel to do the job after he last spoke to me.'

Brown mulled over that, too. 'Yeah, but why? We don't know why he wanted Freddie and Beverley killed and we sure as shit don't know why he might have wanted Strauss killed. At least, I don't but I'm not so sure about you.'

I gave him a look of innocent, lying candour. 'I'm as much in the dark as you are,' I said.

He got off the bed, finished his drink, put the glass on the table and went to the door. 'I know you're holding out on me,' he said, 'but I can't figure out what it is you're not telling me. Never mind. I'll get there and when I do and if it's serious, no more Mr Nice Guy. You understand me?'

I nodded.

'I'll be in touch,' he said and went away. I locked

the door after him and went into the bathroom to plunge my sore, scraped hands in cold water, while I waited for Linda to come back.

The night's drama had happened too late to make the morning papers but the local TV news was full of it or, specifically, full of the aged gunmen. One was a minor real estate tycoon, the other a music publisher and they were both in their late sixties, small bald men with soft tummies which they tried to disguise from the cameras in macho-looking track suits. They were interviewed by the usual Californian blonde, a long-haired, long-legged professional gusher, fairly fresh from whatever factory it is that turns out American TV interviewers by the gross. They stood side by side at the scene of the killing, cradling their shotguns and trying to look like hard men. At this stage it was too early to tell which of them had fired the fatal shot so they both claimed the credit. A man from the DA's office said the death would, of course, be investigated and quite possibly charges would be laid but without actually saying so he made it pretty clear that the two old boys would be released with the grateful thanks of the court ringing in their ears. After all, a DA seeking re-election was not about to jeopardise the senior citizen vote by coming down hard on a couple of the old folks' heroes.

In all this Linda and I received only a passing mention. Harry Brown had promised to keep our names out of it and he did, though only I think because he thought Tommy Bergdorf would like that. We appeared peripherally in the story as a young couple who just happened to be around when the burglar/gunman went berserk. I liked the young but wasn't altogether pleased when one of the old men said he thought, from my accent, that I must be Australian.

'Australian?' I yelled at the TV screen. 'Bloody cheek!'

Linda, who was lying beside me in bed with a swathe of bandage on her cut head, chuckled happily. 'Californians think everybody with a funny accent comes from Australia.'

'I haven't got a funny accent,' I said. 'You're the ones with funny accents. I may tell you that there are those who think I sound just like Michael Caine.'

'No, you don't,' she said. 'You don't sound a bit like Michael Caine. And anyway, even if you did you'd still have a funny accent. Michael Caine has a funny accent.'

'Talking of Michael Caine –' I said but she told me to shut up and listen. One of the old men was describing her as tall, dark, American and very beautiful. 'You hear that?' she said. 'He said I was beautiful – not real-looking but beautiful. Kindly bear that in mind in future.'

Back in the studio the anchorman had picked up the Australian reference. 'Comes to something, huh, when a coupla senior citizens have to rescue Crocodile Dundee.' The junior anchor, who might have been the twin sister of the reporter, burst into carefully controlled uncontrollable laughter. She had to; she wanted to keep her job.

Tommy Bergdorf called me after breakfast, by which time Linda had gone to her office, protesting that she was perfectly all right; her head was a little sore, that was all. The only thing that worried her was whether she would be scarred, though the doctor had assured her she wouldn't.

'You've heard the dreadful news?' Tommy asked. I said I had.

'I simply cannot believe it,' he said and he sounded genuinely distressed. 'It was a burglar who did this?'

'Not a burglar, no. It was a professional hit.' I told him exactly what had happened last night, including the fact that I was the mysterious Australian on the scene.

'Can we find out more about this – this gunman?' he said.

'I hope to later today. I think you'd better keep out of it. The reporters and probably the police will be wanting to talk to you and Freddie and the less you know the better.'

'You mean we might be suspects?' Distress replaced by incredulity.

'Well, Freddie might – if the police don't buy the burglary story and decide it was a hit. Freddie and Strauss were partners, after all. Look, don't worry. If everybody keeps calm there'll be no problem. I'll find out what I can and come and see you this evening, okay?'

He said okay, thanked me and hung up.

I took Linda to lunch at the Hamburger Hamlet on Hollywood Boulevard. This time I paid; it was a lot cheaper than the previous night's meal, as she pointed out rather tartly. By her reckoning – and she reckoned it on a pocket calculator – I owed her at least four more lunches like this before we were quits, which meant I'd have to stay at least four more days.

'You weren't thinking of going back to England

before then, were you?' she asked, a hint of anxiety in her voice. Of course, the anxiety could have been due to the fact that if I left sooner she'd be out of pocket but it pleased me to think there was more to it than that. I ate my hamburger and thought of England and decided there was nothing going on there at the moment that a couple of phone calls wouldn't cope with.

'I thought I might hang around for a few days,' I said.

She leaned across and kissed me. 'Good,' she said and went back to giving her southern fried chicken a hammering. A little later she said, 'Hey, congratulate me. I got a new client today, guy wants me to find his wife. She ran away with the pool man.'

'With the what?'

'Guy who cleans the pool. Apparently he'd been humping her for months, mostly in the Jacuzzi. My man, the client, is really pissed. He says he'd been breaking his ass, working all hours, just to support the goddamn pool and now look how the bitch shows her gratitude.'

'Well, you have to feel a little sorry for him.'

'Oh, sure. He's really broken-hearted. He says he thinks they may have gone to Vegas and he wants me to go there with him to look for them. So I say, what if they haven't gone to Vegas? And he says, well, let's you and me go there anyway. I got this friend runs one of the hotels and he'll give us a really great suite, we'll have a ball.'

'What did you say?'

'I said, you wanna go to Vegas, go to Vegas. I'll stay here and look for your wife.'

'Way to win friends and influence people,' I said.

'The hell with him. You know what he said? He

said he wants her back by the weekend because he's entertaining his boss to dinner on Saturday and if she's not there he's got nobody to cook for him. Whatever happened to romance?'

'Romance', I said, 'died with the twentieth century and women's suffrage and women doing men's work while the men went to war. I'm not saying these are bad things; these are good things. But they kicked the shit out of romance. However, do not despair – there are still some of us who keep a shrine to romance in our hearts.'

She gazed at me incredulously, her chin resting on her hand. ' "Some of *us*?" You mean *you*?'

'Certainly me. And other men. Mostly men, as a matter of fact. Your client is the exception. I mean, take us two. You're the realist. You look upon me as a meal ticket and a handy body on which to slake your lust. But I . . . ah, I look at you and I see glossy black hair and deep blue eyes, legs to be measured in yards and a figure to die for, lean where it should be lean but well-provided with subcutaneous fat where a woman ought to have subcutaneous fat –'

'Subcutaneous fat, what are you talking about?'

'I'm talking about your hips and tits and bum,' I said with dignity.

She shook her head. 'And this is romance speaking? My, my. I thought I was talking to a male chauvinist pig.'

'Let me finish. What I was about to say was that I see all these desirable things on the surface but beauty is only skin deep . . .'

'. . . while ugliness goes all the way through?' she suggested, regarding me with amusement.

'Shut up. Beauty is only skin deep and I look beyond the skin, beyond the beauty, beyond the surface. And beneath these things, even beneath that highly dubious mercenary streak which, incidentally, you really must do something to control, I see fragility, vulnerability, a quintessential femininity. I see true romance, I see Guinevere, I see Héloïse –'

'And if Abelard talked as much crap as you do,' she said, 'no wonder somebody cut his balls off.' And soon afterwards she left me there and went back to work.

I spent the rest of the day keeping up with the latest developments in the Strauss killing. Tommy Bergdorf told me that he and Freddie and Bev had been interviewed by the police and the media but had been unable to say much except that they were distressed, stricken, saddened, appalled, horrified and outraged at what had happened. Such TV news as there was during the barren afternoon wasteland of soaps and game shows bore this out. Tommy and Freddie and Bev turned up on camera to say that they were distressed, stricken, saddened, appalled, horrified and outraged. Strauss's murder was, of course, a big story in California. Generally speaking, Hollywood movie producers expect to be assassinated only by the critics, so a real slaying with bullets and blood came as a very nasty shock to the film community. The perp, the late Willie Viertel, was swiftly identified as a professional hitman out of New York, but speculation as to who might have employed him was guarded. I ached to hear from one of the hyperactive TV clowns who purported to be film critics some kind of speculation that the contractor might have been a cinemagoer enraged to the point of madness by the crass stupidity of *Space Fiends* and its projected sequel but these

TV clowns no less than the movie makers were the creatures of Hollywood and knew to whom they owed their allegiance. So they spoke of the death of Strauss as solemnly as if they were discussing the recrucifixion of Christ.

Only Harry Brown introduced a note of irreverence. He turned up late in the day demanding, unusually for him, coffee. He was working, he said, like seriously working and he didn't drink anything stronger than coffee when he was seriously working. So I asked him what was going on and he said, 'Yeah, well, we found the widow Strauss in Manhattan. A duplex in the low 70s up on Madison. She was so distraught at the death of her husband that she'd taken to her bed. But luckily for her she had a really sympathetic lawyer who was just as distressed as she was and he'd taken to the same bed to offer his condolences.'

'Nice for her,' I said. 'Do you think she hired the hitter?'

'Nah. The New York cops think she was genuinely surprised at her old man's death. I'm not saying unhappy, I'm saying surprised.'

'What about Viertel?'

He shrugged. 'A freelance hitman, eight arrests on suspicion of murder, no convictions. Far as we can tell he worked for anybody who needed a mechanic but with no particular allegiance to any outfit. We checked the gun we found on him but apart from the Strauss killing it was clean. Doesn't mean a lot. What the hell, our late serial killer used at least three different guns. In this country you walk into a candy store you can buy a gun.'

'And Strauss,' I said, 'anything new on him?'

The waiter refilled Harry Brown's coffee cup. The

good news about American coffee shops is that you get as much coffee as you can drink; the bad news is that just as you've got the balance of coffee, milk and sugar exactly as you want it a waiter comes by and ruins everything by pouring more coffee in. Harry didn't seem to mind. 'Born in Switzerland,' he said. 'Zurich, I think. I got the details back in the office. Shee-it, you expect me to remember *all* this stuff? Anyway, he came to the States just after the war, far as we know never went back to Cuckoo Clock Land. Immediate family all dead. And, well, I guess you know about his career in this country.'

'And the Widow Strauss inherits all the loot?'

He shook his head. 'Not quite. We got a copy of the will from Strauss's own lawyer in Beverly Hills. The widow inherits a sizeable chunk but the bulk of the estate goes to a nephew in Geneva. Son of Strauss's older brother. Brother died during the war, fighting for the Nazis, would you believe?'

I started to say something, then stopped and thought and said, 'Under what name? I mean, what name did the brother use when he joined the German army or whatever?'

Harry Brown gave me a curious look. 'How the hell should I know? Adolf Hitler? Hermann Goering? Hans Strauss, Herbert Strauss, whatever his first name was, it began with an H that's all I can remember. Who the fuck cares?'

I said, 'Look, please, tell me what you know about this brother.'

Harry beckoned the waiter over, holding up his coffee cup. 'We don't know much. He married young, in the late 1930s, had a kid. Then the war broke out, he wanted to fight for Germany, his wife thought this was a lousy idea, they separated, he went off to do his bit for the Fatherland and they divorced. What more do you have to know?'

The answer was: quite a lot and yet at the same time perhaps not very much. Karl Strauss's big brother had gone to war, joined the SS perhaps, married – who knows? – some buxom, flaxen-haired Hitlermädchen, had another son and . . .

'You've contacted this nephew?' I asked. 'The Swiss one?'

'Sure. The gendarmerie in Geneva checked him out. He's kosher.' He finished his coffee, waved the waiter away and got up. 'You ready to talk to me yet?'

'Me? What would I have to tell you?'

'That, my friend, is the big question. And I'd like the answer real soon.' He squeezed my shoulder – not a very friendly squeeze; quite a hard one in fact.

As he turned away I said, 'I'd like to know about this brother. Any information you've got, I'd really like to have it.'

He gave me a long, hard look. 'And what do I get in exchange?'

I shrugged, helplessly. 'I honestly don't know. Maybe a lot, maybe nothing.'

'Some swell deal, huh?'

'I'm sorry, it's the best I can offer right now.'

He nodded, thoughtfully, still giving me the hard look. Then: 'Okay. I'll call you.'

An hour later he did. I took a lot of notes of what he said and spent a long time reading and re-reading them and then I went to see Tommy Bergdorf.

18

TOMMY WAS ALONE on his Bel Air estate, if you dis-
counted the two gardeners looking after the
grounds and the butler and two maids taking care
of the house. Tommy, being very rich, did discount
them. They were only servants, after all.

'I'm alone,' he said when the butler showed me
into the study. 'Freddie and Beverley are coming
over later but right now I'm by myself and I welcome the company.' He was dressed in designer
labels attached to a black polo shirt, white slacks
and white sneakers. 'The sun, as you English say,
is well over the yardarm. Can I offer you a drink?'

I accepted the usual champagne and we settled
down companionably in armchairs. 'So,' he said,
'what news?'

'Oh, just this and that,' I said and told him what
Harry Brown had told me about Viertel and the
highly consolable Widow Strauss and then I mentioned the nephew in Geneva.

He frowned, the blue eyes sharp behind the aviator glasses. 'A nephew? I didn't know Karl had a
nephew.'

I nodded. 'Oh, sure. Karl had a nephew all right. The only thing is, I don't think – and this is only a guess, mind you – I don't think Heinrich Müller did.'

He was very still. 'What do you mean, Mr Lennox?' I put my glass down on the occasional table beside me. He said, 'Would you mind using the coaster? That table is rather an expensive piece, an antique, of course. There are not many others like it.' I moved the glass onto the coaster and rubbed the droplets of moisture off the table top with my sleeve. I didn't care; there was no designer label in my jacket.

'What I mean, Mr Bergdorf, is that for a while I thought Karl Strauss was Heinrich Müller. Well, you know that. And, after all, it seemed so obvious. Well, to me anyway – and yet, curiously enough, apparently not to Philippe Pascal. I mean, if he'd come to the conclusion I came to, that Strauss and Müller were the same person, I'd have expected him to put out a hit on Strauss. Don't you agree?'

He gave the idea careful consideration and then nodded.

I sipped some more champagne and carried on. 'So I wondered why. I wondered why he hadn't actually got around to asking me to kill Strauss along with Freddie and Bev. And all this bothered me quite a lot until an hour or so ago when I found out a couple of interesting things.'

'Yes?' He leaned forward, listening eagerly. 'What things?'

'Well, thing one – Karl Strauss was indeed born in Switzerland, not in Germany, and never actually fought for the Nazis.'

'What?' His mouth was open, his hand and glass

paused halfway to it in total astonishment. 'But he told me . . .'

I held up my hand. 'Wait. Karl didn't join the German forces but – thing two – his elder brother, whose name, oddly enough, was Heinrich, did. And Heinrich died, fighting for the Fatherland, in Normandy.'

There was a reflective, frowning, sipping interval. Tommy said, 'So . . . let me work this out . . . the boy, Freddie, was not Karl's son but Heinrich's? Heinrich must have enlisted under an assumed name – Müller – and married a German girl?'

I nodded. 'Seems to fit, doesn't it?'

He chewed thoughtfully on his lower lip. 'And they had a son. Yes, yes, I can see that. Heinrich was killed in the fighting, his wife died in the bombing.' This time it was his turn to nod, vigorously. 'The boy – Freddie – survived and Karl wanted to get him, his nephew, out of Germany and into safety. But . . .' He paused. 'Why should Karl have told me that it was he, not his brother, who fought in the German army? Unless . . .' Another pause before he added on a note of incredulity, 'Unless he feared that I would not do as much for his nephew as I would do for his son? Oh, my God . . .' He shook his head and there was such a look on his face that he could have posed, as he sat there, for a portrait of grief. 'Karl, you were such a fool! You were my friend, Karl, you were my friend! I'd have done anything . . .'

I gave him a small, sympathetic smile. 'I know. Tragic, isn't it? Except that . . .' I took a great gulp of Krug and sighed. 'Except that the whole scenario is wrong. Karl Strauss, born in Zurich, not Berne, spent the entire war in Switzerland. Heinrich

Strauss, also born in Zurich, got married, had a son, joined the *Wehrmacht* as Heinrich Strauss, not Heinrich Müller, got divorced and died 6 June 1944 on Omaha Beach.'

'I beg your pardon?'

'As well you might,' I said, leaning across and tapping him on the knee in a friendly sort of way. 'How neat and convenient it would have been if Freddie had turned out to be the son of either of the Strauss brothers, doesn't matter which. But, alas, he isn't. No way. So that brings us back to the story you told me last night, which is probably quite true except that you switched the identities. It wasn't Karl Strauss who turned up one day in Zurich – it was you. Strauss was already there. He was born there, as we now know for sure. Therefore you were the one who arrived from Germany, not as a deserter from the nasty Nazi Party but on the run from the Allies. Which, naturally, makes you Heinrich Müller.'

He brushed my hand from his knee, rather disdainfully, and contemplated the Hockney on the wall behind my head for quite a long time. 'No doubt,' he said, eventually, 'you can prove all this?'

I shook my head. Of course I couldn't prove it and even if I could it wouldn't mean anything. If he were pushed far enough Bergdorf could even admit it all and it still wouldn't mean anything. Right, he could say, I *am* Heinrich Müller and I deserted from the German army because I couldn't tolerate the Nazis; I kept it dark till now because I was ashamed that, young as I was – a mere boy – I had once been taken in by them. All that would get him by way of punishment would be a round of applause as a man of sensitivity and conscience because there was nobody left to point to him and accuse him of slaughtering the Pascal family. 'No,' I said, 'I can't prove that. But I think it might be possible to prove that it was you who had Pascal and Kaplan and Strauss killed.'

He smiled a little, held up a hand, said, 'One moment, please,' and went to a drawer in his desk. When he turned round again there was a gun in his hand, a .38 as far as I recall, not that it matters much. He put a finger to his lips, walked over to me and, holding the gun against the side of my head, made me stand up the better to frisk me. Then he nodded, pushed me gently back into my chair, refilled my glass and put the gun in his pocket.

'What on earth were you doing?' I asked.

Another smile, a faintly apologetic one this time. 'I thought perhaps you might be wired, Mr Lennox; that some policemen might be sitting outside in a plain van, listening to our conversation. An exaggerated precaution on my part. Do forgive me.' He took a sip of his drink. 'You know, what puzzles me slightly is that it took you so long to associate me – a much more logical choice, you must agree, than poor Karl – with Heinrich Müller.'

I'd thought about that, too. 'I think it was because I didn't want to. I rather liked you. I didn't like Pascal and I didn't like Strauss either, so I suppose I let my emotions lead me. I mean, what the hell, I'm not a detective; I'm just a broken down old prizefighter.'

'You're too modest. You've done rather well as a detective – a lot better than the police, for instance.'

That, too, I had thought about on my way to the house and I knew that I had been a lot luckier than the police. I had found, or been found by, Perry Lance and the police had not. I had had Pascal's files, the reports from the various detective agencies, and the police had not. And perhaps even more to the point, the police, in the shape of Harry Brown, had had a vested interest in keeping Bergdorf out of anything that might have seemed remotely unsavoury. So I accepted the charge of modesty modestly and said, 'When did you suspect that Pascal might be on to you?'

He considered that for quite some time. 'You know, Mr Lennox, I'm not at all sure that he ever was on to me. I learned about his activities and what he was trying to discover only when the private detective, er, Kaplan, approached the adoption agency in New York. You see, that was originally set up as a Nazi front. Oh, certainly it brought innocent German babies to the USA before, during and after the war. But with them came aunts, parents, nannies, uncles – all of them dedicated Party members. And because they came with tiny refugees these people were pretty well above suspicion. So they were easily accepted and moved around and set up little Nazi cells all over the country. At the beginning the idea was to influence public opinion to keep America out of the war. But, alas, that didn't work and then, later, when it became obvious that Germany was going to lose, the objective changed. The plan then was to rescue people who might one day help to establish the Fourth Reich and carry on the work of our glorious Führer.' He said the last bit with such a cynical grin that I knew he didn't believe a word of it.

'You think that's bullshit, too, don't you?' I said.

He laughed. 'Of course it is. I simply used this

organisation just as it hoped to use me. They made me into Thomas Bergdorf, they got me into Switzerland and then they brought me here. I couldn't have done any of it without them. With Karl it was different. He was a Swiss; it was much easier for him to get to America after the war. The organisation and I, we gave him a little help but not much. He was a good Nazi, Karl, much better than I. That's why I was sent to him when I got to Zurich – because he and his family worshipped the Führer, though God knows why. Do you know something, Mr Lennox, to this day I cannot understand how Hitler exercised such power over the German people. Have you heard the story that he suffered from uncontrollable flatulence? I don't know whether it's true but I'm prepared to believe it. More than that – I *like* to believe it.'

'You're saying you weren't much of a Nazi then?'

He shook his head. 'No. What I'm saying is that I wasn't any kind of a Nazi. Oh, I'm not telling you this to impress you or gain your sympathy. I joined the party of my own volition because I was a survivor. In Germany the Nazis had a better time, a higher standard of living and I wanted those things.'

I said, 'So with all your high convictions and principles it didn't bother you to come here ostensibly as a Jew?'

He raised his hands, smiling. 'I welcomed it. I have no religion, Mr Lennox. If it had been easier to be accepted in America as a Buddhist or a Moslem, then I'd have become a Buddhist or a Moslem. But it wasn't, as a matter of fact, my idea to become a Jew. The organisation suggested it. They thought there was a nice irony to smuggling a fierce young

Nazi into the country in the guise of a Hebrew.' He was silent for a moment. 'Of course, it was all done with Teutonic thoroughness. I even had the operation and, for a grown man, that's rather painful. But think about it: which would you rather lose – your foreskin or your life? So I became a Jew, a non-practising Jew, an agnostic Jew. It's never bothered me. Indeed it's been a positive advantage. In America, as in other western countries, the Jews control much of the wealth and if you are wealthy, too, it's helpful to be regarded as one of them.'

I just sat there watching him, listening to him, wondering why I had ever thought I liked him. 'Then as a dutiful, though non-committed, Nazi, when you massacred the Pascal family you were simply obeying orders?'

He tutted at me, exasperated, like a teacher who had been wasting his wisdom on a fool. 'Mr Lennox, please. Of course I wasn't obeying orders. I was scared. Do you understand? I was a young man, not much more than twenty, in a house full of people who hated me and the men with me. When Pascal *père* reached towards that cupboard I thought he was reaching for a gun, so I shot him. And my men were as young as I was and as frightened as I was and so they started shooting as well. It was as simple as that. It wasn't Nazi zeal that made us wipe out that family – it was panic. Afterwards I was sorry about it; not remorseful – remorse is out of place in wartime – but sorry. However, there was nothing I could do to make amends, so I forgot about it until the organisation told me that Pascal was trying to find me, or at least Freddie. I'm still puzzled about that. What on earth had made him, suddenly, start looking for me?'

I told him everything that I knew about Pascal and his obsessive quest. Tommy listened attentively, almost sadly, as if he felt for Pascal, empathised with him. 'Strange, isn't it? There was a man of talent, a man who could have lived a full, interesting life and instead he wasted it on something as empty as vengeance. Of course, I didn't know too much about this. Kaplan turning up in New York, asking questions, came as a shock. You see, the organisation nurtures fond hopes that I shall become at least some kind of deputy Führer when the Fourth Reich takes over America. These people are quite mad, you understand. But they believe, and they have ample funds and powerful friends, and they were anxious to protect me. So they investigated Kaplan and that led them to Pascal and they asked me about him and I told them how, as a good Nazi, I had executed his family of Maquis sympathisers and terrorists. And that was when it was decided that Kaplan and Pascal should both be, well, terminated with extreme prejudice, as our noble CIA puts it. The organisation sent me Mr Viertel and, since the serial killer was then zealously going about his business, it was decided that he should be given the credit for disposing of Messrs Kaplan and Pascal. Mr Viertel did it rather clumsily, though I believe the police were taken in. You, however, were not.'

I shook my head. 'I couldn't stand the coincidence.'

'No, I can see that. At the time, of course, I didn't know about you.'

'I'm very relieved, otherwise I imagine Mr Viertel might have been asked to terminate me as well.'

He smiled. 'Perhaps. The question never really

arose because by the time I did find out about you, it was rather too late to do anything. A pity. A great, great pity. Because if I had asked Mr Viertel to turn his attentions to you, poor Karl would still be alive today. I liked Karl. Oh, he bored me rigid, of course, with his fervent Nazism. Do you know, right to the end he was still eagerly looking forward to *der Tag*.' He shook his head, smiling slightly; a man who believed in nothing but himself and his own survival; a man who had even used Hitler and the Nazis to his own ends and was now, no doubt, using the Republican Party in the same way; a man to whom any kind of conviction in others was a source of amusement and mild wonder. 'But unfortunately in the end poor, dear Karl had to go, too. I wasn't happy about it, believe me, but if you'd talked to him and started knocking him about the way you knocked my son about I'm quite sure he'd have told you everything and that would decidedly not have been in my interests.' He smiled sadly and heaved a little, regretful sigh. 'What I'm curious about now is what you're going to do. Nothing violent, I'm sure. I don't think you'd kill me as some sort of romantic act of retribution. You're not the kind of person who could coolly plan to murder someone.'

'Oddly enough,' I said, 'I did once.' He gave me a look of surprise and, for the first time, respect. 'But you're right in a way. I wouldn't do it again. Not unless you did something that really upset me. No, what I thought was I might have a little chat with Freddie, tell him all about his dear old dad. He still thinks you adopted him, doesn't he? I imagine he'd be quite interested to learn about his real background.'

He sat very still for a moment, then: 'If you say one word about me to Freddie or Beverley, I will certainly have you killed and I will also have your pretty girlfriend killed.' That made me sit still, too, because I knew he meant it. We stared gravely at each other for a bit until he said, 'I think it's what is known as a standoff, Mr Lennox.'

And then, suddenly, Freddie and Bev were in the room. Neither of us, I think, had heard their car pull up or heard them come into the house. They just appeared and stopped, Bev looking surprised to see me there, Freddie scowling, asking, 'What the hell are you doing here?'

'Mr Lennox is just leaving,' said Tommy. He got up and I got up, too. 'We've been having a nice little talk. Mr Lennox, or rather his clever little partner, managed to locate that tape and they very kindly destroyed it, didn't you, Mr Lennox?'

'Yeah?' Freddie said. 'You got evidence of this? You see him destroy it? Jesus, I wouldn't take his word for it.'

'Oh, I believe him,' Tommy said. 'I have the utmost confidence in Mr Lennox and his discretion.'

Bev said, 'What partner?' She was looking at me, frowning.

'Did you not meet her?' Tommy said. 'An extremely pretty young woman, a private detective here in Los Angeles. But, alas, I believe her health is apt to be a little frail. Isn't that so, Mr Lennox?'

I ignored him. Bev said, 'Where did you meet somebody like that? What's her name?' Was there just a hint of jealousy in her voice, her look? No, I don't think so. There was only curiosity. 'It's a long story,' I said.

'And unfortunately there's not enough time to tell it now,' Tommy, smiling, put his hand genially on my shoulder. 'We really can't keep Mr Lennox any longer.' He stopped, laughed and said, 'Oh, but dear me, I'd almost forgotten what Mr Lennox came for – his fee.'

Freddie said, 'His what? His fee? You mean Beverley's good old buddy from way back then is hustling you for money? Dad, don't give him a single lousy penny. It's a con, don't you see that? There probably never was a tape. He's just been setting us up.'

I watched them all, watched Bev's reactions. 'Bobby? Is this true? You're asking for money?' She looked embarrassed, ashamed for me and no doubt that's what Tommy had intended.

He said, 'Well, naturally he's asking for money. The labourer is worthy of his hire. And, Freddie, your suspicions don't do you credit. I believe Mr Lennox has worked hard on our behalf.' He had an open cheque book on the little table and was bending over it with a pen in his hand. 'I think the sum we agreed upon was 10,000 dollars, was it not?'

'Ten thou!' Freddie said. 'Dad, for Chrissake . . .'

Tommy finished writing the cheque and handed it to me. 'There. Your services have been much appreciated, Mr Lennox. And now, if there's nothing else, the butler will see you out.'

I glanced from him to Freddie to Bev. Tommy was smiling, Freddie was sneering and Bev looked as if the last illusion she had ever held had just received a vicious kick in the balls. I took the cheque, glanced at it, nodded and then tore it up into a dozen little pieces and put them in the ashtray.

'Fuck you, Müller,' I said.

Tommy just froze. 'I warn you –'

But anything else he planned to say was cut short by Freddie yelling at me. I don't think he'd heard me say 'Müller' but he'd certainly heard the 'Fuck you' and he'd seen me insult his old man by tearing up the cheque.

'I'm going to kill you, Lennox,' he said and came at me, swinging. I had to admit he had guts – not much sense, but a lot of guts.

'Leave it out, Freddie,' I said wearily, and popped him on the nose again with a fast left jab. It was getting to be a habit. He yelped and sat down suddenly on the sofa that, conveniently, was just behind him. Blood was trickling from his nostrils into his mouth.

Bev said, 'Bobby! How could you . . .' and then she was on her knees beside him, cleaning up his face with the silk Hermès scarf that she'd been wearing round her neck and spilling words of consolation in his ear. 'It's okay, darling, it's okay. Poor baby . . .' And then she turned to me and said, 'Get out of here, Bobby. Just get the fuck out.'

So I did, without even waiting for the butler to show me where the door was. I didn't say goodbye either; I didn't think it was necessary. 'Get the fuck out,' seemed to say it all.

Linda joined me for dinner at the hotel, still complaining about her new client, the one whose wife had run out on him.

'He keeps on about Vegas,' she said. 'There's no evidence she's ever even thought about going to Vegas but that's where he says we got to go, him and me. Shack up there and look for her.'

'Get rid of him,' I said. 'How could you possibly have any faith in someone who wants to go to Vegas? Vegas is the anteroom to hell. When you die they send you to Vegas while they work out which particularly nasty level of purgatory you're going to occupy for the rest of eternity.'

'You can't have any rest of eternity,' she said, shovelling pot roast into her mouth. 'Eternity has no limits, ergo –'

'Ergo!' I said and leaned across to shake her hand. 'You don't know how happy I am that you and ergo have finally made up.' And at this point Harry Brown came and joined us. We didn't invite him; he just came into the restaurant and joined us, beckoning to the waiter to bring him a glass so he could help us drink our wine.

'British Airways flight tomorrow,' he said. 'Leaves LAX at six.'

'What about it?' I said.

'That's the one you're on.'

'Pardon?'

He let a sip of wine roll around his mouth, nodded appreciatively and said, 'Tommy didn't tell you? You're going back to London.'

I thought about it. 'Hold on. What are you saying here – that Tommy is giving me twenty-four hours to get out of town? Who does he think he is – John Wayne?'

'Might as well be. Got even more power than ever the Duke had. He just says you and he don't get along and he'd appreciate it if you went back where you came from like as soon as possible.'

'And you're the boy to see it happens?'

He nodded. 'Except that "boy" is not a word I like too much. Very few gentlemen of colour do.'

'What did he say about Linda?'

Harry looked puzzled. 'He didn't say nothing about Linda. Why should he? He can't run her out of town even if he wanted to. She was born in this country, which is more than he can claim.' He finished his wine in one long swallow. 'Tell you what I'll do, don't want you to think we're inhospitable over here, I'll come by about four, four-thirty, give you a ride to the airport. Save you a few dollars.' He got up to leave. 'Till tomorrow then.'

I reached up, put my hand on his arm. 'Sit down, Harry, pour yourself another glass of wine. There are one or two things I have to tell you about Tommy Bergdorf.'

Quite a long while, at least another bottle, later Harry said, 'Well, well, so that's what you've not been telling me all this time.'

'What was there to tell? Oh, all right, most of it was to tell and I should have told you, I admit that. But the important stuff, like who Bergdorf really is, I didn't know myself until today. And I still can't prove any of it.'

'But he admitted it all to you?'

'Yes, of course, he did. You think I'm lying?'

He shook his head. 'No. In a bizarre kind of way it makes sense. Thing that bothered me about the serial killer, in his apartment we found stuff tying him in with all the victims except Pascal and Kaplan. Now I understand why. Well, well.'

'So what are you going to do?' I said.

'Do? What can I do? You got evidence? No. Nobody's got evidence. Whatever he did, Tommy's home and dry here. I'm not saying I like it. I got no more time for the Nazis than you do. As I recall they were none too kind to the brothers. But look at it logically. Unless Tommy has a brainstorm and confesses, there ain't a damn thing to be done. No way we could ever tie him in with Willie Viertel.' He thought about it, nodding and sighing and sucking his teeth. 'Well, I'm glad you told me at last but . . .' Another sigh as once again he finished his wine.

I said, 'So what now? You just carry on taking your retainer from Tommy as if nothing had ever happened, right?'

He looked at me with that cold, hard cop's stare. No matter how often you've seen it it always has the same chilling effect: it makes your kidneys flinch in anticipation of the rubber truncheon or the well-directed boot.

'You know something, Bobby?' he said. 'I was just starting to like you. It wasn't easy but I was working at it. Don't make me stop now. Have a good night, get your packing done, I'll see you about four . . .'

And Linda, who had been busily eating and drinking and listening and saying nothing, said, 'Jesus, you know what makes me really mad? We let the motherfucker have that tape. If I'd known then what I know now I'd never have sold it to him. Never. Well, not for that price anyway . . .'

'Tape? What tape?'

And I sighed and said, 'Yes, well, I didn't mention the tape, did I?'

We had got through a third bottle and Linda had had the pecan pie and we were all on the coffee when Harry said, 'Well, kids, it's late and this is your last night together in LA so I won't keep you away from your bed any longer.'

I said, 'Hey, hang on, what are you going to do now?'

'Me? Well . . . it's not *that* late. I thought I might drift up to Bel Air, have a word with Tommy.'

Linda said, 'You bastard. You crooked bastard.'

And Harry grinned and said, 'Yeah, life's a crock, isn't it? You just can't trust anybody.' And then he left.

'Our last night, huh?' Linda was wearing a bath towel at the time, the skin above and beneath it all pink and glistening.

From the bed I said, 'Looks like it.'

She dropped the towel and got in beside me. 'Will I be safe when you've gone?'

'I think so, so long as you don't say anything to anyone. Tommy's not a fool. He knows that if anything sudden happened to you I'd kill him.'

'Yes, but what if something sudden happened to you first?'

'I'll leave word in London that people should let you know right away and then you're on your own.'

'Oh, thanks,' she said bitterly.

'It'll be okay. Tomorrow I'll write to Tommy, tell him I'm going to leave copies of a letter addressed to Freddie and Bev with at least half a dozen different lawyers and they'll all be given instructions that if either you or I should die unexpectedly the letters will be in the mail immediately. He won't like that. He really doesn't want Freddie to know anything about the good old days in the Third Reich. Or about what happened to Pascal and the others. It'll work – trust me.'

She snuggled up against me. 'You wouldn't really kill him. You couldn't, could you? It's just talk.'

'If anything happened to you,' I said, 'I'd kill him all right and I think he knows it. I've killed somebody before and for the right reason I could do it again.'

She propped herself up on one elbow. 'You – *what*?'

I said, 'Shut up and switch off the light. We haven't got all night here.' Which was stupid, really, because all night was exactly what we had.

19

AT BREAKFAST SHE SAID, 'Are you really going back to London tonight?'

'I think it's best. It'll be good for Tommy to think he's frightened me away, stop him getting nervous and doing something silly.'

'And has he? Frightened you away, I mean.'

'No. I'll be back. As soon as things have settled and everyone's calmed down.'

'You like it here, huh?'

'No, not much. I know better places than Hollywood and LA. But I like some of the people.'

She leaned across the table towards me, holding her coffee cup in both hands close to her mouth. 'Oh, yeah? Which people?'

'Well, you can't expect me to be specific. Right now I can't think of which people. I just know there've got to be some people around here that I like.'

'Okay.' She put the cup down, patted her lips with the napkin. 'Then I might as well go to Vegas.'

'Go to Vegas,' I said. 'But you'll be sorry.' I walked her out to her car and she kissed me and clung on to me for a long while and said, 'When will I see you again?'

'Lunchtime. Butterfields. I'll book.'

'Idiot. I mean after today.'

I eased away from her, the better to look at her. 'You really want to see me again?'

'Of course I do. You still owe me two thousand dollars.'

'Ah. Yes, well, it's actually because of that that I'm getting out of town.'

'I knew it. So I'll tell you something, friend – you're not back here within a month with my two grand *I'll* send a hitman after you and you better believe it.'

'I believe it,' I said and we kissed again. I was still standing there, grinning, and watching her car disappear along Sunset when Harry Brown said, 'You got lipstick on your nose.'

I wiped it off with my handkerchief. 'Isn't there anywhere a man can get away from you? Christ, you'd think you'd be safe enough standing all by yourself in a bloody car park. Anyway, it's not nearly four o'clock yet, it's not much more than nine and I haven't even started on my packing.'

'Relax. I just want to take you for a little drive, show you some sights.'

'You what?'

'Shut up and get in the car.' So I did and in his unmarked police car he drove west along Sunset and through the big gates into East Bel Air, telling me who lived in which house and what their criminal records were, if any, and ignoring me when I asked where we were going. For a while I thought he was taking me to Tommy Bergdorf's place but he drove past it without a glance and we went on

293

up higher into the hills and turned into the drive of a pink and white bungalow sitting on about a quarter of an acre of land.

'Who lives here?' I asked.

'Some movie director. Makes horror flicks. He's in Spain making one now. There's nobody home. Come on.' He got out of the car and I followed him round to the back and across the lawn to the fence and found myself looking down at the Bergdorf house.

I said: 'What . . . ?'

'Don't ask so many goddamn questions. There's something I want you to see.' He glanced at his watch. 'Any time now.'

We stood in silence for a few minutes, admiring Tommy's sweeping, lovingly tended grounds. Way over in the distance a gardener was pruning something but otherwise there was no sign of life. Then a plain white van came up the drive, went around the house and stopped at the side door. Two men got out carrying what looked like a large picture covered with a cloth. One of the men I had never seen before but I knew the other one. Even at that distance I could recognise his build, his walk and his dark curly hair. It was the man who had brought me the invitation from Carlo Minelli, who had met me at the door, taken me through the house and then shown me out when I left.

'What the . . . ?'

'Don't talk. Just watch.'

A Mexican maid came to the door. The dark man, the one I knew, spoke to her and she nodded and let them in. The door closed again and for a few minutes nothing else happened. Then the two men came out again and the dark one went round to the passenger side of the van, paused, looked straight in our direction and held up a small rectangular package in a brown envelope. He waved it once in the air, just above head height, gave the thumbs up with his other hand, then he got into the van and it moved away.

Harry said, 'Goodbye, Tommy, it was nice knowing you,' and walked swiftly back towards his car.

I trotted after him, saying, 'What on earth was that about?'

'Let's just get out of here, okay? In a little while this is not going to be a good place to be. There are going to be cops swarming around here like flies on a dead dog.'

He drove down the hill in the opposite direction to the Bergdorf place, taking a twisting, winding route that finally brought us back to Sunset through the west gate of Bel Air.

I said, 'I know that man, the one who waved the package at us. I met him at Carlo Minelli's.'

Harry nodded. 'Yeah. Paulie. Good kid. Just forget you ever saw him.' He didn't seem at all surprised that I even knew Minelli, though I had never told him. We drove on west along Sunset and after a while I could hear, faintly, the sound of police sirens behind us. When we reached the Pacific Coast Highway we drove into a restaurant parking lot and Harry turned off the engine. 'Let's go walk on the beach a little,' he said, 'nice day like this.'

We walked about a hundred yards until there was nobody remotely within earshot and then we stopped and stood looking at the Pacific. 'I love the ocean,' he said. 'Always have.'

I said, 'Screw the ocean, what happened back there?'

He loosened his tie and turned his face up towards the sun, eyes closed. 'What happened back there was that Tommy Bergdorf suddenly became the late Tommy Bergdorf.'

I let that sink in for a moment, fishing around inside myself to see if I could detect any sense of shock, or horror, or grief but none of those seemed to be on duty. I wasn't glad Tommy was dead but I wasn't sorry either. I just accepted it. 'Why?' I said.

'Because of the tape. The tape in the brown envelope Paulie was waving at us? The tape you told me Bergdorf put in the safe in his den?'

I shook my head. 'I don't understand. Or, at least I think I understand but I'm not sure. Paulie went in there, killed Tommy and took the tape, right? But if he did that Minelli must have told him to. How did Minelli even know there was a tape?'

'Because I told him.'

'You told him? Right. Which means you're on Minelli's payroll as well as Tommy Bergdorf's – pardon me, the *late* Tommy Bergdorf's. Tell me, is there any part of you that isn't sold to somebody?'

He turned and looked at me. 'Why, you want to buy a piece?'

'Just tell me what's going on, will you? After all, in a way I already appear to be an accessory to a murder. Knowing some more isn't going to hurt.'

He nodded. 'You're right. Anyway, you're not going to tell anybody and if you did who'd believe you? Not the cops, that's for sure. So, okay, here's what it's all about: after I left you last night I went to see Carlo, told him about the tape, what was on it and how Bergdorf was planning to use part of it to hurt Peter Vincent. He asked me how and when he could get hold of the tape and I told him. I told him this morning was good because this morning was when the butler and one of the maids went to market and there'd be just one maid left in the house didn't speak English too well. Carlo was very grateful.'

I skimmed a stone out over the ocean. It bounced once and then sank without trace. 'And no doubt he showed his gratitude in the time-honoured fashion.'

Harry Brown sneered at the pathetic effort of my pebble and skimmed one of his own. It bounced at least four times before vanishing into the heat haze that hung over the gentle waves. 'How did you guess? Well, anyway, I put all his gratitude in my pocket, had a drink with him and then I went to see Tommy.'

'After all that you went to see Tommy?' I said. 'To tell him what?'

He seemed surprised. 'To tell him nothing. What should I tell him? Goodbye? No, it was pay day and I figured if Tommy wasn't going to be around much longer it made sense to collect what was owing to me.'

I chewed this over for a bit. Then: 'Why?' I said. 'Minelli told me Peter Vincent is going to be the next Governor of California.'

'You can bet on it.'

'And the next but one President of the United States.'

'Very likely.'

'But Vincent's a crook. Bergdorf was going to use the tape to expose him, destroy him politically. Now Minelli's got the tape and he'll use it to get an even stronger hold on Vincent.'

'I imagine,' Harry said.

'And it's okay with you if a Mafia-controlled crook becomes President of the United States?'

He sighed. 'Ever since I can remember all our

presidents, with one or two exceptions, have either been crooks or assholes. And between a crook and an asshole, I'll take the crook. At least with a crook there's a chance you can figure what he's going to do next but with an asshole, who knows? Even the asshole doesn't know. Look at Reagan. When did he ever know what he was going to do next?'

We were both quiet for a while, watching the ocean rolling in, sparkling and blue and peaceful as it ever gets. 'There is just one more thing,' I said. 'Why did you tell Minelli? You didn't have to. You could have gone on as before, putting Minelli's money in one pocket and Tommy's in the other. Now you've lost one of your pay-masters.'

He'd obviously considered that already. 'Well, yes and no,' he said. 'Tommy's gone, sure, but there's still Freddie and Freddie can use a friend even more than his father could. Besides . . .' He reached up and stretched in the sunshine. 'I'm still a cop. Well, part of me anyway, the part that's not sold. And I don't like people hiring murders done in my town. Tommy overstepped the line and I couldn't let him get away with it.'

I couldn't believe it. He was sincere; he meant what he said; that's what I couldn't believe. I said, 'Boy, do you have double standards. You disapprove of Tommy hiring a hitman but you can still stand by and watch while Carlo Minelli has him blown away?'

He said coldly, 'That was different. That was business. Besides, one killer wastes another killer, so what? Who's to care? There's just one less killer in the world, is all. But Tommy . . . Tommy was wasting citizens, taxpayers, civilians if you like. That's what makes it different.'

I didn't point out that he had no proof of Tommy's activities except what I had told him. I didn't think such niceties would bother him. He obviously had his own code and though it was one that baffled me it seemed to satisfy him. He said, 'Let's get back to Hollywood.'

We drove in silence until we got to the Strip when he said, 'Anywhere special you want to go?'

I looked at my watch. 'Butterfields. I'm meeting Linda for lunch.'

'You really hit it off, you two, huh? Lucky man. That is one very pretty lady.' A couple of minutes later he pulled up outside the restaurant and stopped the engine. 'I'm sorry,' he said.

I shrugged. 'That's all right,' taking it as a kind of blanket apology for all the dreadful things he had done or connived at in the last twelve hours or so. 'Sorry' wasn't much but then there wasn't really a lot he could say.

'What I mean, I'm sorry for telling you Willie Slate carried you that night. It was the truth but . . . I shouldn't have told you. You have the right to your own illusions.'

'Oh well,' I said, 'makes no difference now. Like the man said, we've all passed a lot of water since then. And besides I knew about it a long time ago. A friend of mine, a bookie, told me.'

'Yeah? Well, anyway . . . you had heart. Willie said you had heart and he's a man who knows.'

'Sure does.' I saw Linda come out of the hotel across the road where she had parked her car and walk down to the pedestrian crossing and wait for the light to change.

Harry saw her, too. 'There's your lady,' he said. The light turned green and Linda started across the road. Harry leaned over and shook my hand.

I said, 'What's this – goodbye?'

'Could be. I have an idea I'm going to be kinda busy for a while, helping to investigate the murder of that much-loved, much-respected citizen, Mr Thomas Bergdorf. Not, of course, that you know anything about that yet, do you?'

'Me? How should I know anything? Tommy's dead? What a shame.'

He laughed and opened the door for me as Linda came, smiling, towards us. 'Look on the good side,' he said. 'At least now you don't have to be on that plane tonight.' And then, chuckling to himself, he drove away.

Halfway down the steps to Butterfields Linda stopped and clutched my arm. 'Have you heard the news? Tommy Bergdorf's dead, murdered. It was on the car radio.'

'Good God,' I said. 'When did this happen?'

'This morning, like just before ten. Thank God I'd already paid his cheque into my account.' She stood very close, looking into my face. 'You . . . you didn't have anything to do with it, did you? I mean, you didn't do it for me, for, for us?'

'Me?' I said. 'I've been with Harry Brown all morning. Since you left after breakfast. We looked at the ocean and walked on the beach. You can ask him.'

She blinked at me incredulously. 'You walked on the beach with Harry Brown? The Bergdorfs' tame detective? Why?'

'He wanted to talk. About boxing. He's a big fight fan, a friend of Willie Slate's.'

'Who?'

'Man who beat the shit out of me once. I'll tell you about it one day, when you've annoyed me and I want to get my own back by boring you to death.'

She looked relieved. 'Well, that's okay then. I mean, if you were with a homicide cop . . . you could hardly have a better alibi.'

'Exactly,' I said. 'I'm not going to tell you I'm sorry about Tommy. Frankly, I think he had it coming but the very suggestion that I might have known something about it – I'm really quite shocked that such an idea could have crossed your mind.' And we went on down to lunch, me carrying my chin high in affronted dignity.

An hour or so later – 'You know something?' I said. 'I'll be glad to get out of this town. Everybody eats too much. I don't know how you manage to burn it off but I haven't taken any exercise in days and my clothes are getting tight. I can't wait to get back into a gym.' But that was after lunch, at the coffee stage, when finally we'd exhausted the topic of Tommy's murder and all the fruitless speculation about who might have done it. The police theory, she said, having heard it on the car radio, was that the motive had probably been robbery. Tommy had been found, shot through the head, at his desk and his safe was open and empty.

'You know what that means?' she said. 'The killers took the tape.'

'They'll probably look at it and throw it away, just think Tommy was a dirty old man who kept a naughty home video in his den.'

'Yeah.' But I could see her working out all the

angles, trying to decide whether it was a good thing she had sold it to Tommy before he was killed or whether it might have been worth more if she had hung on to it. I think I managed to persuade her that she had made the right move and indeed I believed it. True, Carlo Minelli might have paid her twice as much or even more but on the other hand he might simply have taken the tape and sent Paulie round to kill her.

'That client of mine?' she said. 'Guy who thought his wife had run away with the pool man? He got it all wrong. She didn't go with the pool man at all. Oh, she'd been screwing the pool man okay, but that ended a month ago. He just gave her a ride to the Beverly Hilton for old times' sake.'

'You've found her?'

'Of course. I told you – I'm a good detective. She's shacked up with a basketball player, would you believe? He's seven foot tall and she's five-one. Can you imagine them in bed? If he lay on top of her she'd just vanish. Her face would be around his navel and he'd be murmuring sweet nothings into the pillow.' She shook her head, imagining it.

'Love will find a way,' I said.

'Hmm.'

'Did the client pay you?'

'Oh, yeah. But I don't think he wants her back any more, not now he's arranged to take his boss to a restaurant on Saturday. Anyway, it was the idea of her going off with the pool man that really annoyed him. The basketball player he's not even mad about. He seemed quite pleased if anything.'

'Famous is he, the basketball player?'

She nodded. 'Even I'd heard of him and I hate sports. My client seems to think it gives him a kind of kudos, his wife running away with a famous person.'

We were silent for a while, a good comfortable sort of silence. Then she said, 'He still wants me to go to Vegas with him. Not this weekend, the next.'

'Can you afford the time?'

'I don't see why not. I'm fresh out of clients.'

'Nothing to stop you then, is there?'

She shrugged. 'I guess not.' We sat with our elbows on the table, our chins cupped in our hands, gazing seriously at each other. 'He's not a bad-looking guy,' she said. 'Matter of fact he reminds me of Sean Connery, only smaller and with more hair.'

'Funny that,' I said, 'because I look like Michael Caine. I mean, before he made all the money and put on the weight.'

She laughed, really quite hard, a genuine, amused laugh. I was hurt. 'No, you don't,' she said. 'I told you that already. You're not a bit like Michael Caine.'

'You didn't say that. You said I didn't sound like Michael Caine.'

'Well, you don't look like him either. I've never seen anyone who looks less like Michael Caine.'

'What about Harry Brown?'

'Even he looks more like Michael Caine than you do.'

'That's what he said.' Now I came to think about it the only person I'd ever met who said I looked like Michael Caine was Arnie and what did he know? He never watched regular movies, just video nasties and Michael Caine didn't appear in those. There was a very real possibility that Arnie wouldn't even have recognised Michael Caine if he'd walked up and introduced himself. 'Do you fancy Sean Connery?' I said.

She nodded. 'Every woman does. He has balls.'

'Then perhaps you'd better go to Vegas with your Connery lookalike,' I said. 'See if he has balls, too.' She was still staring deeply at me, her chin in her hands. I sighed. 'Be a pity, though. You see, I had a different idea. I thought you might come to London with me.'

Another nod, a little cagey this time. 'What for?'

'Well, it's my mother, you see. I think she's worried that I might be gay.'

'Hah!'

'Indeed,' I said. 'You may well say "hah!". So I thought that if I turned up with someone like you . . .' I gave another sigh. 'But there's no point even talking about it, is there? Not if you're going to Vegas.'

'Vegas?' she said. 'Who wants to go to Vegas? I'll let you in on a secret, my friend, Vegas is the anteroom to hell.'

'Is it really?' I said. 'I've never heard that.'

'Take my word.'

'In that case,' I said, 'you'd better come to London, hadn't you?'

And she said, 'Yeah, all things considered I think I'd better. I mean, if it's going to make your mother happy . . .' She was quiet for a moment, nibbling thoughtfully on a forefinger. 'Do you still have the hotel room?'

'Sure. Why?'

She shrugged. 'I just thought, if I'm going to have to go all the way to London, put my hand on my heart and swear to your mom that her boy's okay, I really ought to check you out at least one more time.'

I gazed at her in open admiration. 'You're a mind-reader. I was just going to suggest the very same thing. Shall we go?'

And she said yes, so we went.